WATCHING YOU

A gripping crime mystery full of dark secrets

GRETTA MULROONEY

Published 2017 by Joffe Books, London.

www.joffebooks.com

This book is a work of fiction. Names, characters, businesses, organizations, places and events are either the product of the author's imagination or are used fictitiously. Any resemblance to actual persons, living or dead, events or locales is entirely coincidental. The spelling is British English.

ISBN 978-1-912106-96-7

For Hilary.

They are suffering. They're going to suffer more. Much more. I will rack up their fear as and when I want. The changes have been rung. Ding ding! This round is mine. It's my finger on the misery switch now.

There's no urgency. I've been subject to other people's rules and whims for long enough. My old man. Foster parents. Social workers. Teachers. Care homes. 'Move here. Move there. Do this. Don't do that. Hurry up. Eat that. Leave that alone. Don't you ever listen? Stop causing trouble. You're a bloody nuisance. Waste of space.'

I'm in no hurry now. I'm in control. I can take my time and enjoy the process. If life is all about costs and payoffs, I've paid enough. Now it's my turn for full payback. That means hard cash too. Sit back and enjoy. Sweet like honey.

I've thought this through for a long time. Researching. Planning. Slowly adding fuel to my anger. Relishing the resentment. The observing and waiting has brought its own rewards.

Finally, I've reached the place where I can stake my claim. Even the score.

It's satisfying to play the long game. Tease and change the rules and tactics when I feel like it. Watch them wriggling, agonising and wondering.

Sometimes I think I'll never want the game to end because of the satisfaction I get. I know it has to one day. I'm not sure yet how I'll trigger the end. With fireworks and a big bang, anyway. A grand finale. I'll wait and see. I'm flexible. Imaginative. Patient.

My life has been messy and unpredictable. Now they're finding that their lives are. They're discovering what it's like to be scared and wondering what might happen next. To be in someone else's power. Will that person be cruel to you or kind? Stroke your hair or slap your face? Feed you or keep you hungry? Let you in or lock you out? What mood will they be in today?

The pleasure, the warm feeling deep inside comes from the watching. The anticipation. Playing another unexpected hand.

Suffering and damage. They feel good.

It's all a bit of a treat.

Sweet like sugar.

CHAPTER 1

The young man explained that his son had been abducted two years ago, his voice quiet in the small stuffy space. It was mid-afternoon on a hot, oppressive late summer's day. A breath of breeze stroked the faded curtain opposite Tyrone Swift. The shifting fabric fragmented the light so that the man's face was at times half shaded.

'It was a day like this. Hot and bright. I left him in the pushchair for a couple of minutes, while I took the shopping indoors. We had a little porch outside the front door so he was okay out of the sun. I had shut the gate. It was a quiet, safe street and there was no one around. My phone rang and I saw it was work so I stopped to answer the call. I was no more than a couple of minutes but when I went to fetch him, the pushchair was there but he'd gone.'

'How old was your son?'

'Just over six months. His name is Oscar. The police searched for ages. Nothing. Nothing from that day to this.'

The young man's name was Thomas Maddox. He had a rounded face, satiny skin and large, dull amber eyes flecked with hazel chips. Straight, mouse brown hair brushed back from a high forehead. Swift was puzzled.

Maddox had phoned him at his office, saying he needed a private investigator. He had asked to meet to discuss some worrying anonymous emails and had forwarded an example to Swift:

The north wind doth blow and we will have snow.

Did you learn that when you were small? I did. That old north wind was always blowing for me. Oh, poor old Thomas, do you feel the north wind chilling you? It's nipping at you now. There might well be a gale, all in good time. It might rip through your life.

Swift had looked at the sender: whome@randommail.org. An internet search had informed him that Random Mail was a disposable, temporary email address that made the sender invisible if used with a high-tech browser. The tone of the message was certainly offensive.

'I'm sorry about your son but I thought you wanted to consult me about anonymous emails you've received?'

'Yes, of course. I'm not making myself very clear. It's just that I wonder if they're in some way connected to Oscar.' Maddox spoke in an indistinct, uncertain voice. He cleared his throat. 'I'll show you a couple of others. See what you think.'

He reached for an iPad and tapped the screen. Swift scanned the two emails. They had been sent from the same address:

Poor old Thomas. Sad bastard. I've been reading about you. Hearing things about you. You do seem to have had bad luck following you. So many unfortunate things have happened. People can't understand it. I can see why. Perhaps you were born under an evil star. I'm sure you must think that sometimes. I suppose I should make sympathetic noises because I know all about loss too, but I can't. You see, I've suffered because of you and your grandfather. Maybe you know about me, maybe you don't. I suspect you don't. But ignorance is no excuse.

This was followed by:

Oh, Thomas, when your cherished one is no longer with you, it will be icy cold inland and icy cold on the shore.

Maddox twitched the thin, flower-patterned curtains across the narrow window to shield them from the slanting arrows of sun. Dust motes danced.

'When did you start receiving these messages?'

'The beginning of April. I've had five altogether, one every couple of weeks more or less.'

'You have no idea who could be sending them?'

'No.'

'You don't have any friends with a perverse sense of humour, who think this kind of thing might be funny? A practical joker?'

'Absolutely not.'

Swift scanned the emails again. 'Have you replied at all?'

'No. I thought of it but then I was worried that they might be some kind of phishing and if I replied, I would be hacked. I changed my account password after the second one.'

'Have you shown them to the police?'

'Yes. I contacted the detective who led the inquiry about Oscar. He had just moved to another job so I spoke to a DI Cheng. She looked at them and asked if I had annoyed someone. She said to let her know if I got any more and especially any with content that's directly threatening or that mentions Oscar. She was going to talk to her boss about it. She said she'd get back to me. It always seems to take so long.'

'I know it must be hard, waiting for a response. Police work can take time.'

A strand of hair fell on to Maddox's forehead and he brushed it back slowly. 'If there is any chance that this is about Oscar . . . if someone is trying to tell me something . . . What do you think?' He raised forlorn eyes to Swift.

'I have no idea. What I've read is odd but indirect. Are the other two emails similar?'

'Yes, insinuating things about grief. As if the person knows about me or is observing me. They make me anxious, which is the point, I suppose.'

'And have you annoyed or upset anyone?'

'Not that I know of. Maura's really anxious about the emails. I feel bad for her.'

'And Maura is?'

'Maura Haskin, Oscar's mother.'

Maddox looked at the floor and chewed at the skin around the nail of his right index finger. All his nails were bitten to the quick, sore looking and grimy. Swift flinched as he noticed them.

Maddox continued. 'We split up a while after he was taken. Maura said she could never forgive me for leaving him. I couldn't blame her. I'll never forgive myself so how could I expect it of her. We gave up our flat. Neither of us could bear the memories. That's why I've ended up here in this caravan. A friend loaned it to me until I can sort myself out. My grandfather suggested we get a private investigator when these emails came. He says the police take too long and never seem to get results. Then we decided we should ask the investigator to look for Oscar too. I wish in a way that we'd done that a while ago but of course, we kept expecting the police to make progress. My grandfather said he would pay. I can't afford it. Maura was keen, she said it was the least we could do. My grandfather found you and said you looked sound.'

'Oscar was your only child?'

'Yes. We had planned to have three but . . . Maura is seeing someone else now but she says she won't have any more children. I certainly won't. I wouldn't trust myself.' He wiped his hands on his jeans and stood up, switching on a small desk fan. 'I'm sorry; I haven't offered you a drink.'

'Water would be fine, thanks.'

Swift felt trickles of sweat on the back of his neck. The fan was noisy and ineffective. He moved it nearer while Maddox fetched water, the floor creaking as he walked to the adjoining kitchen. The living area they were seated in was at the front of a small caravan, parked on a shabby site in south London. The caravan was cramped and featureless with stained dark grey carpet and a cheap metal coffee table. A couple of Pollock and Hockney reproductions hung crookedly on the walls. Thin Indian cotton throws were draped on the seats. A clothes airer with shirts drying on it was propped behind the door, next to a tiny upright piano. Maddox had been playing the piano when Swift arrived, the sounds of *Hickory Dickory Dock* drifting across the browning grass. There was a handsome pale oak desk wedged into the space between the living area and the galley kitchen, half blocking it. It held a laptop and a row of books. Swift leaned forward and looked at the titles: *The Skilled Representative*, *Advocacy: The Rules and Boundaries*, *Being a Champion*, *Choosing Your Battles*. An open box of medication lay on the table, alongside several empty, stained mugs, a sticky plate with the orangey remains of what looked like beans on toast, a bag of liquorice and a half-eaten, large slab of milk chocolate.

Swift sat back against the hard, narrow cushioning of the bench seat, stretching his long legs out. All caravans smelled the same. Slightly sweet but with a hint of something mouldering, and this one also held a whiff of blocked drains.

'What do you do for a living?' Swift accepted a plastic beaker of water. It was warm and tasted metallic.

'I'm an advocate. I work for a charity called All about You. We support people who need help to have their say in life. People who want to raise their problems with government organisations, hospitals, doctors — any areas where they run into difficulties.'

He seemed a nervous, earnest and shy young man. Swift's first impression was that he had a soft centre. The vacant heaviness of his eyes suggested the effects of medication. His skin looked clear and healthy but he was carrying too much weight, with rolls of pudginess around his waist and hips. Swift imagined him sitting here, staring into space, munching chocolate and easing his misery with drugs. He wondered how effective he would be at representing others. As if reading Swift's thoughts, he shrugged and added:

'I'm not sure I'm all that good at what I do. I get tongue-tied sometimes, especially with council bigwigs. I've had to work hard at being assertive. But I've had a few successes so I suppose I must have some talent for it.'

Swift thought that talking yourself down was rarely a useful tactic in life. He wasn't sure what to make of Maddox, his haunted gaze, the tatty caravan on this scrubby site, the piano playing, the strange emails or the missing son. The man was articulate but diffident and down at heel. Swift was curious.

'Can I see the other emails?'

'Sure. They're all in the same folder. Does that mean you'll help us?' He had an imploring smile.

'Let me take a look at the emails and check a few things out with you.'

The two remaining emails read in a similar fashion:

Hey there, Thomas, have you discovered that grief feels like fear? You might find that truth feels like fear too. Time will tell. You see, I've got a bone to pick with you. You've taken things from me. Things that were rightfully mine. Left me feeling sore and angry. I said before that I couldn't offer sympathy but it was bad about your boy. Not for you but for him. It's a crap thing to happen to a child, even if his family are deceitful bastards.

I wonder if you're looking, Thomas. I've been looking all my life and guess what I found? You must be bewildered. I'll tell you eventually. You'll find out what you've done to me.

'Are you generally called Thomas? Not Tom or Tommy?'

'No, Thomas. So whoever is sending these knows that.'

'Have you considered it might be your ex, Maura?'

'No, no, I haven't. She wouldn't do something like this.'

'You're sure? She might feel bitter towards you.'

'Maura's not like that. She's never underhand. She's direct. If she has something to say, she comes out with it straight to your face. And she'd never know how to set up an anonymous email address.'

Swift sipped more water. It was the school holidays and children were playing outside. A ball banged against the door and a high voice called 'Sorry, mate!' Maddox jumped at the sudden noise and nibbled again at his fingernail.

'Tell me more about the day your son was taken.'

Maddox was wearing a short-sleeved shirt. He rubbed his forearms as if he was cold. 'It was a Tuesday in August. Two years ago last week. We had a ground floor flat in Wanstead. We both worked part time, Maura and me. We shared the parenting. She's a hairdresser. I was at home Mondays and Tuesdays. I had taken Oscar shopping for some groceries. He hadn't slept well the night before and he had been crotchety that morning. Being in the pushchair and on the move always calmed him. I was hoping he would fall asleep and he did. I walked to the supermarket with him, and then headed home. We got back about noon. I took the bags through to the kitchen and as I said, I had a brief phone call. When I went out to the porch to get Oscar he had gone. I ran out and looked up and down the road but no one was there.' He stroked his throat. 'We worked out the parenting that way because we agreed we didn't want anyone else looking after our child. In the end, he'd have been safer at a nursery than with me.'

Swift made no comment. He knew Maura must have thrown that allegation at Maddox more than once. 'The police inquiry came up with nothing?'

'Nothing that helped. They searched the area, had some calls from people saying they had seen Oscar but none of them led to anything. It was a quiet street. No one had seen or heard anything. The person who took him must have had a car, to be able to vanish that quickly. The police said that too. They think it must have been planned. They interviewed people at the playgroup Oscar went to and checked offenders who had taken children before. It was no good. There was a woman who lived somewhere nearby: Suzy Mulligan. The police talked to her because she'd taken a baby once before. But they said she had nothing to do with Oscar. She came to the flat and spoke to Maura after the police had seen her. It upset Maura; I came home and found her there. Maura was in tears.' He lapsed into silence. His breathing sounded ragged.

'Are you okay?'

'Yes. I was just remembering. At least I could still put my arms around Maura then. The police have kept the case open and they review it now and again. I suppose that should be of some comfort but it isn't. I used to call them every week, hoping for good news, any news, but then I gave up.' He pressed his right thumb against the heel of his left hand. 'I fell apart afterwards. Couldn't work for months. I still can't function without anti-depressants. I feel so alone.' He closed his eyes for a moment. 'It's the not knowing, you see. Life now is like a horrible dream state. I dread these emails but they give me a kind of hope as well.'

'It's possible that is the intention. There seem to be hints of it. But it could be someone acting cruelly and using your loss to hurt you for another reason.'

Maddox drank his water, cradling his glass in both hands. Swift noticed he had dainty feet for a man of above average height. He was wearing grubby white plimsolls with no socks and his ankles looked oddly naked. Swift felt a stab of compassion.

'I feel I want to say to you . . . oh, I don't know . . . you're pretty experienced, aren't you . . . your website says you've worked in Interpol and the Met. I mean, you must have come across some odd things, heard some strange stories.'

'Not a lot surprises me.' Except his own peculiar path through life, that often surprised and baffled him.

'No, I suppose not.' Maddox pressed his thumb into his hand again.

Swift looked through the dusty back window at a girl erecting a tent. Her bare brown feet were planted firmly in the parched grass. There had been no rain for weeks. Just endless glaring sun and burning skies. The air was thick and tarry. He could taste petrol fumes and frying food. On hot days like this, he often felt drowsy and sluggish and thought it was probably hay fever. A doctor had once said he could be tested to determine which pollens he was allergic to but he didn't see the point. He could hardly spend the summer indoors with the windows shut and curtains drawn, which seemed to be the main advice for hay fever sufferers.

He looked back at Maddox. 'Just tell me what's on your mind.'

'It's . . . well . . . for quite a while now, I've felt as if there was something destructive in my life. Something following me around like a malicious shadow and making things go wrong. Like a curse, almost. Like it says in that email. There have been times I've stopped in the street and looked behind me. Oh I don't know, as soon as I start to say it I sound crazy, paranoid. I know I'm on tablets for depression but I don't think I'm a complete head case. I expect you're sitting there thinking I am and looking for a quick exit. I saw a counsellor after Oscar was taken. He suggested I was focusing my feelings of bereavement on things and events as a way of shutting them out. I came away from him feeling even more upset. I never went back.'

Swift took a breath. He had no idea how disturbed Maddox was but he sounded like a man who was capable of ordering his thoughts and emotions. He thought it was best to try to keep things concrete.

'You say things have gone wrong. Give me some examples.'

'Okay. Three years ago, someone riding a bike at speed came up on the pavement and ran me over. It was dark, the bike had no lights and it might have been an accident but they didn't stop. I lost two teeth and sprained my wrist. A while after that I had my wallet and passport stolen. Then I had a car taken a bit later. A couple of months after that, I found both my cats dead in the street, run over. Our flat was broken into just after Oscar was born but nothing was taken. Maura said it was as if someone had placed a hex on me. Then when Oscar vanished . . . I said all this to the police and they checked that I'd reported the incidents, but they seemed to have been unconnected. The break-in interested them because nothing was stolen. They thought it might have been someone checking the layout of the house. A while after Oscar was taken, I was at the gym and someone forced my locker open and took all my clothes and my bag, even my shower kit. Then my rucksack vanished from a café when my back was turned. It had sheet music in it, my own compositions and I had no copies. That hurt. Last month I came home and found my bike had been stolen. I had padlocked it at the back of the caravan but someone had used a bolt cutter. I reported those incidents to the police as well. They were sympathetic but they've never got anywhere with finding who's responsible. And now these emails.'

He sat with his hands dangling between his knees, staring at the floor. His body drooped. Swift felt uneasy about getting involved with Maddox. This was quite a mix of misfortune, persecution and anguish. He wasn't sure he wanted to engage with so much grief and loss. He had enough anxiety to deal with about his own child. On the other hand, keeping busy was a kind of therapy and the situation was thought-provoking.

'Thanks for listening, anyway. At least you haven't given me that pitying, wary look I get from people. You know, *he's clearly not right in the head but best to humour him*. I'm used to that.'

Swift looked around at the evidence of a wretched life and decided. 'First of all, I should think you're entitled not to be right in the head after your child was abducted. Secondly, I have no idea if the abduction is related to your bad experiences or the emails. Thirdly, I will take a look at the situation.'

'Thank you.' Maddox let out a long breath, as if he had released a terrible tension.

'I think you said your grandfather is paying my bill so I need him to sign a contract. I need to talk to him as well.'

'He wants to meet you as soon as possible anyway. I said we would arrange it if you were willing to take the case. He lives in Kent, near Tunbridge Wells.'

'What about your parents?'

'My mum died when I was four. I never knew my father. My grandfather brought me up. He was widowed before I was born. I'm his only grandchild.'

'Will Maura talk to me?'

'I'm sure she will. I'll email her. Thanks again, thanks so much. I read that you've been successful with some very difficult cases.'

Swift was seizing up from sitting on the narrow bench. He rose, rubbing his lower back. At six feet three, his head almost scraped the caravan's ceiling. 'I have, yes, but there are never any guarantees. We'll need to talk more, take a look at the details of your life and who knows you. It would help if you could send me a timeline of all these unpleasant events that have happened to you. Don't be tempted to respond to any of these emails. Forward me all the ones you have and let me know immediately if you receive another one. If the same person is responsible for the emails, the accident and thefts you've experienced, then they know where you live now. Keep an eye on your security. Lock the door and windows at night. By the way, I enjoyed your piano playing.'

'Oh, yes. It's my comfort, I suppose, always has been. I hoped once I might play professionally but I was never quite good enough. I used to play *Hickory Dickory Dock* to Oscar. It sent him off to sleep. I still play it every day. Just in case.' Maddox reached out a hand and picked out a few notes on the keys. 'I hope that he is alive and okay but I'd rather he was dead than suffering or being abused by someone.'

'Is that Oscar in the photo on the piano?'

'Yes. It was taken a week before he vanished.' Maddox handed him the photograph.

He looked down at a dark-haired plump boy. He was giggling and waving chubby fists in the way of happy babies everywhere. 'Is it okay to take a photo of this with my phone?'

'Sure.' Maddox waited while he photographed it, then looked at his son and placed the photo back gently with both hands. 'Have you got children?'

'Yes, I have a baby daughter, four months old.'

'You're a lucky man.'

The simple, direct sentiment struck home. 'I am, yes. I'll be in touch.'

Swift left the caravan and skirted a game of football and a man hanging out washing. He heard the piano again. A folk song, he thought, although he couldn't recall the name. He headed through the deep blue afternoon to the scrubby path that led out of the park. A plane ploughed a furrow high overhead while a woman wearing rubber gloves picked up litter scattered outside the site shop. It had wire mesh over the windows, reinforced glass in the door, graffiti scrawled on the pebbledash walls and a large sign warning that CCTV was in operation. A hard looking, bare chested man came out holding a wriggling toddler in one arm and two heavy bags of shopping in the other hand. The door slammed after him. He cleared his throat and spat on the ground as he walked away.

Thomas Maddox had chosen a rough, depressing place to live. He seemed so inoffensive. It was hard to imagine that he had made anyone angry enough to torment him. Yet there was always more beneath the surface of every life once you started digging.

In Swift's last investigation, a guilt-ridden murderer had said he was searching for the courage to kill himself. Swift had some inkling of the resolve Maddox must need to get from day to day, navigating the ordinary business of a bereft life that no longer made sense. He was struggling himself to understand life's absurdities. A sick worm turned in the pit of his stomach when he thought of the hospital appointment he had to attend with Ruth in Brighton the following day. He raised his face to the insistent sun, as if to gather and store strength.

* * *

The audiology clinic room was full of bright posters, glossy leaflets and photos of smiling children wearing hearing aids. There was a bowl of tiny, gaily coloured lollipops on the window ledge. Swift sat beside Ruth holding Branna, their daughter. Ruth had a hand on his arm. Dr Chopra sat opposite them. She was a kind, softly-spoken woman. She was confirming what they already suspected, that Branna was deaf. Swift felt as if he had temporarily lost his own hearing. The doctor's words were muffled and echoing. Muted, underwater sounds.

'The further tests have demonstrated without doubt that Branna has a moderate to severe hearing loss. This is permanent. We won't know exactly how much hearing loss there is until she is older. I understand this is difficult for you. The first thing I want to say to you is that the Branna you know now, after this diagnosis, is the same Branna you brought in here. She is the same little girl.'

He looked down at his daughter. His own grey eyes looked back at him. She was staring at him with a determined gaze and working her mouth as if she understood and was displeased. He wanted to tell Dr Chopra that what she had just said was banal nonsense. This was the same Branna and an entirely different Branna. But the woman was doing her best. Ruth's grip on his arm tightened. Her voice trembled.

'What do we do? What can we do for her?'

'We recommend hearing aids as soon as possible so that Branna's speech and understanding can develop in line with her other milestones. I'd like you to come back next week for measurements and impressions to be taken. When she is a little older, we may recommend cochlear implants. These are electronic devices that are placed in the ear during surgery.'

Dr Chopra said she understood that this was a difficult time. She talked on about how much could be done, the use of lip reading and sign language, support groups. It was helpful to talk to other parents, share concerns and progress. There would be a designated nurse to answer their questions and help them monitor Branna's development. She placed a hefty pack of leaflets on the desk for them. Swift held his daughter's gaze.

'Can she hear me now, talking this close to her?'

'To a degree, yes. It's good to look directly at her, as you have been doing. But most sounds will be indistinct. Hearing aids will help enormously. There is no reason why she can't achieve everything she wants in life with your loving help and support.'

They drove to a café along the seafront in Brighton. It was another still, baking day, the light glaring on the concrete. They didn't speak. Branna had fallen asleep by the time they parked and Ruth placed her in the shade between them in the café, snug in her seat.

'I can't eat,' Ruth said. 'Just a coffee.' She ran her hands through her short butterscotch hair and stared out at the sea.

Swift ordered two coffees. Every time he saw Ruth, he felt the familiar pleasure and pain of loving her. The usual delight and torment. He wanted to take her hand but she looked remote, lost in her own thoughts. Her face was pale, gaunt almost. He wished she would eat something.

'I can't help thinking this is my fault,' she said at last. 'I've been reading about the causes of deafness. There is no genetic history of it between us. One article said that stress during early pregnancy might be a reason. I certainly put Branna through plenty of that, leaving Emlyn, going off to Devon, not getting enough rest, not eating properly or taking vitamins in the early months. That's probably why she was premature as well.'

'Oh Ruth, if we're going to look to apportion blame, I need to step forward and so does your husband. But guilt and blame won't help Branna.'

Their complicated history sat between them like an unwanted guest at the table. He had been engaged to Ruth before she left him more than six years ago and married Emlyn Taylor, setting up home in Brighton. For a long time, Swift had lived a half-hearted, twilight life, burying himself in his job at Interpol and rowing his grief into the Thames. Taylor, a barrister, had developed a rare and aggressive form of multiple sclerosis. When Swift and

Ruth met again at a party, they had started seeing each other in London for lunches and walks. He had supported her through a miscarriage and the anguish of dealing with her sick husband. He and Ruth had slept together again just once and she had got pregnant. Driven by rage and jealousy, Taylor had conducted a campaign of harassment against Swift through a petty criminal. This had resulted in the death of Kris Jelen, the woman Swift had been seeing at the time. Ruth had left her husband in great distress and for months, no one had known where she was. She had returned to Taylor shortly before Branna had been born prematurely, at eight months.

He loved Ruth still. It tormented him, this love. It was a burden and he thought he should be able to put it down. He grew exasperated with himself for his inability to separate from her. He had known Kris Jelen for just a few months before she died and he had been fond of her. He never compared Kris to Ruth but always in the background was the knowledge that no other woman had come near her.

The sea and sky were a pure, faultless blue, the air invigorating. It was the kind of shimmering day that would usually gladden the heart. Outside the restaurant next door, there was live music. A smoky-voiced woman was singing about feeling good. There was the gleaming smooth veneer of things, Swift thought and then the murky, snarled undercurrent and you never knew when it might tangle and trap you.

'This is all such a mess. Branna deserves better than this.' Ruth sipped her coffee, frowning.

She was thin, too thin, her shoulder blades jutting from her sleeveless shirt. There were new worry lines at the corners of her eyes. As well as coping with Branna, she was supporting Taylor, who was on trial for Kris Jelen's death, charged with encouraging a crime.

He did take her hand now. 'Ruth, whatever it is, we all made this situation. Now we have to make the best of it. We do the best we can for Branna.'

She squeezed his fingers. 'I know. I know you're right. It's just that these things keep going round inside my head and I can't seem to stop them. I try to focus on Branna and I know that I can transmit my anxiety to her. Then I feel even guiltier. We are a strange pair, you and me, bobbing on the tide, flotsam and jetsam. People looking at us here now would have no clue. They would think we're a couple with their baby and that we'll be taking her home when we've had our coffee. Dr Chopra would have thought that.'

Well, he thought bitterly, if you hadn't played around behind my back, if you hadn't cheated on me and run off with Taylor, we could be that couple. We would be having the marriage we planned. Our lives could be straightforward instead of this thorny mess. Branna would be with both her parents. He looked at his daughter. Anger and resentment were no good for her. He forced himself to sound confident. 'We are a couple with our baby. Just not the usual kind of couple.'

Ruth gave him a faint smile and raised an eyebrow. 'Who wants to be run of the mill?'

That was more like the Ruth he had known. 'Exactly. Why not break the mould?' It was best to talk like this, he thought, instead of raking over the past and worrying about what couldn't be changed. Best to act and speak with bravura, to pretend they were celebrating their difference.

Ruth lifted the tiny glass saltcellar from the table and rolled it from side to side. She shook a few grains on to her finger and licked them. 'That's good and bitter. Gives me a kick where I need it.' She replaced the salt next to the pepper, aligning them. 'You look tired, Ty. Your eyes have that tight look.'

'I worry. I'm okay. You focus on you and Branna.'

'I feel as if I've messed up your life. Messed with your feelings. I've brought trouble and sadness to your door. I'm sure that is what your family and friends think. I'm sure it's what you think.'

'Oh, I reckon I'm capable of finding my own trouble, Ruth. People can think what they like. You know that rarely bothers me. Yes, of course I am angry sometimes. Angry and sad. But we just have to deal with what there is.'

'Ty . . . Branna's deafness is definitely what there is. The hearing aids should be a big help. The sooner she has them, the sooner she'll be used to them.'

Branna snuffled, yawned and kicked her legs. Her dark, downy hair was like a dandelion clock, sticking up. Swift bent his mouth to her ear.

'You're like a little duckling in a nest,' he said.

She wrinkled her nose and kicked again. He wondered if she had heard him.

CHAPTER 2

Swift took a train to Tunbridge Wells. He bought a coffee from the trolley that rumbled along the aisle, the wheels nipping at ankles. He had arranged to meet Thomas Maddox and his grandfather, Gabriel Maddox, who lived at a place called High Hawksford.

'He runs a holiday business,' Thomas had explained on the phone. 'He said he can fit you in on Saturday morning, if that's ok. I spend some weekends there, helping out. You can't miss where he lives, it's Hawksford windmill.'

Swift sipped the coffee, grimacing at the harsh flavour. He'd known it would be a mistake as he handed over the money. At least the train wasn't busy and he had legroom. The day was intensely hot and a tannoy announcement had already informed him that the air conditioning wasn't functioning. He rolled up his sleeves and opened another button on his thin cotton shirt. A smartly dressed woman sitting across the aisle was on her phone, answering questions. She was nervous, her voice loud. He guessed she was talking to a recruitment consultant as she discussed her experience and skills, mentioned where she lived and confirmed her full name, date of birth, email address and phone number. Swift could see that she was oblivious to him listening in. He thought about the anonymous emailer. Gathering information about someone could be easy enough. The train approached a station and the woman exited, still talking.

He googled Gabriel Maddox as fields sped by and saw that he owned a company called Smell the Roses. It specialised in unusual holiday homes around the High Hawksford area: *quirky and special breaks in the beautiful rural peace of the Weald of Kent.* You could book converted railway carriages, treehouses, luxury cabins and huts with hot tubs, restored army trailers, static gipsy caravans, a chapel, an oast house, a folly and a selection of tipis and yurts with sky decks.

We are all about peace, relaxation and tranquillity. We provide an experience that is second to none and our friendly team is always on hand to make your stay as wonderful as possible. So phone us, drop in any time for a chat and best of all, come and join us for a break from the hurly burly.

There were glowing five star reviews from previous customers and photos of smiling holidaymakers. If you liked that kind of thing, it looked classy and well organised.

He saw that he had received an email from Ian Wareham, a colleague he had worked with during his time in the Met. Wareham was a computer expert now working in fraud and had helped him with a previous case. Swift had phoned him, describing the emails Thomas Maddox had received and forwarding one to him. Wareham's response was, as always, succinct:

No direct threats here but I believe the officer overseeing the case is looking into the emails. Very complex to trace sender. Will be using public computers. Using false information and address and a portable browser that masks by sending through lots of servers. An expert might get a successful trace after months but no guarantee. So, if it's actioned, it will be a long haul.

Swift had expected the response. The email sender had skills and was a tactician. He sat back and watched the countryside unfold, listening to Tony Bennett duet with Lady Gaga. He wondered again if he should move to Brighton, be on hand to help with Branna and support Ruth. A private investigator could work from any base. But his context was London and always had been apart from a brief period of his life when he had worked for Interpol in Lyon. London was where his family, friends and contacts were. And his old and trusted companion and confidant, the Thames. He couldn't imagine living near Ruth and her husband, hovering on the edges of their lives. They might feel encroached on and the truth of it was he didn't want to be near Taylor. He had never met the man and had no wish to. He felt such animosity towards him, he stayed well away. He sneezed, rubbed his itchy eyes and used his eye drops.

A fifteen-minute taxi ride from the station took him past an orchard, a large Tudor manor house and a farm shop with punnets of raspberries and baskets of apples set out for sale. Then along a narrow, tree-lined lane flanked by pretty cottages with white wood cladding. The air was fresher than in London but the heat was as intense and the taxi seat was scorching.

'You booked into Smell the Roses?' the taxi driver asked. 'If you are, you're travelling light.'

'No, just a visit. I suppose you take a lot of customers there.'

'Oh yes. A popular destination. Bloke who owns it hasn't always been popular around here, mind.'

'Gabriel Maddox? Why is that?'

'There was a row about him buying up land, expanding his business. Some locals got up a petition but he got his planning application through. I don't know him personally but I've heard he doesn't take any prisoners. Of course, there was talk of bribery and corruption. Mind you, there's snobbery involved because he started as a market trader in east London. Some people think he's a jumped-up barrow boy. I'm a Londoner originally myself. I'm not complaining. It's good for my trade. More power to his elbow, I say.'

The driver carried on, talking about how the countryside had changed in the last twenty years. Swift half listened, nodding along. Suddenly, the windmill's two sails loomed on the horizon across the fields. They were black and elegant against the cloudless sky. Shortly after, they passed a wide entrance with a hand painted sign by open red iron gates:

Smell the Roses
R & R Starts Here
Leave Your Cares Outside the Gate

Another half mile along the road they came to the windmill. It was painted white with long charcoal framed windows on the first two storeys and round windows like portholes on the third. It sat behind high gates at the end of a long, paved driveway, on a low hill surrounded by a semi-circle of beech hedges. The taxi driver got out and pressed a buzzer on the gates, which opened noiselessly.

Thomas Maddox appeared from the side of the windmill, hefting a plastic box of cleaning materials. He wore his plimsolls, denim shorts and a sleeveless white T-shirt that was too small and rode up over his fleshy waistline. His face had a sheen of sweat and he was puffing as he approached.

'I won't shake hands. I'm a bit grubby and smelly. I've been cleaning some of the accommodation. Saturday's one of our changeover days.'

'Is that how you help at weekends?'

'Mainly. Sometimes I check bookings, order repairs. Whatever is needed, really. Gabe gives me a list.'

'Is that what you call him?'

'Yeah. He's never wanted to be called grandad, says it would make him feel ancient. He'll be in his office. Come on in.'

The wide front door had huge iron hinges and rows of metal studs, so that it resembled the entrance to a castle. A small, square hall inside opened into a huge light-drenched space, which held the kitchen and a dining area, an expanse of gleaming white appliances, grey marble and pale elm. The bare brick walls were hung with prints of cinema posters and wire sculptures. Thick black beams supported the ceiling. Wide, open tread metal stairs led to the next level. Swift followed Thomas across a polished woodblock floor, through a door at the side of the kitchen and along a short corridor to another room at the back. Thomas tapped lightly as he went in.

'Gabe, Mr Swift is here.'

'Good, good, because this email situation is ratcheting up!'

Gabe Maddox stood up from behind a curved beech wood desk and came forward, hand held out. His grip was brief but firm. He wore jeans and a cream linen jacket over a black T-shirt. His bronze hair fell in corrugated waves from his long, equine head to just above his shoulders. Swift thought it looked dyed. He radiated energy although his face was closed, his narrow eyes watchful rather than friendly through rimless glasses. He smelled of limes.

'Pleased to meet you,' Swift said.

'Well, you're very tall. That inspires confidence. Why is that, do you think?'

'I've no idea.'

'No, well, take a seat. You too, Thomas. Now, our anonymous postie has contacted me. I've received one of these emails this morning. Want to see it?'

He spoke pugnaciously, as if he was issuing a challenge or a test. His accent was refined cockney. He took his glasses off and twirled them. His eyes were a remarkable colour, an intense blue-green.

'Yes, I'd like to see it.'

'Right. It came to my business email so there's no mystery about that. The address is on our website.'

Swift waited while Maddox senior fussed with his laptop. The room had one window at the back, looking out on to a hedge. It was furnished with red leather sofas and armchairs, a glass topped coffee table and the beautiful beech desk. Three of the walls were brick, the fourth painted a pale orange. Abstract modern paintings and sketches of fruit and geometric shapes covered one wall and a montage of holiday properties featured on the wall behind the desk. Unlike the train, the room had air con and was deliciously cool. Gabe Maddox cleaned his glasses with a monogrammed hanky, turned the laptop round and watched as Swift read. The email had come from the same address as those sent to his grandson.

Dear oh dear, Gabe, I see you've gone and got yourself a private eye. Not a good move. How do I know? I keep my own eyes on people. I'm always alert. Nothing gets past me. I've been busy but now I've introduced myself properly to Thomas, I was about to get around to you so here I am. I would say that once upon a time you didn't treat me too well. Was it in a business deal? Or was it to do with Thomas? Have a think. I'm good at biding my time. That's part of the satisfaction. I'm well qualified in hanging on in there. Lovely place you've got, by the way. You must be raking it in. Nice for some. I'm worried that you might not be able to escape the hurly burly there for much longer.

Swift pushed the laptop back and looked at Gabe. 'It hasn't taken your emailer long to find out about me. Have you told people you've employed me?'

'I haven't kept it a secret. Neither have I broadcast it.'

'I've probably told people. I can't really remember who,' Thomas mumbled.

'Well, he or she might be accessing your emails or phone calls or watching you, Thomas. I'm no computer expert but you should both check your software for viruses and change your personal email passwords. Phone hacking would be pretty sophisticated so I think it's the least likely option. I've spoken to an ex-colleague who is a specialist on such matters.' He explained what Ian Wareham had said. 'Do either of you know anyone who has those skills?'

They both shook their heads. Thomas was holding the plastic cleaning box on his lap as if it gave him comfort.

'Well, Mr Swift, your CV is impressive. You appear to have robust experience and credentials. I'm impressed that you've solved some crimes that the police failed to deal with. What are you proposing to do about this joker?' Gabe Maddox leaned back in his leather office chair, arms folded, peering over his glasses.

Swift looked at him for a long moment. 'Who didn't you treat well?' he asked.

'I beg your pardon?' The older man frowned, pursing his lips.

'The email refers to your mistreatment of this person. Do you know what that's about?'

'No idea. Not a clue.'

Swift looked at Thomas. 'Any idea?'

He stroked the handle of the box. 'No.'

Gabe Maddox picked up a slim gold pen and twirled it through his fingers. 'If you're alive, you've mistreated people sometimes. I don't care for anonymous digs. And I don't like someone hiding their identity and being familiar with me, calling me Gabe, trying to alarm me.'

'Are you alarmed?'

He made a movement with his hand as if he was batting away a fly. 'Very little alarms me, Mr Swift. I'm too long in the tooth, seen too much. I was very alarmed when my grandson managed to mislay my great grandson and I still am.' Swift saw Thomas flinch and sink down in his chair. Gabe continued. 'I'm *annoyed* by these emails. I want you to stop the annoyance. Do you think this joker has anything to do with Oscar?'

'I have no idea but that's what you're paying me to find out. I don't think this person is a joker. There is intent, planning and knowledge here. I think that you or Thomas must have crossed someone, made someone angry. It will help me if you think carefully about that. You need to be honest with me. Have you fallen out with anyone, sacked anyone or do you have any employees who might be holding a grudge?'

'I'm a businessman,' Gabe Maddox said truculently. 'I've spent my life doing deals, buying, selling, and hustling. I'm sure I must have crossed people and rubbed them up the wrong way. You can't make omelettes without breaking eggs. But I can't think of anything that would make someone resort to this rubbish or go after Thomas. Fair but firm; that's my motto. I haven't sacked anyone and I'm not aware of anyone who works for me being pissed off. It's not in my interest to mistreat my staff.' The pen twisted in his fingers. 'I hope you're not one of these people who take the moral high ground, thinks doing business means doing the dirty.'

'Hardly. I run my own business. Why do you have the same surname?'

Maddox tossed the pen down. It bounced off the table. His grandson bent to pick it up and replaced it. The man certainly had a confrontational style.

'Thomas's father was never on the scene. My daughter was raped by a stranger and got pregnant. She lived with me and when she died, I looked after Thomas. Hence the surname. Why is this relevant?'

'I never know at this stage what's relevant. I just ask questions. Some of them might be painful or annoying, but they can be productive.'

'Oh, you're not causing me any pain. I see where you're coming from. I don't have to like you to employ you.' He sat forward, hands folded on the desk.

Swift nodded. 'Of course. And I don't have to like you to accept your money.'

There was a moment's silence, and then Gabe Maddox laughed. Swift could see he had passed a test. He didn't mind the man's posturing and belligerence as long as he wasn't concealing anything. For now, Swift wasn't sure about that.

'I prefer people who speak directly, no pussyfooting around,' he told Swift. 'Now, Thomas, didn't you say you'd thought of someone you crossed swords with in that excuse for a job you do?'

Thomas fiddled with a cleaning cloth, stroking it between a finger and thumb. 'Yes, I did. There was a man, last year. He complained about me. It was all sorted, though.'

'Okay, I'll need to get some details from you,' Swift told him.

Gabe Maddox stood up, his chair spinning around. All his movements suggested leaving the starting blocks in a race. 'Thomas, why don't you go and finish whatever you're doing, and then you can talk to Mr Swift, say in about half an hour. I'd like a brief chat with him now.'

It was an order. Thomas nodded and left. His grandfather watched him go, head to one side. He must have been in his late sixties but with his slim, compact torso, confidence and vigour, he seemed younger than his grandson did.

'I just don't know about that young man,' he said. 'He lacks drive and he's woolly headed. I wonder what will become of him. Now, Mr Swift, would you like to come to the top of my windmill? The view is spectacular and we can talk up there.'

'Fine with me.' It was the first time Swift had been in a windmill and the man clearly wanted to show off and talk, but on his terms.

Maddox led the way, rapidly explaining as they went up the stairs that he had decided to furnish the windmill in three different styles: the ground floor modern, the middle floor Jacobean and the top floor Victorian.

'It was built in 1812 and it's Grade II listed. On the middle floor here we have three bedrooms, a sitting room and bathroom.'

He opened the door to the sitting room. The overall impression was of a murky gloom, despite the large windows. Dark square panelling covered the lower walls to waist height with crimson paint above. An impressive fireplace was surrounded by more dark wood, carved with running deer. It was inset with indigo and crimson tiles and fronted by an ornate tapestry with trees, grapes and foliage. Geometric wood panels covered the ceiling, edged by Tudor roses. The pendant lights were candle-shaped with diamond lozenge patterns in the glass. A large, dark red and brown rug depicting a pastoral scene of nymphs, cherubs, deer and birds covered the dark oak floor. Heavy pewter urns stood on the mantelpiece as decoration.

'Impressive?' Maddox asked.

'Very.' Swift thought it would be like sitting in a room in a National Trust property.

Maddox seemed satisfied by the response. 'On we go, then, up to my Victorian den.'

The top room was entirely circular, with four small round windows edged with squares of green glass. Dark green paper featuring lighter green leaves and large white swans covered the walls. Above the dado rail, the wall and ceiling were painted a ruby red. Green fringed standing lamps stood behind a couple of plump purple velvet armchairs with button backs. The fireplace had green and white tiles featuring the same swans as the wallpaper and had been fitted with a wood burning stove. Faded, patterned rugs covered the polished floor and stuffed animals under glass domes sat on top of a mahogany cupboard. There were two red squirrels clutching acorns, a monkey sitting on a branch, an owl, some goldfinches, a ferret and half a dozen butterflies pinned to a long stick. Swift found them repulsive.

'This is where I relax,' Maddox said. 'Glass of whisky, Dean Martin playing and a view over my estates. Come and look.'

He beckoned Swift to the rear window. As far as the eye could see, there were fields dotted with trees, bushes and hedges with small pockets of yurts, tipis, tree houses and the other types of holiday accommodation offered. A river meandered along a field boundary, glittering in the sun. It was a tranquil, pastoral scene. Maddox handed Swift a pair of binoculars.

'You can get a better look through these. I like to keep a close eye on everything.'

The binoculars were powerful. Swift could see that each dwelling had space and privacy. It was an upmarket outfit. At the far right of the nearest field was a long, low timber-framed building with a children's play area beside it.

'What's the timber building?' Swift asked.

'Showers, laundry and a small shop selling basics. Also houses a front office, with brochures, information about the area and suchlike, and staff to help with any problems.'

Maddox took the binoculars and scanned the horizon. 'I've run lots of businesses in my time, taken the odd punt that didn't work out. But generally, I've made a success of whatever I turned my hand to. I'm good at telling which way the wind is blowing, where to put my money. This place is the jewel in my crown. I planned the site meticulously. It's high quality, top end of the market. No petting zoos, bars, entertainment or games machines. Simple but classy. Vehicles have to park at the far end of the site so there's no noise nuisance. It's deep quiet here at night under the stars. We're booked solid all year round. I have to admit, it's a little gold mine.' He gestured around him, chest puffed. 'Not bad for a boy who grew up in a bombed out street in Bermondsey with paraffin heaters and an outside lavvy, eh?'

Swift glanced at him. He was an interesting mixture of vanity, abrasiveness and childish approval seeking. Apparently not a man to examine his motives or his conscience. 'I can see you've put a lot of work into this.'

'Certainly have.' He gave Swift a nudge. 'Know what I do sometimes, when I'm up here late at night on my own? I take a piss out of the window. I find it very satisfying. Primal urge, marking my territory from up high.'

'I presume you check there's no one below?'

'Yes, well.' Maddox grew abrupt again. 'Let's sit down for a few minutes. Before you talk to Thomas again, there are some things I want to say.'

They sat in the deep armchairs. Swift chose one with its back to the unnerving stuffed animals. The sun sparked on the odd orange glints in Maddox's hair.

'You need to understand Thomas is a dreamer. He was like that as a child, always in a world of his own. Absent-minded. Still is. Misplaced his child, then his partner. He prats around at that charity job in London, advising whingers and moaners. Seems to have some pathetic notion of doing good in the world. A bleeding heart. As far as I can make out, none of the punters he helps wants to do a day's work and he spends his time getting handouts for them. Finding ways for bloody immigrants to milk the taxpayer. Probably illegals, most of them. And he lives in that skanky caravan surrounded by benefits scroungers, petty criminals and layabouts. I've asked him to move back here, help with the business, get his life back on track but he won't.' Maddox shook his head impatiently, rubbing the arms of the chair.

'Maybe what he's doing is his way of getting his life back on track.'

'As if! Oh, I know, I know I can be a bit full on. But you have to make something of yourself in life, make your mark.' He made a fist and punched the air. 'Then he has this idea that someone has been sniffing around him for a long time, causing him injuries and the like. I don't know what to make of all that. The police have looked into all the incidents and they haven't linked them. Not that I place much faith in the plod. It's a strange business but Thomas always had an over active imagination, got it from his mother.'

'What happened to your daughter, when she was raped?'

Maddox leaped up, straightened a silver cigarette case on the mantelpiece and sat down again. He had the same feet as Oscar. Small, balletic.

'She went to a party in London. We lived there then. I'd been a market trader but I got myself started in property development. I took a look at the future and saw that the housing market in London was going to go mental. No flies on me. I still own six properties there. Absolute goldmines. Anyway, Julie was seventeen, she got plastered, and some bloke dragged her behind the bushes in the garden. She woke up in the morning and couldn't remember anything much except being raped. Then we found out she was up the duff.'

'Did she go the police?'

'Yep, but they weren't too understanding. Different times back then, eh? She'd get tea and sympathy now, post-traumatic stress counselling and whatever. It didn't help that she couldn't recall anything; the party was full of all kinds. The girl she went with was paralytic and couldn't remember anything either. Anyway, then she was expecting Thomas. I wanted her to have an abortion, tried my best to persuade her but she wouldn't. I'd been widowed the year before so we made a new little family. Then she got cervical cancer. She never had much luck, my Julie. So, I got on with things, as you do. Anyway, that's old history, nothing to do with this crap we're getting.' He shook his head, as if ridding himself of the memories.

'What about resentful exes? Your wife died a long time ago. You never remarried?'

'No, never wanted to. I've had a few relationships here and there. As far as I know, there are no women out to get me.'

The more time Swift spent in Maddox's company, the more he was inclined to think that the man was so egocentric and conceited, he would be unlikely to realise that he had upset someone. 'What's your view about Oscar? Do you think he is alive?'

'Haven't a clue. The police have been useless. Lots of questions and no results.' He jabbed a finger at Swift. 'We're pinning our hopes on you now. Let's hope your methods pay off. They have before, or so I've read. You'll need to live up to your publicity.' He glanced at his watch. 'I need to wrap up now.'

'One more question. You said you don't know who would want to send you an unpleasant email but I understand you've caused some protests in the local community.'

'Who told you that?' Maddox asked sharply.

'The cab driver.'

'Oh, right. What can I say about the tree huggers and Nimbys? There were some squawkers when I wanted to extend the development and I bought another field from an old guy. Petitions and such to the council. I might get in the way of a couple of badgers or stoats or some wildflowers, all that guff. I played it straight and they didn't like it that I won the day, put rumours around about me bribing people. I'm no saint, but I didn't bribe anyone. You always get begrudgers. I don't see why that would be linked to Thomas or Oscar, though.'

'That's a fair point but I have to consider all angles.'

'Fine. Talk to the naysayers if you want. I wish you joy of them. They'll bore you to tears with their global warming claptrap. I don't buy into any of that bullshit. The world's always changing and it looks after itself. I love hot weather, me. Brings in the punters! I've signed the contract you emailed. Stella, my PA will give it to you. I'd appreciate regular updates from you. I like to keep an eye on what my money is buying.'

Maddox sprang from his chair and went lightly down the stairs in front of him. A woman was making coffee in the kitchen. She wore her long brunette hair in a plait with two wooden pins like knitting needles securing it. She had a broad, pleasant face, full-lipped, and wore a belted, full-skirted lavender dress of some soft material. A gauzy pale pink scarf was looped about her neck.

'Stella, this is Mr Swift, the detective,' Maddox said briskly. 'The contract's on my desk. Have you got those details about the site in Hereford for me?'

'I've emailed them to you. Can I get you a coffee?'

She was soft voiced with a slight lisp, her manner placid. As she looked at Maddox, Swift sensed something unspoken lingering between them.

Maddox smiled at her, his closed, intense expression relaxing for a moment. 'Not for me, Star, got to get off. Mr Swift would probably like one, yes?'

'Please.' Swift said. 'Then I'd like to speak to Thomas.'

'Okay, he should come wandering back soon, if he remembers the way. See you!'

Maddox left a citrus trace in the air. Stella tutted. She had a slight over bite that was attractive.

'He'll meet himself coming backwards one day,' she said. She heaped coffee into a cafetiere and brought the kettle back to the boil before pouring on the steaming water. The rich aroma filled the air. Her movements were quiet, measured, and stately almost. She fanned biscuits on to a plate and took two mugs from hooks on the wall, placing them carefully on a tray. Swift thought she would provide a balance to her employer's darting impatience. He guessed she smoothed his path and any feathers he had ruffled.

'Star?' he asked.

She nodded. 'Oh, you know, "Stella for star." Gabe started calling me Star as soon as we met.'

'How long have you worked for him?'

She picked up a tray and gestured to the long steel and glass table that filled one side of the room, asking him if he would like to sit. Her dress swayed as she moved, rippling over her full hips. Swift pulled a chair out for her and she sat down, sweeping her skirt deftly beneath her.

'I've been with Gabe for about eight years. We actually met through the local business circle, at the annual dinner. Then he asked if I would like to come and work for him. So, here I am.'

'When you say you've been with him, do you mean in more than a work relationship?'

She turned gentle, pale eyes on him, colouring slightly, and touched the knot of her scarf. 'You ask very direct questions!'

'I know. I think I was born nosy. I suppose that's why I was drawn to a career where I could ask questions and get away with it. Sometimes it pays off. I didn't mean to embarrass you.' Swift took a biscuit. It was treacly and delicious, filled with almonds.

Stella held his gaze. 'I believe you. Yes, it is more than a work relationship. I have my own house locally but I stay here for part of the week. I'm Gabe's partner as well as his PA. I oversee the day-to-day running of the business. We have a good-sized team and I coordinate, deal with any problems.'

'And is it a happy team? You're not employing someone with an axe to grind?'

'I'm sure that's not the case. I certainly don't know of any discontent and I think I would hear if there was any. It's a fairly stable team, too. We hardly ever lose anyone. I think that shows this is a good place to work.'

'How many people do you employ?'

'About forty in total. That includes cleaners, gardeners, maintenance, and office and shop staff. Some are part time, of course.'

'Did you and Gabe get together fairly soon after you met?'

'Yes. He and Thomas were living in the little chapel that's a holiday place now. I helped him turn this windmill into a home. It was in a terrible state of disrepair and we spent hours working out how to do it up. It's been a terrific project, a labour of love, I suppose, planning and engaging an architect, builder, carpenters. Dust, dust and more dust! I've enjoyed myself with it, particularly with the interior design. I did lots of research and we visited stately homes to look at décor and get ideas. It is wonderful to see a neglected building turned into a beautiful and unusual place to live. I love entertaining here, welcoming people in. You could say I've put my heart into it. My heart and soul.' She spoke with intensity, looking around. 'Did Gabe tell you it's a listed building?'

'Yes, he did. I can see how much care and attention have been paid to it. So, do you own part of all this?'

'No, I don't. As I said, I have my own house. I wouldn't have the kind of money needed to plough into this project.' Her tone indicated she didn't want to pursue the subject.

Maddox had made no mention of having a current partner, even when Swift had asked him, or her contribution to the renovation. He had referred to Stella only as his PA. Swift had the impression that he saw the place as his own domain. He wondered if Stella was aware of that and if so, how she felt about it. She had put a lot of effort into making a home she didn't own. He sensed a sadness, a tension lingering beneath her composure. He drank the last of his coffee. 'Presumably you know about the emails to Thomas and his grandfather?'

'Yes. I've seen the one Gabe received. It's unpleasant.'

'Any ideas?'

She sipped her coffee, shook her head. 'No, no ideas. I can't think of anyone we know who would want to do that.'

Swift's cushioned chair was deep and comfortable, with armrests. The sun had moved, leaving the kitchen in warm shade, just tiny stipples of light on the pots of sage and basil on the window ledge. Stella was gazing at the table. Like him, she sat very still. If felt as if they were mirroring each other.

'I understand that Mr Maddox ran into some opposition when he was developing the business and bought more land. That might have annoyed someone enough to get vicious.'

Her eyes were deep set, with a trace of pale blue make-up on the lids and tiny lines on the skin beneath. He put her in her mid-forties. She picked up a biscuit, then replaced it. Her nails were short, her hands square and large, jarring with the femininity of her dress. His observation had made her uneasy.

'Well, goodness, that was a while ago. It would be a long time for someone to bear a grudge.'

Swift changed tack. 'You have known Thomas a long time. Do you know of anyone he has crossed?'

'Thomas? Hardly likely. He's a shy man and very gentle. How could anyone dislike him?'

Swift thought that possibly his grandfather disliked him as well as loving him. 'He's very unlike his grandfather. I picked up on some friction.'

She fingered the scarf at her neck again. 'What family is without friction? It's true that they are very different, those two, but Gabe would do anything for Thomas. He really does love him.' She seemed to drift away for a moment, her brow wrinkling, and then continued. 'He would like him to live here again but Thomas won't agree. I think he's punishing himself by living in that awful caravan, doing penance for Oscar. He's lost everything: his baby, then his partner.'

'Maura? What is she like?'

Stella smiled. 'A dynamo — or she was, until Oscar was taken. I was, am, so fond of her but she drifted away from us after what happened. She and Gabe got on well. She used to trim his hair. She was so good for Thomas, she gave him direction and impetus, boosted his confidence. Of course, after Oscar went they were both in pieces. Thomas is so flat these days, and sad. That's partly the effect of the anti-depressants he takes. I don't think he should be using them for so long but his doctor keeps prescribing them. We don't hear from Maura now. I think she has another relationship and I expect the memories associated with us were too much for her.' She smoothed the belt of her dress. 'She isn't sending spiteful emails, if that's your angle. Maura's not a brooder. Do you think you'll be able to get to the bottom of it?'

Her perfume was light and floral. Swift was reminded of evening scents in a garden when the heat of the day has faded.

'Maybe,' he said.

'You're very economical with words and good at getting people to talk. Gabe said you have a sound reputation. You seem quietly confident. Are you married?'

'No. Almost, once.'

She nodded. 'I'm divorced. It still feels like a failure. Here comes Thomas. I'll fetch your contract.'

She kissed Thomas on the cheek as she glided past him. He nodded at Swift, running a hand through his hair.

'Sorry I was so long. I lost track of time. You've had coffee, then?'

'Yes, thanks. Are you having one?

'No, I'm fine. I don't drink it, it makes me jittery.'

Swift stood, put his mug on the tray and carried it to the grey marble worktop by the deep white sink. 'Maybe we could talk while we have a walk. I'd be interested in looking around, if that's okay.'

'Yeah, sure.'

Stella returned with the contract in an envelope. 'It's been good to meet you, Mr Swift.' She patted Thomas's shoulder.

* * *

It's good to have them guessing. On the hop. Sweet feeling.

The private investigator is an interesting move. I hadn't thought of that. But that's fine, makes it more of a challenge. Means they're really worried, watching their backs. Bide my time and see what this Swift is made of.

It's like catching fish. You cast a line now and again and wait for a bite. You start with little ones and then you land a big one.

Thomas was an easy catch. Too easy in a way but satisfying all the same. He's Gabe's Achilles heel. Good to get Gabe going now. The big man in the swanky home. Lord of the manor. King of all he surveys. Interesting web he's woven. Interesting games he's playing. Thinks he's untouchable, too smart to be caught out. Careful, Gabe. You might get rumbled. Gabe is where it all started.

Sometimes I laugh to myself in the dark. I lie in bed and the frame shakes as the ripples of laughter swim up through me. Tears of laughter. Hunting and snaring make me so happy. Better than hiding. Better than crying and sniffling in the night hours. I've spent enough years doing that, making sure my old man didn't hear me. 'Stop that bloody snivelling or you'll get a bloody good wallop!'

What would he make of me now? He always told me that I was a pathetic specimen. I wouldn't amount to anything. That was a laugh, looking at him with his face all covered in sores and his arms full of needle marks. Crawling around looking for the next fix. Towards the end I could smell him before I saw him.

The long, stinking years of childhood gave me lots of scope to practise my talents. Develop my style, my credibility, staying under the radar. Get a liking for the taste of revenge. All those little victories and the good feelings.

Other kids got given things. I had to take them for myself. When I was treated badly I made sure I got my own back. I started when I was seven, when my old man was too sozzled to look after me. That was my first care home and the cleaner couldn't work out where her purse had gone. There were foster carers whose pets died suddenly. Lots of wallets vanished along the way. A couple of social workers lost bracelets and rings. There were teachers who couldn't find their packed lunch, their briefcases, and their leather jackets. Stuff to eat, stuff to sell, money to buy food. That was something like happiness. That was feeling better.

My old man used to tell me it was a dog eat dog world. Well then, I'll be top dog.

I'm on a roll now. Even the old man would have to admit I've got this spot on. Bullseye. It's amazing how gullible people are. So easy to manipulate them. Pull the wool over their eyes. The secret is to smile, to lie and tell them what they want to hear.

I've got them doubting, looking around them. In the palm of my hand. Sweet.

CHAPTER 3

It was almost noon as Swift and Thomas Maddox stepped outside. The heat was growing and expanding. Thomas smelled sweetly acrid, a mixture of cleaning fluids and sweat. They went around the back of the windmill and along a narrow path to a tall wooden gate. On the other side was a wider gravel path flanked by large white stones, which led to the holiday site. The place was beautifully tended with some grassy areas filled with wildflowers. Shrubs, hedges and white wooden fences formed boundaries. Wooden benches and seats sat under trees with the odd picnic table and children's swing. Sprinklers sprayed on lawned areas, freshening the air. They walked in silence for a few minutes. Thomas seemed lost in his own thoughts.

'Tell me about your relationship with your grandfather.' Swift ran his fingers over a lavender bush, releasing its medicinal scent.

'He's been more like my dad, really. He can sound a bit abrupt and critical but he has always been kind to me when it matters. His bark is worse than his bite. I know I try his patience. He used to get cross with me when I was a child because I was always daydreaming. He's always on the move, wheeling and dealing, looking for opportunities. That's his element and he loves it. His energy is amazing. He's hoping to develop more holiday places like this one. He would have liked me to go into business with him but I haven't got what it takes. I am like my mum, apparently, she was a bit of a dreamer, head in the clouds. I see Gabe looking at me the way Maura does now, as if I'm someone he has to put up with in his life. I don't understand why Gabe's got one of these emails now. None of it makes any sense.'

They passed a long railway carriage, painted in red and gold and surrounded by ceramic pots of flowers with a hot tub to one side. Swift thought that Thomas must have found his grandfather hard going, especially when he was younger. He would be alarming and overwhelming to a sensitive child. Thomas had a generous, forgiving nature. Gabe Maddox was lucky in his grandson, even if he didn't know it.

'Who is this person who got upset with you at your work?' Swift asked.

Thomas stopped and bent to retie a lace. He had a tiny bald patch on the crown of his head. 'His name is Philip Asher. He was a client I helped. I hadn't been back at work long and I was out of the loop, still feeling my way. Philip was a dancer and he had a fall that left him with a brain injury and problems with walking and balance. I was working with him on a dispute he had with the council about adaptations to his flat. He made an allegation about me.' He sighed, and stopped again on the path. 'He said I kissed him and asked him for sex.'

'And did you?'

'No. I've never been attracted to men. He withdrew the allegation a couple of weeks after he made it. You know, I found him hard going from the minute I met him but I felt sorry for him because his career had been devastated overnight. I didn't realise how manipulative he is. I made the mistake of agreeing to meet him in a bar near where he lives. He was insistent, said he was lonely and his old friends didn't have time for him. He had a lot to drink, and then he tried to kiss me and wanted to hold my hand. I refused. He became nasty and aggressive, started shouting at me, saying I was prejudiced because he's disabled. I should never have agreed to meet him socially. The following week, he phoned my manager and made a complaint. I'd been suspended and an investigation had started, then Philip said it had all been a mistake.'

'So you kept your job.'

'Yes. I got a ticking off and had to go on a day's training about client boundaries. My manager discovered that Philip had made complaints about his GP and a nurse in the past and I think there was some other stuff as well. I was stupid. I know that. I had also stupidly given him my personal email and he did send angry emails to me and my manager but they stopped after he withdrew the complaint. My manager decided he should be directed to a different advocacy service. I assume he got a new advocate and went back to his battle with the council.'

'Have you still got the emails he sent you then?'

'No. I deleted them.'

'Did you tell him about Oscar?'

Thomas nodded. 'Another mistake. I was feeling down one day and he asked me if I was okay. He turned that against me as well, when he complained. He said I'd tried to burden him with my own problems when I should have been focusing on him.'

'He sounds a treat. He also sounds like a possible candidate for these emails.'

'I don't know. Philip can't focus on anything for long. I don't think he would have the ability to put those emails together, connect thoughts in that way. And I doubt he'd have the skill to anonymise them.'

Maybe not, Swift thought, but he might have found someone to do it for him. Manipulative people could be very persuasive. 'I'll need to talk to him given what you've told me,' he said. 'I'll look him up. You don't need to give me any other details about him. We don't want you in any more trouble at work. I would like to speak to your manager sometime, though. Just to see if there's any other background on Asher.'

Thomas looked relieved. 'Just so that you understand, his injuries have caused irritability and fatigue. You'll probably find him very difficult, but bear that in mind.'

They continued past the small whitewashed chapel and a wooded area of tree houses, then back along the river's edge towards the windmill. Their route took them near the car park, where half a dozen people were arriving and lifting cases. On the far side of the car park, a woman was putting something in a car boot. As she straightened, she saw Thomas and waved cheerily. He waved back. She got into the front passenger seat of the car, beside a man wearing a broad brimmed straw hat and sunglasses.

'That's April, one of our cleaners,' Thomas said. 'She's like a tornado when she gets going. I'll give you a lift to the station if you like. I have to get a few things in town.'

On the way to the station, Swift thought about the emails he had read, their teasing and allusions to the missing child. He guessed that there was more to the Maddox family than he had so far been told.

'You're not tempted to move back here to live?' he asked Thomas.

The young man drove with a tight grip on the steering wheel. 'No. Gabe is such a strong personality, so dominating. He can't help it, it's just the way he is. It took me a long time to get away from him and build some confidence. I don't want to go back to that. It would be the easy option but he'd take over and run my life for me. One of the reasons I miss Maura is that she acted as a kind of buffer between me and Gabe and now she's not there, I have to keep my independence.'

Swift was glad that Thomas had some backbone beneath the malleable appearance. 'I want to look into the protests over the land your grandfather bought. Any idea who I should contact?'

Thomas was pulling up outside the station. He yanked the handbrake and turned sideways, shielding his eyes with one hand. 'The woman who organised the protest is Sonia Gath. Thing is . . . can you go carefully there? She's Stella's daughter so it's all a bit problematic.'

'Stella's daughter! How does Stella manage that conflict?'

Thomas massaged the base of his thumb, kneading into it. Swift thought he must have been taught it as a stress reliever.

'I don't know. We don't talk about it. She looks upset sometimes but she doesn't discuss it with me. I suppose she and Gabe must talk it over.'

'Do you know Sonia?'

'I've met her. She's a very unpleasant person. Aggressive. Not a bit like Stella.' He put the car into gear, clearly not wanting to talk any more.

Swift bought a sandwich and a bottle of water while he waited for the train. Gabriel Maddox and Stella had failed to mention a family connection with the protest against him and yet they must realise that Swift would find out. Perhaps they didn't like dealing with the discomfort or just pretended the problem wasn't there. Swift contemplated the phrase, *we don't talk about it*; it usually meant that there was a minefield of family tensions to be explored.

* * *

Swift rose early, at six thirty, wanting to row before the heat of the day set in. He kept his boat at his rowing club, *Tamesas,* which was ten minutes from his house in Hammersmith. He ate a bowl of muesli, dressed in an old T-shirt and shorts, then walked fast through the empty streets, the light already bright enough to warrant sunglasses.

After a quick warm-up, he got on the water and sculled for about ten miles, slowly at first, then building speed and slicing through the calm, full river. His lungs filled with the fresh morning air and he felt the surge of wellbeing that the Thames always brought him. Rowing was his passion and his consolation. The long, rich history of the river and its fascinating wildlife put human striving and fretting into perspective. The river was living, ever changing and enduring. On this stretch, the tideway, it was enriched by the daily surge and ebb from the North Sea. He slowed down to watch a grey seal on the far bank, rolling and stretching. It looked fat and he guessed it was a pregnant cow, ready to pup in the autumn. The sky was turning from the palest mauve to deep blue as the sun burned away early mists. A swan stared at him angrily as he passed by, ruffling its wings in a wide arc. On the other side of the river, a passenger boat ploughed along. He slowed again, wiping sweat from his face. His boat rocked gently on the water as he ate a banana and had a drink. The long, ridged scar on his right thigh ached and started to tingle. He massaged it with a thumb, soothing it.

This morning, Ruth was taking Branna to have her hearing aids fitted. He was going to see his daughter again soon and he couldn't wait. He missed her. He tried not to think about the fact that Emlyn Taylor saw her every day. She would be used to his face and presence. Taylor had promised that he would not come between them and that Branna's welfare would always be a priority. Swift didn't trust the man or believe in his promises. Ruth had miscarried their own baby and now Taylor was sharing his home with another man's child. He had been subject to fits of anger before and might be again. His illness was savage, blighting his life, frustrating him and skewing his judgement. Swift worried about the sick man's unpredictability.

He fought off the bleakness creeping through him, taking deep breaths. As soon as Branna was old enough, he would bring her on the river, show her its treasures and mysteries and tell her about its history. He hoped it would captivate her the way it did him. He would tell her that once, over thirty million years ago, it was a tributary of the Rhine. Londoners had worshipped their ancient gods by it and Old Father Thames was its very own river god. Once a year, the river was blessed from London Bridge and it had been called 'a string of pearls' because it linked so many famous and wonderful places. He would sing *Sweet Thames, Flow Softly* to her. Suddenly he wondered if her deafness would affect her ability to sing. There were so many things he didn't know about hearing loss. He must educate himself, and fast.

He pulled his sunglasses down and raised his face to the sky, listening to the soft slap of the water against the boat. Thoughts of his child led to that other missing one. Thomas Maddox must spend hours wondering if his son was alive and hoping that if he was, the person who had him was being kind to him. Why would someone take the child and wait for nearly two years before sending emails? Possibly someone willing to play a long game and who derived satisfaction from holding all the cards. If that were the case, it would suggest a deep and bitter anger towards the Maddoxes. An anger that was intensely personal. He had thought about the gender of this emailer. The tone and style of the messages suggested a man and he decided to go with that gut feeling.

He glanced at his watch. He had an appointment to see DI Abby Cheng at eleven thirty and before he met her, he wanted to visit the street where Oscar had lived. He turned the boat and followed a flock of vivid green parakeets back towards Hammersmith.

* * *

The street where Oscar had been abducted was residential and quiet, just as Thomas had described. The houses were 1930s, semi-detached, substantial. It was mid-morning, there were no pedestrians and half a dozen parked cars. The air was exhausted and stewed. Swift could feel the heat of the pavement through the soles of his shoes. He looked at the porch where Oscar had been asleep in his pushchair. There were no gates to the houses and it would have taken only a minute or so to undo the baby's safety strap and carry him to a waiting car. Swift knocked at doors around the house where Thomas and his family had lived. There were no replies until he rang the bell of a red front door on the opposite side of the street. A middle-aged woman with a cheerful smile appeared and listened as Swift showed her his card and explained why he was calling.

'Were you living here two years ago?'

'I don't live here, my son and daughter-in law do. I helped them move in around then. The place was so dirty, you wouldn't believe it. I was busy with my rubber gloves. I used to see that man, Mr Maddox, with his baby. I didn't know him, as such, except to smile to. He seemed so nice. His wife, too. That little boy was never found, was he?'

'No.'

'Dreadful. You don't expect something like that to happen in this kind of neighbourhood. It worries you, wondering who might be prowling about. I know these days you read that most awful things happen in families but when I was young, we were taught about "stranger danger." It seemed as if it was a stranger who took that baby.'

'No one knows, even now.'

'Well, I was glad my son hadn't any children then, although they're expecting now.'

'Were you here the day Oscar was taken?'

She settled a hip against the doorframe. 'I was in the house here, vacuuming. That poor man hammered on the door, looking for his son. He was frantic, asking if I'd seen anything. I'm afraid I hadn't. I was upstairs, at the back. The police asked me as well. I made him a mug of tea and took it to him but he was so beside himself, he dropped it and the mug smashed. I've never seen a man so distraught.'

'You hadn't noticed anyone around in the days before?'

She shook her head. 'Sorry. I mean, you get people walking around, bits of traffic but nothing unusual. Of course, I was only visiting the area then so I wouldn't have known who was a local and who wasn't. I still don't, even though I come here frequently — that's a city for you, isn't it? And we were busy with comings and goings. It was awful around here for weeks after the baby had gone, with the press and TV hanging around. People didn't know what to say to the couple. What can you say? Is he alive, do you think, that little boy?'

'I don't know.'

'No . . . well . . . it doesn't bear thinking about.'

He left her a card and tried a few more doors with no success. He strolled to Wanstead Flats, where he was meeting Abby Cheng by one of the ponds, noting that there was a busy dual carriageway nearby. She was waiting for him as he approached.

'I got a shock when I first came to work here,' Abby Cheng told him. 'I had no idea I would see cows near the middle of London. Apparently, there are ancient grazing rights on the common land.'

They sat outside a café by one of the larger ponds on Wanstead Flats, and ordered coffee and muffins. A small herd of russet coloured cows grazed on the horizon. Nearby, a woman and her children were sailing a remote control model boat on the water. It surged and turned as they danced among the dry gorse and broom, shrieking with excitement.

'Thanks for meeting me,' Swift said. 'I gather you're not on duty this morning.'

DI Cheng was wearing jeans and a sleeveless blouse with flip-flops on her feet. Her glossy coal black hair was short and spiky, her eyes bright and darting, like a robin's. She seemed approachable and friendly, unlike some of his previous encounters with Met officers. There were quite a few who disliked sharing information with a private investigator and particularly one who had been one of their number. Also, his cousin Mary Adair was an Assistant Commissioner in the Met and if they found out, this often made officers wary, thinking that he was trading on a family connection.

'I'm on a late shift today,' she said. 'Good to be able to soak up some sun.'

'I've met Thomas Maddox and his grandfather, looked at the emails they've received and heard about Oscar. I've agreed to look into the situation.'

'I took over the Maddox case just a couple of months ago but I've read through the file and I spoke to Jon Stanmore, who was in charge of the original investigation. It's a serious failure for us that the child wasn't found.'

'Can you see any gaps from back then?'

She dusted crumbs from her fingers. 'I can't see that we missed anything and Jon has a sound reputation. We checked on missing children nationwide, looking for patterns. There were dozens of interviews: family, friends, neighbours, networks. We looked at records of paedophiles and similar crimes. CCTV was no help. There's a dual carriageway near where they lived and the nearest cameras weren't working. We thought Oscar must have been driven away to have vanished so completely and so fast and the carriageway provided a speedy exit.'

'Thomas Maddox mentioned a Suzy Mulligan. He said she was eliminated from enquiries but then visited Maura and upset her. Do you know anything about her?'

'I read that she was interviewed. She came across as a pathetic young woman. Lived in Forest Gate and was involved in petty crime with her brother. A couple of not very bright low lives who've been in trouble since they left the cradle. She'd had a stillbirth, a daughter when she was seventeen and she took a baby from a maternity unit a couple of months later. That was three years before Oscar vanished. Different kind of scenario and the baby was found within days because Suzy was showing her off to people — not the sharpest card in the pack. She'd looked after the baby well, within her abilities. She got a community sentence and had to see a psychiatrist. She was checked out but she didn't take Oscar. I didn't know she'd visited Maura Haskin.' Abby stretched her legs out, crossing her ankles. 'I'm not convinced that these emails are related to Oscar's disappearance. They allude to it but they're vague and anyone could easily find out about the abduction and use it if they've got a gripe. There was a lot of press coverage. Seems to me like someone has a grudge against the family, especially now the grandfather has received an email too. I talked to my guv'nor. He's up to his eyeballs in targets and spreadsheets as usual. He said that as long as I don't use too much of our budget, I can liaise with our techies to see if we can get information about the sender. It's not easy and it'll take time. We don't have that many IT specialists and they're busy.'

'You've seen all the emails received so far?' Swift flicked a tiny piece of the rather dry muffin to a sparrow who was loitering nearby.

'Yes. I spoke to Gabe and Thomas Maddox yesterday.'

'I just have a feeling that they *are* connected to Oscar,' he said.

'You know, when Oscar vanished we thought that a ransom demand might be made. The grandfather is a wealthy man. When none was forthcoming, it left the investigation stymied. The case was entered on HOLMES, so the information is out there. You used that when you were in the force?'

'Yes, several times.' It was the central database used by police across the UK to store and compare information about major incidents.

'Right. Well, any similar cases should draw attention. I checked it yesterday. Nothing. Complete blank. My brief is to keep a watchful eye and see what we can track with these emails but you know how busy we are and the statistics about this kind of abduction. It's likely that Oscar is dead and was murdered soon after he was taken.'

'What about the break-in before Oscar vanished, do you think that was linked?'

Abby sipped her latte. 'It was a theory at the time, that the abduction was planned. Someone prospecting and doing his or her homework. But there's no evidence, no fingerprints. It could have been a random snatch, someone driving along that road who saw Thomas leave Oscar outside. Random opportunism does happen, especially with kids. I read that Thomas Maddox talked about someone wanting to harm him and he told me more when I spoke to him. There's a record of some unfortunate things that happened to him. When we talked, he came across as a very nervous man. Some people do have bad luck; my grandfather used to say, "good fortune may forebode bad luck, which may in turn disguise good fortune." He managed to escape Chairman Mao but was then hit by a car near Leicester Square so I suppose he proved part of the proverb.'

Swift smiled at her dry humour. 'I believe in luck up to a point but listening to Thomas Maddox, his experiences could add up to someone intending him harm. Someone patient, wanting to watch him suffer, enjoying spinning out the punishment. Some of the references in the emails might support that.'

'You may be right. All I can say is that our investigation found nothing to link those previous events to Oscar. We cross referenced the accidents and thefts carefully. I understand that Thomas Maddox must feel desperate and people clutch at straws when they're in that state. The emails are unpleasant but there's no direct threat and they're probably from someone working out resentment. I'd say that Gabe Maddox has mixed it with quite a few people in his time. You or I could read up about Oscar's abduction and write those emails. I'm doing my best but I have to let the techies get on with their tracking. As usual, there aren't enough hours in the day.'

Swift could see that she was struggling to make headway with the Maddox case. He understood. Her workload would be immense and there would be cost and time restraints.

'How long have you been a private investigator?' Abby continued.

'A couple of years. I worked in the Met and then Interpol and I felt jaded. I was posted to investigating sex trafficking. The work was harrowing and often got no results. Plus I was stabbed in the leg during an investigation and enough was enough. My great-aunt left me her house so I decided to work for myself.'

'I read that you've had some good outcomes. You must have been an effective Met detective. It's a pity we lose people like you. Tenacious, determined.'

'That's kind of you. Not all Met officers are so well disposed to me.'

'Hmm, well, I've worked with a few plodders. Do you ever regret leaving?'

'Never. I choose my work. I go rowing when I want. I've had a few sporting injuries I could have done without, but then I was attacked when I was with Interpol so swings and roundabouts . . . The only thing I miss sometimes is being able to bounce ideas off colleagues. How long have you been in the force?'

'I joined at eighteen, so fourteen years. I want to work on a murder squad. Hoping to make DCI next year.'

He thought she might well make it. She was intelligent, articulate and confident. He shifted in the plastic chair and caught his breath as his lower back twinged. It had been tender since earlier in the year, when a brothel owner had kicked him, and he had pulled it earlier as he got out of his boat.

'Back pain?' Abby asked. 'The curse of the tall person.'

'Yes, it's not too bad. Partly an old injury and I twisted it this morning.'

'Go and see my brother, let him stick needles in you.'

He pressed his hand into his back. 'Your brother's an acupuncturist?'

'Jerry Cheng. He has a clinic in Pimlico. Works wonders, honest, and I should know, my people invented it. I'll send you Jerry's number.'

'I've never tried it, I might see him.' He got up carefully, gently flexing his hips.

'Let me know if anything interesting comes your way about the Maddox family. I don't like unsolved cases and I'm not too proud to refuse assistance from a private investigator.'

'Right. In the meantime, would you be able to get me an updated picture of how Oscar might look now? I presume you can access the technology.'

She grinned, her cheeks dimpling. 'I can see you're a man who likes to strike a deal. Okay, leave it with me.'

As he crossed the gorse and grass to the bus stop, he saw he had an email from Ruth. He stopped under the shade of an oak tree to read it.

Here we are with our new equipment with customised decoration. Branna was wonderful and made no fuss. What a girl. She kicked a lot just now when I spoke to her so I think the aids are already making a difference.

There was an attachment with a photograph of Branna wearing her tiny hearing aids. They looped around her neat ears, transparent plastic inset with blue and yellow stars. They didn't look as cumbersome for her as he had feared. He felt an overwhelming surge of sheer love. He rested a hand against the tree trunk for a moment, pressing into the coarse bark and then walked on.

* * *

Swift was driving to a baby-naming ceremony in Clerkenwell with Cedric Sheridan. The baby belonged to Swift's cousin Mary and her partner Simone. Cedric was his good friend and his sitting tenant, living on the top floor of the house in Hammersmith. Swift's great-aunt Lily had left him Cedric with the house, stipulating in her will that Cedric should live there as long as he wished. Cedric was in his late eighties but his upright posture, thick hair and insatiable curiosity about the world belied his age. He looked natty in a raspberry shirt and dark green linen suit. Swift was recycling the outfit he had worn to Mary and Simone's wedding — grey trousers, a shirt with a mandarin collar and a burgundy waistcoat. It was the most expensive clothing he possessed. Mary usually referred to his style as shabby chic because he often wore frayed shirts and jeans. He did appreciate quality fabrics and styling and knew the colours he liked. It was just that he rarely thought about shopping, except for food and rowing equipment. Kris Jelen had helped him choose the outfit. He could see the airy shop in Marylebone where she had led him and Cedric. She had already scouted the territory and knew what she was after. The waistcoat was a garment too many for the heat of the day but he knew that she would have said it completed the look and she had told him the colour complemented his eyes.

'Kris would approve of you wearing her choice.' Cedric echoed Swift's thoughts.

'I think so. She's the only woman who has ever chosen clothes for me. Hopefully it'll see me through social occasions for some time to come.'

They settled into a companionable silence. Swift thought of Kris, the way she blew her hair back from her forehead, her skill on her sewing machine, the incredibly sweet Polish desserts she prepared. She had failed to turn up for Mary and Simone's wedding the previous December and he had been angry with her, not knowing that she was lying strangled on the floor of her flat. Emlyn Taylor's trial was due to end soon. He was unlikely to receive a custodial sentence because of his ill health. At least the man who had squeezed the life from her body was behind bars.

Swift still felt a leaden sense of guilt about Kris's death. He had asked her out because he found her attractive and because Ruth had walked away from him again, not knowing that she was pregnant with Branna. Kris had been working as a waitress in the restaurant where he used to meet Ruth for lunch. After she died, he wondered if his motive for starting an involvement with her was because she was part of his context with Ruth. Kris had formed a link in a chain to her. The thought troubled him. Kris had died because she knew him and he would never forgive himself for that. He had known her for such a short while and at times, the relationship seemed unreal. Some nights she was there in his dreams and he would wake, confused. Then he would remember the faces of her anguished parents, sitting bewildered in a tatty room in a police station, struggling to understand what had happened to their daughter. She was gone, her body taken back to Lodz in Poland and buried there.

He became aware that Cedric was tapping his fingers on his knee and shifting in his seat.

'You okay there?' Swift asked.

'Hmm? Oh yes, yes. Actually, Ty, I've been thinking. I hardly ever use this car. I would like to give it to you. I'm sure you'd drive it regularly and there's little point in it sitting in a garage most of the time.'

'That's very generous, Cedric. But you could probably get a reasonable amount if you sold it.' It was four years old, a burnt-orange Mini Cooper convertible. Swift borrowed it sometimes when his work took him out of London, in return for doing odd jobs for Cedric.

'I don't need the money, dear boy. I'd rather you had the use of it. And I thought . . . now that you will want to see Branna regularly, you could get up and down to Brighton, buy a child seat and all the paraphernalia the young need these days.' He laughed. 'My mother used to bung me in a wicker basket in the back of her car. She had a Crossley tourer — they were all the rage at the time.'

Swift had been thinking that he might buy a car so Cedric's offer was timely and he liked driving the Mini. He wondered if Cedric's son, Oliver might object when he found out. Oliver was a surly character who paid infrequent visits to his father and usually only when he wanted money. Still, it was up to Cedric what he did with his belongings.

'If you're sure. Do you want to think about it?'

'I have thought. I am quite sure. We can sort out the paperwork. I have only one condition.'

'Which is?'

'That I meet Branna soon. It's a shame she couldn't come today.'

'I know. But she's only just been fitted with her hearing aids and Ruth thought a lot of people might be a bit overwhelming for her. Maybe she's being too protective, I don't know. I have to trust her judgement and I can understand that she worries. Why don't you come to Brighton with me next week?'

Cedric clapped his hands. 'Lovely. A seaside spin! I haven't been there for years. I used to take Oliver sometimes when he was little: a walk on the pier, a ride on the dodgems and ice cream. If only he was so easy to please now! Sometimes I think it can't have been good for him, having an older father. Maybe I was selfish, having a child in my fifties. His mother was so keen for a baby and I was too.'

Cedric's wife had left him and taken Oliver to live in France. She had been killed in a car accident many years later but Oliver had decided to blame his father for being an absent parent. Swift knew that Cedric harboured deep feelings of guilt about his son and dwelt on his failures as a father. Parenting was certainly tricky, although Mary and Simone seemed to have adapted to it with ease.

They lived on the top floor of a four-storey building that had been a Victorian workhouse. Their apartment had a wide balcony running the length of the property on which they grew flowers and vegetables in the summer. There were around thirty people gathered in the living room and on the balcony, sipping champagne and paying their respects to Louis, who was a big baby with a halo of dark hair and a benign expression.

Joyce, Swift's stepmother, was holding Louis to her cushiony bosom. She was a vision in a royal blue dress emblazoned with gaudy yellow roses. She beckoned vigorously to Swift as he accepted a glass of wine from his cousin. Mary laughed and nudged him.

'You've been summoned. Gird your loins.' She imitated Joyce's fluting voice: '*Oh Ty, now when are you going to find someone you can settle down with?*'

'Behave,' he told Mary sternly, smiling over at Joyce.

He approached her with his usual mixture of feelings. Guilt, because he didn't see her often enough, and touchiness because she always commented on his single status and asked him personal questions he disliked. Swift's mother had died when he was a teenager and Joyce had married his father not long after. She was a friendly, well-meaning, overwhelming woman who tried too hard and invaded Swift's space. When his father died, he found himself left with Joyce as an extra, uncomfortable family connection. It wasn't Joyce's fault that his mother had died too young and that she was alive. Yet he couldn't help occasional childish feelings of resentment. There she was living in the home he had grown up in. She had redecorated it in her own gaudy style and made it her own. His father had left the house in trust to him, with Joyce allowed to live in it until she remarried or on her death. That was fair but it didn't stop him feeling that she was usurping his mother's place. If Joyce was aware of this, she never showed it. It didn't help that she often expressed disappointment that he had given up an important career to take up private investigation. Despite his successes, she regarded it as a seedy, low status occupation.

'Ty, darling, it's been too long.' Joyce beamed up at him. 'But you're as handsome as ever! A sprinkling of silver at the temples, I see. Quite distinguished: a touch of the George Clooney.'

'Not as young as I used to be, Joyce. Hallo, little Louis.' He touched the baby's warm hand. Louis gave him a sleepy look and yawned.

'Isn't he gorgeous?' Joyce dropped her voice. 'I know it's not possible but I think he looks like Mary.'

Given that Louis had been conceived through sperm donation and Simone was his mother, this was indeed impossible.

'He's a muscular boy,' Swift said.

'Would you like to hold him?' Joyce promptly handed him the baby. 'But Tyrone, are you really all right? Your eyes look a little inflamed.'

'Hay fever. They'll settle down once autumn gets underway.'

Joyce stood on tiptoe to get a closer look. 'Have you tried honey?'

'Honey? Wouldn't that make my eyes even stickier?'

Joyce clicked her tongue. 'You eat the honey, silly. I've read that if you use honey produced locally to where you live, it can relieve allergic reactions. The pollen collected by the bees you see, like treating like. I believe it's called immunotherapy.'

'I haven't heard of it. I'll look into it.'

'You must take care of your health, especially now that you're a father with big responsibilities. And Branna, how is she? Mary told me about the audiology clinic.'

Louis was warmer than his daughter as well as heavier. He smelled of fabric softener whereas Branna smelled of milky biscuits. Swift would never have imagined that he would become attuned to baby aromas. 'Branna has hearing aids now, just got them. She's doing fine.'

'What a shame you couldn't bring her. And Ruth, is she coping?'

'As best she can.'

'Such a difficult, complicated situation, Ty. I do feel for you. All of that trouble with Ruth and that terrible business with Kris. You haven't had much luck with love, that's for sure. I wish some lovely woman would snap you up and look after you. Clara, one of my golf partners, has a gorgeous daughter, Rosie. She divorced a year ago and she would love to meet someone. She says it's difficult once you're in your late thirties because all the men are married, bitter after divorce or gay. She is highly intelligent, an economist. I thought that maybe you could both come to dinner. Just a small, informal affair, I know you don't like fuss. But you know, sometimes you do have to make your own luck.'

He found Joyce's earnest gaze and the way she patted his arm excruciating. The thought of being snapped up and looked after appalled him. He focused on Louis as if the baby might help but he had decided to doze. 'Maybe, we'll see. I hear you're going on a cruise soon,' he dodged deftly.

Joyce sighed. 'Oh, you're an impossible man, always well defended. Be careful, it can get lonely on the mountaintop. Yes, I'm looking forward to the cruise: the Rhine and the Danube. I'm going with a couple of friends from the golf club. You must come and see me when I get back and please bring Branna. I'm dying to meet her. I am her stepgran, after all.'

Mary appeared at his elbow and winked at him. 'Can I kidnap Louis? We're about to gather in the living room for the naming.'

It was a simple affair and touching. Simone and Mary read poems, and then Simone spoke about the choice of name. Swift knew that they had debated a number of options. He watched Simone, thinking that motherhood had improved her. She was a volatile, chippy person and they had crossed swords in the past. But since Louis's birth, she had mellowed and seemed more at ease with herself and the world. She brought a fervour to everything she did in life, whether it was her work as a forensic pathologist or motherhood. She still liked to bombard people with her opinions though. When she became pregnant, she started a blog about exercise and nutrition for expectant mothers. The last time Swift had seen her, she had held forth about baby routines and diet, advising him that setting bedtimes, awareness of baby's cues and carefully planned weaning were crucial.

'We decided on Louis to honour my grandfather of the same name,' Simone explained. 'He married my grandmother, who came here from Barbados, against the wishes of his white parents. They tried money and angry words to persuade him to leave her but he stood his ground. They disowned him and never spoke to him again after the marriage. Heaven knows what they would have made of me, their mixed heritage, gay great granddaughter.'

Mary laughed and raised her glass. 'Here's to tolerance and Louis and long may he prosper!'

They all raised their glasses and drank. Swift spoke to some of Mary's family and to Simone's brother, who was a chef and had provided delicious canapés. Simone quizzed him at length about Branna's deafness, asking him questions he didn't know the answers to, telling him about websites he had already consulted and offering reassurance he didn't want. She introduced him to a friend of hers called Tilda Harrison, a woman with an expressive smile and quick wit who made him laugh with her descriptions of her colleagues. Mary found him a while later on the balcony and hugged him. She was almost as tall as he was, and dear to him. They had sometimes been taken for brother and sister: both slim with dark curly hair. They had helped each other through life's trials. He put his arms around her and breathed in her sweet scent. She led him along the balcony to a tub of tomato plants and pulled a deep orange fruit for him.

'Try this. It's called Sun Sugar.'

The baby tomato was warm and burst sweetly on his tongue. 'Delicious.'

'I know. I can't stop eating them. As soon as I get home, I head for them and grab a handful. Next year I'll plant loads.' She handed him a couple more.

'I wasn't sure what a naming ceremony would be like,' he said. 'That was lovely and a moving story about Simone's grandfather.'

'In the end, Louis was the obvious choice, a fitting way of dealing with what was a terrible injustice in a family. It's hard to believe that parents could reject their own son in that way and deprive themselves of contact with their grandchildren. The irony is that they focused on their other son who did marry the "right" kind of woman but the marriage was childless. They must have had moments when they wished they had been less single minded. Simone says from what she's heard, they never expressed regret. They were the kind of people who go through life convinced that their beliefs are the right ones.'

'Sometimes I wouldn't mind not being troubled by doubts. Simone looks good, you both do. I can't help comparing how she looks to Ruth. She's got careworn and thin. I worry about her. She's very anxious with Branna, doesn't want to let her out of her sight and of course the hearing problem is an extra concern. I've asked to bring Branna to London for the weekend sometime soon but Ruth says she's too little. I do understand and she's her mother, she knows best.'

Mary nodded. 'Becoming a parent is overwhelming. Give it time. Maybe once her husband's trial is over life will settle a bit. She knows you're there, that's the main thing. Just hang on in and do what you can.'

'Sensible Mary.'

She slipped an arm around his waist. 'You've often been the voice of reason for me. Tell me, was Joyce trying to match make?'

'Of course. She was bigging up an economist called Rosie.'

'She means well.'

They smiled at each other and simultaneously spoke a phrase their Irish grandmother had been fond of: 'The road to hell is paved with good intentions.'

CHAPTER 4

Maura Haskin had told Swift she could meet him after work, around six o'clock. She lived now in a flat in Walthamstow, in a terrace just off the high street. The heat was building each day as August drew to a close, radiating from house bricks. The air grew stiller and drier as the temperature headed for ninety degrees. Weather forecasts spoke of the dominant Azores high and a sweltering plume of air from the continent, mixed with Saharan dust. Tabloid headlines screamed about soaring thermometers and a monster heatwave. In this busy, congested part of the city, the air was fume laden. Pedestrians moved slowly, clutching bottles of water and clinging to any tiny patches of shade.

Swift was early so he stopped at a tiny café selling freshly squeezed fruit juices and bought a lime and pineapple with ice, rolling it against his forehead and along the back of his neck before drinking it. He sat on one of the high stools by the window and phoned Cameron Blakemore, Thomas's manager at All about You. He explained his involvement and said he had found Philip Asher's details and was going to ring him.

'I know you'll be governed by data protection,' he said, 'but this stuff that Thomas Maddox and his grandfather are receiving is nasty. Is there anything you can tell me about Philip Asher?'

Blakemore sighed audibly. 'I can't share details about our organisation with you. Let's just say that I decided I didn't want our agency to continue working with Mr Asher when I found out some further information about him. He caused problems for some colleagues in the health sector. Malicious would cover it and that includes emails. Not anonymous, though. Also, I spoke to the manager of a dance company he worked with. He was involved in arguments and there was physical violence with another dancer. He left before they could sack him. He certainly leaves trouble in his wake.'

'Were the police ever involved?'

'Not that I know of. Since his accident, of course, professionals tend to give him the benefit of the doubt because he did sustain significant injuries.'

'Do you think he would be capable of planning and sending unpleasant emails?'

'Okay. Let me choose my words. I met him twice. I would say that although he is disabled, Mr Asher would pursue anyone he imagined he had a grievance against. Also, he is adept at getting others to encourage and help him. I'd say he is also susceptible to suggestion. I hope your meeting with him goes well.'

Swift thanked him and saw that he had an email from Nora Morrow.

Hallo from Dublin. My mother can't even lift a kettle for now so I am general housekeeper/nursing assistant/cook etc. I don't like to leave her on her own for long so am a bit stir crazy, although catching up on novels and teaching myself Pilates via YouTube. Shocked to find my mother cheats at cards. Send news from London. I see on the forecast that you are broiling. How is Branna and have you a juicy case I can help out with to keep my skills polished?

N

He had met Nora during a previous investigation. Earlier in the year, she had helped him and Cedric to assist a young Syrian woman, Yana Ayo, who had been living on the streets. She was a DI in the Met and they had mistimed acting on a mutual attraction — he distracted by Ruth, Nora getting together with a man who had eventually rejected her for a job in New York. Now she had taken a leave of absence and returned to Dublin for a while to care for her mother, who had had a hysterectomy and lived alone. Hearing from her lightened his mood. He thought of her easy, straightforward manner, her natty trademark string ties and quick, direct way of talking. He sent a brief reply:

Good to hear from you. On my way to an interview, will talk more later.

Ty

He finished his drink and left the café. It was rush hour and the pavements were thronged with long, weary queues at bus stops. Swift weaved along, waving away a woman who asked him if he had made a will, dodging a man collecting for amputees and stopping to stare in the window of an old-fashioned hardware shop where you could buy individual dusters, flypapers, metal buckets and mousetraps. Such places were rare and reminded him of visiting his grandmother in Ireland. She used to send him regularly to Kelly's emporium for a single candle, a wire brush, a twist of sugar in a small brown bag or one bar of unwrapped green soap. Kelly's had smelled of hen food, yeast and heating oil. He closed his eyes and could see himself standing there, money clutched in his hand. He had dreaded seeing Mrs Kelly, who had a whiskery chin and a booming voice. She was always there, elbows propped on the counter, holding court and chatting to women customers. She always commented on how tall he was growing. She would declare that people might mistake him for a girl because his curls were so long and her female audience would titter obligingly. Sometimes he thought that he let his hair grow bushy in defiance of Mrs Kelly's gibes.

He paused to look at a vegetable stall, admiring the jewel colours of peppers, stacks of plantains and yams, piles of root ginger and bunches of coconuts and okra. Reggae music thumped from an open window, almost drowning the hooting and screeching of traffic. A man leaned out, his dreadlocks hanging over the windowsill, smoking a spliff. The sun flashed and struck light splinters on the mirrors in the window of a bathroom fitter. He heard a couple of women speaking French. He was reasonably fluent and listened as they discussed the Somalian restaurant they were going to visit that evening. He sought sanctuary from the heat and clamour in an air-conditioned bookshop where he browsed through a paperback about ocean rowing and was hooked enough to buy it.

When Maura Haskin answered his ring, he thought she looked like a pint sized Cleopatra, a petite woman with gold streaked straight black hair, cut level with her chin and a thick fringe above dark eyebrows. Her heavy eye shadow and liner couldn't conceal the unhappiness in her gaze. She took his outstretched hand in both of hers.

'I'm so glad you've got involved. I hope you can help us.'

He had heard that intensity, that awful hope in voices before. 'I hope I can,' he answered gravely.

She lived in a first floor flat and he followed her up the narrow stairs.

'I'm warning you, my place smells of fish. I'm starving, didn't have time for lunch so I just pinged a haddock pie in the microwave. Hope you don't mind if I eat as we talk.'

He said that was fine with him. The fish smelled pungent in the small flat, which had a galley kitchen opening on to the living room. A vase of pink and white roses gave off a musky scent that mingled strangely with the haddock. He watched as Maura tore the top off her pie, grabbed a fork and sat down next to him. She wore a striped shirt over a black skirt and gold and jade bangles that chimed on her arm as she raised her fork. She took a mouthful of food and sighed.

'Run off your feet today?' Swift asked.

'Tell me about it. My junior called in sick with flu. Who gets flu in this weather? I started at eight and only had time for a coffee and a biscuit at one. I had two complicated jobs, a colouring and a straightener. They took ages. Then a woman came in, saying she wanted a Kate Middleton style but complained it wasn't as full and glossy as the princess's was when I finished. Well, I'm pretty good at my job but I'm not a magician and she had such thin, lank hair, it was a struggle.'

'What did you do?'

'Put a load more volumising spray in it. It'll go flat as a pancake when she washes it. Ugh, I'm sure I just swallowed a tiny bone. That's not on in a fish pie, is it?'

He agreed it wasn't as she forked through the rest of the meal, checking suspiciously for bones, then eating rapidly but leaving it unfinished. He had never seen anyone demolish food so fast yet with so little enjoyment.

'That was nothing to write home about,' she said. 'Fancy a glass of wine? I've got a white in the fridge and I'm gasping for one now.'

He said he would. She had a charming smile and a confiding way of talking, as if he was an old friend. He thought this must be useful in her trade and wondered if it was her natural style or if she had cultivated it. Her feet were bare and nut brown, her toenails painted alternately gold and silver. As she handed him a large glass of wine, her tiny gold earrings swung from side to side and he saw that they were Egyptian-style and looked like a queen's profile.

'I only know two Egyptian queens,' he said. 'Hatshepsut and Nefertiti — which is on your earrings?'

'Nefertiti. Clever of you to notice. I suppose you would, though, being a detective. If I dropped one at the scene of a crime it would be a clue.'

He smiled and sipped his wine. It was light and not too sweet.

'I'm into Egyptian stuff at the moment.' Maura took a deep draught of wine and sighed softly. 'I like trying out different styles and it interests the customers.'

'That reminds me a bit of Gabriel Maddox, with his windmill and different eras on each floor.'

'How is Gabe? Haven't seen him for ages.'

'He seemed okay.'

'And Stella? I miss Stella. She was a bit like a mum to me, really kind. My mum's dead so it was nice to have someone like her around.'

'Stella is fine. Gabe had an email similar to the ones Thomas received.'

'Yes, Thomas rang to tell me. I'm so relieved Gabe has taken you on. Maybe, you know, maybe you'll find something out.' The light vanished from her face as her thoughts turned to her son.

'I'm sorry about what happened to Oscar.'

She took another drink and nodded. 'Yes. My Oscar.' She seemed to dwindle in her chair, her voice dropping. 'My perfect little Oscar. I still wake up in the night thinking I can hear him. I've read that mothers can identify their own baby's voice from birth and I could hear his in the hospital. They put him in a little side nursery because I had to have stitches but I knew it was him the minute he cried. I could never leave him crying, like some parents do. It would have seemed so cruel, letting a helpless baby stay upset. I used to put him in a sling while I did the housework, keep him snug against me.' She placed a hand against her heart. 'I work long hours to get through and make life bearable. When I'm working, I don't think about him, at least not too often.' She gestured at her face. 'The make-up's a distraction, it fills the time, thinking about it and putting it on. I imagine that it's gluing me together. Sometimes I don't know how I stay sane. I mean, how can I paint my face and sit and eat and drink when I don't know where my boy is? Ross says I work too hard but that's what helps me.'

'Who is Ross?'

'He's my partner. My lifebelt. He's helped me so much. I was thinking about suicide when I met him. You know, reading about ways to do it. I wanted to stop the pain.' She ran a finger around the rim of her glass. 'Ross just kept talking to me, made me realise I had to keep hope alive. I wish sometimes that Thomas could meet someone new, someone he could confide in and rely on. He still rings me, almost every week, wanting to talk about Oscar and I wish he wouldn't, I can't bear it. Sometimes Ross is here and it feels awkward. I know Thomas is grieving. I know he wants me to say I forgive him and I can't. I suppose that sounds awful.'

'It's how you feel.'

'I feel sorry for him but I don't want to see him and talking is hard. It brings back the anger, churns it all up. He still wants me to advise him. I do sometimes. I told him not to go back and live with Gabe, or work for him. I knew that would be disastrous for Thomas. Gabe is such a strong personality. Anyway, you don't want to hear my troubles. Another glass?'

'I'm fine with this. I'm fine with you talking, too.'

She had put the bottle inside a cooler on the coffee table. She poured herself another. 'What do you make of the emails? Do you think they're anything to do with Oscar?'

'I don't know at this stage, it's too early. Do you know of anyone who would want to hurt Thomas or his grandfather?'

The dark make-up made her eyes look bruised. 'I don't. It's not me, I can assure you.'

He believed her. She had an emotional candour that didn't fit with the taunting messages. 'What about these strange things that have happened to Thomas? Some of those took place while you were together?'

She nodded. 'They were upsetting and they seemed odd. I could never work out if he was having a lot of bad luck or if something else was going on. He used to get really down about it but why would someone do all that for so long before sending these emails? It doesn't make any sense. I know Gabe had some run-ins with protesters down in High Hawksford. People got very angry although I can't see why that would involve Thomas, except that he helps out there. I suppose you'll look into that?'

'Yes. I understand that Stella Gath's daughter led the protest. That's complicated.'

Maura held her feet out and flexed her toes. 'My pins ache, standing all day. Most hairdressers end up with varicose veins or neck problems. Sonia, that's Stella's daughter. She's a keen environmentalist, all about being green and saving the planet. I met her just the once and that was once too often but I know there's no love lost between her and Gabe.'

'Tell me more about when you saw her.'

Maura pulled a face. 'It was soon after Oscar was born. We had taken him to the windmill one weekend for a visit. I was with Thomas and Oscar in Tunbridge Wells doing some shopping when Sonia barged up to us. She started shouting at Thomas, saying he should be ashamed of his family, making money by destroying nature. Oscar was frightened by the noise and started crying so I moved away. People were staring and Sonia was shoving leaflets at them while she ranted at Thomas. In the end, he walked away. He was shaking. We were both upset. Sonia had a stall in the town centre with a petition for people to sign so we abandoned the shopping and went back to High

Hawksford. Thomas told Gabe about it and he just laughed, said Sonia was a nutter, fit for the funny farm. Stella wasn't there that day which was just as well. Sonia has always refused on principle to go to the windmill and it must be hard for Stella, being piggy in the middle. She's a lovely woman. Too good for Gabe.'

'I thought you got on well with Gabe? Stella said you did.'

She yawned. 'I did. We don't have much contact now. Life has changed. We always hit it off but I didn't have any illusions about him. Stella is devoted to him and he knows that and trades on it. Don't get me wrong, I think he genuinely loves her but I don't think one woman would ever be enough for Gabe. I'm pretty sure he plays away.' She sat up. 'Maybe that's who you're looking for, a scorned woman out for revenge. I have thought about who took Oscar and I hoped it was a woman. I don't know why that idea helps but it does. I suppose I think a woman would be kinder although I know that's not necessarily true, from the awful things I read sometimes. You know, that awful woman, Rose something . . .' She clenched her hands together.

'I think you mean Rosemary West.'

'That's it. The things she did. She was a monster.'

'It's probably best not to speculate, although I know that's very hard. Do you know for a fact that Gabe had other relationships?'

She shifted in her chair, pulling her skirt down. 'There's something I could tell you but I wouldn't want Stella or Thomas to know. It would be hurtful and it's water under the bridge and nothing to do with the emails or anything.'

Swift finished his wine. He wanted another but put the glass down. 'Okay, I understand. Go on.'

'One time when I was at the windmill with Thomas, a couple of months after we met, Gabe made a grab at me when we were alone in the kitchen and kissed me. Tongue in mouth job, too. I mean, my boyfriend's grandad! It was Christmas time and we'd both had a drink but I was furious.'

'What happened?'

'I smacked his face. He apologised straightaway, said he'd had one too many and he was out of order. Told me I was right to smack him and offered to let me do it again so we ended up laughing. He never tried anything on again but I saw him flirting with female guests around the place now and then. He just seems like that kind of man. A bit of a peacock, you know. Very figure conscious, gets his hair dyed, and wears contact lenses to make his eyes that lovely sea green. He never likes to be reminded of his age.' She fiddled with an earring. 'Gabe's used to always getting his own way. He's so persuasive. I reckon he could sell seawater to sailors. He's one of those people who thinks he calls all the shots in life.'

'And does he, usually?'

'Yes, I'd say so. He's been very successful. He's wealthy and has a beautiful home. He snaps his fingers and things happen. I don't mean to speak badly about him. After that one incident, he was always kind and considerate to me. Probably kinder to me than he is to Thomas. They rub each other up the wrong way and Gabe gets cross with him. I know he only wants the best for Thomas but he's too full on sometimes, a bit of a bully.'

'You don't know of anyone else Gabe Maddox might have annoyed?'

'No, although of course I've only seen him now and again. There's his father, he fell out with him years ago and never contacts him but I don't think a man in his nineties would be sending horrible emails to his son and great grandson.' She reached out to fill her glass again.

'Gabe Maddox's father is alive?'

'Yes, Wilfrid. He's ancient. I don't know where he lives. I never met him. Thomas is fond of him and visits him sometimes but Gabe doesn't know that. Talk about secrets!'

Swift filed that away for further consideration. He felt himself slouching in the heat and straightened up. He heard his back click. 'I don't want to upset you but can I take you back to the weeks after Oscar was taken? I understand that a woman called Suzy Mulligan visited you after the police had spoken to her. Could you tell me about that?'

Maura shook her head. 'Oh, that poor woman. It did upset me but she was in a right state. She told me about what she'd done, taking a baby from the hospital after hers was born dead. She was so distressed, saying she hadn't been in her right mind at the time and she would never have taken another child. She said she had to find me and see me because she couldn't bear to think I suspected her. She was a tiny, thin little thing. Sad looking. I think she still wasn't mentally stable when she came to our door. We ended up crying our eyes out together. The police said she had nothing to do with it.'

He said nothing, thinking that it would be worth checking her again. It seemed odd and insensitive that she had sought Maura out. A woman was calling Maura's name from below on the street. She went to the open window and raised a thumb.

'That's Pru. She lives downstairs and she's always locking herself out. I won't be a minute.'

She rummaged in a jar on the kitchen counter and found a set of keys, then vanished downstairs. Swift thought about what she'd said concerning the other, more senior Maddox. He was interested in what the family were failing to tell him.

The room was close and hot. He stood, pulling his shirt from his body, pressing his lower back and rotating his hips. Maura's chairs were thinly upholstered and hard. He looked around at the neat, spick and span room. It was unfussy, painted in a matt, pale pink with a dark red carpet.

There was a pile of hairdressing and celebrity gossip magazines on the coffee table. A collection of green and yellow glass bottles stood on a wall shelf and a semi-circle of large blue and orange silk fans hung around the opening to the kitchen. There were no photographs or books and very little evidence of Maura's personality in the room. Neither was there any sign of a masculine presence. Swift sat again, wincing.

'The forecast says tomorrow's going to be the hottest day for ten years.' Maura came back in and slumped in her chair. She took a magazine and flicked it in front of her face. 'I keep meaning to buy a fan. Ross said he'll get one when he's back.'

'Ross doesn't live here?'

'No, not all the time. He stays with his dad in Bromley but he travels a lot for his work so he's often away. We're planning to buy a place together in a while. I rent this flat and my lease runs for another year. I see him a couple of evenings a week, depending on his work. We talk on the phone every day.' She glanced at her watch. 'He rings about eight.'

He saw her expression brightening as she anticipated the call. 'I won't keep you much longer. Can you tell me why Gabriel Maddox and his father don't talk?'

'I don't know any details and Thomas always steered clear of the subject. He visits his great grandfather now and again but I had to promise never to mention it to Gabe. They're a funny bunch. I expect Thomas will tell you more if you promise not to discuss it with Gabe.'

She went to drain the wine bottle into her glass, and then stopped herself. 'I mustn't have any more. Ross tells me off if I overdo it, says alcohol can be a depressant and that's the last thing I need.'

'He has a point. It can be such a comfort as well, though. Too comforting sometimes.'

She nodded. 'Like a comfort blanket. Oscar had one, white and gold with tigers on. He was always clutching it.

It vanished with him. I do console myself with that. He had it with him, something familiar. I wonder if the person who took him realised that and knew it might help keep him quiet. I've still got some of his things. I suppose some people might think it's morbid but I had to keep them. I take them out now and again, when I'm on my own.' She rose and opened a cupboard next to the window, lifting out a white wicker box. She sat with it on her lap and took out some of the contents: a couple of soft toys, an old-fashioned rattle, a cloth book, a lemon and blue baby grow, a white sunhat and a photo album. She pressed the baby grow to her face. 'This was in the laundry basket when he was taken. I never washed it. It smells of Oscar.'

He couldn't speak, just looked at her hands stroking the cloth. Branna's distinctive smell was already so familiar to him. He knew that even when he was an old man he would recall it.

She opened the photo album and looked at a couple of pages. 'You might think it's funny that I haven't got any pictures of Oscar around the place. I just can't bear it. It's too hard, being reminded of him. Here, would you like to look?'

She offered Swift the album and he took it, turning through the pages. Dozens of photos of the little boy during his first six months: in his cot, in his pushchair, in the arms of his parents, with Gabe and Stella at the windmill, playing with cuddly toys. He looked content.

Maura welled up and rubbed her eyes. 'Don't mind me, it's the tiredness and the wine and this bloody nonstop heat.'

He handed back the album and sat quietly as she reached for a tissue and blew her nose. She sniffed resolutely, carefully replacing the items in the box and putting it on the floor beside her chair.

'I know why I keep going, why I get up and go to work, why I bother to eat and don't swallow a bottle of pills,' she said softly. 'It's because I hope that one day

Oscar will be back with me and I have to be ready for him. I have to wait patiently and keep well so that I can look after him and make up for the time we've missed. I know I have to hang on in there.'

'I'm glad you feel like that.'

'Thanks. You're kind. You used to be in the police, Thomas said. You have a policeman's eyes.'

'What are those?'

'Oh, you know, watchful, steady. Don't give anything away. Oh, ignore me, I'm blabbing on.'

Swift thought she needed peace and quiet after a long, hot day on her feet. He rose. 'I will let you know if I find anything hopeful.'

'Thanks.' She stood, her eyes still misted. 'I hate this endless summer. I want it to be winter, hard and cold. Dark, frosty nights so I can go to bed early and leave the world outside.'

He knew that feeling. It was how he had felt when Ruth left him. As he went back out into the evening glare, he could still see Maura's Cleopatra eyes, the heavy make-up failing to conceal the haunting sorrow.

* * *

Swift was in the cool shade of his basement office early the next morning. Great-aunt Lily had been a chiropractor and had used the basement of her house as a treatment room. She had occasionally worked on Swift's back for him, when it had suffered from strenuous rowing. Her long, sinewy fingers had prodded and stretched bones and muscle, easing out the aches. Friends had pointed out that if he refurbished the basement, he could rent it out at an astronomical rate but he preferred to keep his self-employment records down there as well as using it for the occasional client meeting. That way, he maintained some barrier between his job and the rest of his life.

Thomas Maddox rang just as he settled at his desk, planning to review and make notes on what he had learned about the Maddox case to date. He felt that so far, he had no grip on who might be behind the emails, never mind Oscar's abduction. Thomas sounded tearful.

'Gabe's been attacked. He says he reckons it was random, just bad luck but I don't think so. I have that feeling about it, the one I've had before. A feeling of dread. I'm sure it's the same person.'

'Did he tell you what happened?'

'It was last night. He was taking an evening walk down one of the lanes near the windmill. Someone came at him out of the trees. He's got cuts and bruises, he says. Told me not to make a fuss.'

'Have the police been involved?'

'I don't know. It was Stella who called to tell me. Gabe was getting annoyed, said we were making too much of it.'

'Okay, I'll call him.'

'It's the same person, isn't it?'

'Possibly. Let me talk to your grandfather. Keep looking after your own security in the meantime. By the way, I need your great grandfather's address.'

A pause. 'How do you know about him?'

'From Maura. I believe you visit him.'

'Yes but . . .'

'I know, Gabe doesn't know about the visits. Look, Thomas, if you're serious about engaging me and you want me to make progress you have to tell me things. I can't work with people who conceal information. I have to talk to all your family members because whatever the reason is for these incidents, I believe it lies in your family. Do you understand?'

'Yes, okay. Do you want me to come and see Gramps with you?'

'No, I'd rather talk to him alone. How old is he?'

'Ninety-three. His sight is a bit poor.'

'Let me guess — you don't know why he and your grandfather don't communicate.'

'No, neither of them will say. Whatever happened, it was years ago, when I was little. I know that Gramps was at my christening because he's got a photo so it was some time after that. I started visiting him when I was in my teens. He lives on his own and I wanted to make sure that he was okay. I get on well with him.'

'And just to check, Thomas, I do now know about all your family members? You haven't anyone else in a cupboard or anyone you've forgotten to mention?'

'That's everyone. Sorry about not telling you before. I don't like getting on the wrong side of Gabe. It's like treading on eggshells.'

Swift took a phone number and address for Wilfrid Maddox. So many people in this extended family not speaking, disapproving of one another, avoiding questions and telling one another things. Gabe Maddox was at the centre of it all — a powerful, dominant man with a sharp tongue, pulling strings, throwing his weight around, causing dissension. A man who tried his luck with women without any qualms. Swift had a hunch that whatever was going on here, Gabe Maddox was somehow at the root of it. He was about to ring him when he saw that Gabe had just forwarded another email:

Hi Thomas and Gabe, the cosy Maddox family. Life has been comfy and secure for you both. Not recently though. You must wonder what might happen next. You might run a tidy little empire, Gabe, but I wonder if the foundations are crumbling? As for you, Thomas. You haven't amounted to much in the end, have you? A bit of a disappointment to your old grandad. He must think you haven't cut the mustard. You'll be forwarding these emails to your detective.

Hallo, Mr Swift. I expect you'll have spoken to Maura by now. Working your way through the cast of players. There I am, waiting in the wings. When will I make my next appearance?

Swift had wondered if the emailer would engage with him. He had thought it likely. The man was angry, manipulative and attention seeking. There was something about the bragging tone that indicated a need of acknowledgement. It might prove a useful weakness. He wouldn't respond. That would hopefully irritate him and frustrate the game. He called Gabe Maddox who sounded tetchy.

'You've seen the new email?'

'Yes, but first of all tell me about last night. Thomas rang me. You were attacked?'

'Oh, you don't need to be involved in that,' he snapped. 'It was some young druggie, I expect. Came up behind me from the edge of the lane, punched me in the back and on my ear and nicked a couple of fivers from my back pocket once I hit the ground. Luckily, I hadn't taken my wallet or phone out with me. I was just breathing the evening air for half an hour.'

'Do you walk that route regularly?'

'Now and again. Look, I know Thomas thinks this is our emailer but I don't agree. It was an opportunist. There are awful problems with drug dealing around here, especially since the scuzzy eastern Europeans started sneaking in. Those Romanians are the pits. And bored youth, apparently. Some young bloke needing his fix and mugging a guy. When I was young I was always too busy grafting to get bored.'

'It was a man? Did you see him?'

'I'm sure it was a bloke but no, I didn't see him. It all happened too fast and he ran off once he had the money.'

'Are you badly injured?'

'Nope. My vanity hurts the most. I've got a cut on my nose and bruises where I fell. I got checked out. And no, I haven't told the police. Waste of time and I've a full diary this week.'

'You should report it.'

'No point. There are regular stories in the local papers about drug related muggings. The police are overwhelmed as it is. At least the bastard didn't get much for his trouble.

Now, you don't need to waste any more of my time or your own on this. I'll take more care when and where I walk. What do you make of this latest email?'

'More of the same. More insults and power play. He's trying to start a conversation with me, too. I won't respond and make sure you don't either.'

'Hmm. Bloody bastard.'

'I want to speak to Sonia Gath. I've left a message for her. You didn't mention her name, or that she's Stella's daughter.'

'I assumed Stella or Thomas would tell you. She's completely loopy, that young woman, but I don't think she's got anything to do with this garbage.'

'Why is that?'

'Oh, you know, she's virtuous, principled, high-minded. She'd want to lecture me face to face about the error of my greedy capitalist ways, not sneak around.'

'There is something else you didn't mention. Your father, Wilfrid Maddox.'

'My father! What's he got to do with anything?'

'I don't know. Possibly nothing. But it's always helpful to have a full family picture.'

Maddox's tone grew cold and flinty. 'My old man is probably gaga by now. He's irrelevant. I don't see him. And before you ask why not, we had a falling out a long time ago that has nothing to do with this. I have another call coming in. Keep me posted. I want to hear as soon as you think you know anything.'

Gabe Maddox was being evasive but Swift had no idea why. He wasn't convinced that last night's attack was a mugging. You didn't usually employ a private investigator if you had things to hide. He brewed a coffee and gathered his thoughts.

There was an insistent *coo coo* from pigeons who roosted on top of the chimney pot and occasionally threw twigs and seeds down into the fireplace. The noise was louder in the sitting room but travelled down the flue to the unused grate in the basement. Sometimes he liked the background babbling, at other times it irritated him and he went into the garden and clapped his hands loudly. This morning they were annoying him but he tried to blank out the sound.

He sat with his coffee and ran his hands through his hair. Time to recap and sift. Swift knew the first law of forensic science: *every contact leaves a trace*. This was harder to decipher with email but no one could write without revealing something about themselves. He wanted to think about the purpose of the emails and what they divulged about the author. He printed them all, laid them out on his desk in chronological order, and read them again. Then he read them aloud, listening to the tone and nuances. He printed off the events timeline that Thomas had sent him, sipped his coffee and made notes. First of all, he listed what he knew, deciding to give the sender an identity that suited the activity. He chose W for the Watcher. Then he continued to what he didn't know:

What is the mistreatment W refers to?

How real is all this — harassment and annoyance or serious intent?

Who is the real object of the emails — Thomas or Gabe?

He sat back and listened to the pigeons, and then looked up contact details for Sonia Gath and Philip Asher and made calls. Sonia's phone went to voicemail. A man, deep voiced, answered Asher's number.

'Yes.'

'Is that Philip Asher?'

'Yes.'

'Hallo. My name is Tyrone Swift and I'm a private investigator.'

'Yes.'

There was no intonation. He wondered how damaged the man was and if he could sustain a conversation. He seemed to have communicated well enough with Thomas Maddox and his employer. Swift explained why he was calling and asked if he could arrange a meeting with Asher in person.

'Why?'

'As I mentioned, Thomas Maddox has had some worrying emails and I would just like to check a few things out with you.'

'You accusing *me*?'

'No. It would just help to meet you.'

'I don't have to meet you. I know my rights. I don't have to talk to anyone.' He spoke slowly and suspiciously, with pauses.

'No, you don't have to meet me.'

There was a tapping on the other end of the line and the faint drone of a radio or television in the background.

'I don't know. I need to take advice. I don't want to be taken advantage of. I'm a vulnerable person. You do know that, don't you?'

'Okay, I understand. I'll call back in a couple of days for your decision.'

'Yes. I have to be careful. People twist things that I say and tell lies about me. I've had bad experiences. People try to pull the wool over my eyes. I will consult my advisor.'

'I have no intention of—' The line went dead. He wasn't hopeful about obtaining an interview with Philip Asher. The man sounded paranoid.

He opened his laptop and emailed Nora Morrow, copying and pasting the Watcher's emails to her.

Hi Nora, me again. I don't want a good brain going rusty so tell me what you think of these emails. It's a case I'm working on. Anonymous emails have been sent to grandfather and grandson, separately at first and now simultaneously. Grandson's child was abducted two and a half years ago and I think there's a connection. Any insights about the sender are welcome.

Hope your mother is well soon. Branna is okay but I have yet to see her sporting her new hearing aids.

Ty

He finished the dregs of his cold coffee as a large twig and clumps of moss fell down the chimney. He decided that the pigeons were due to find another roost.

* * *

When my old man died, it was the happiest day of my life so far. I can still remember the surge of pleasure when I saw him lying on the filthy floor, needle stuck in his arm, cold as cold. Gone to the great drug den in the sky. Oh, joy. Oh, hallebloodylujah.

I'd helped him on his way. Doubled his dosage for him when he wasn't looking. Nobody suspected. Another druggie gone. They overdosed every day. Good riddance. I was devastated, sobbing for my dad. The policewoman put her arms around me. She smelled of roses, made me a cup of tea. I got the most sympathy in my life then.

The freedom. The relief. It was as if I was breathing properly for the first time.

But there are other days now that are almost as happy. Soon there might be an explosion of happiness. The anticipation is almost too much.

The best times of the day are when I've eaten a good meal and I'm full, contented. My old man always kept me hungry. Spent the money on drugs and booze. I used to cry from hunger pains. That doctor who found that I had rickets had been amazed. He said it was a nineteenth-century illness. They diagnosed the rickets the first time they took me away from my old man. But they always gave me back when he turned on the charm, promised to reform. I've inherited that. The charm, the easy smile, the way with words.

Even in this heat, I love warming foods that sit comfortingly inside me. They blot out the memories of hunger for a while. They have to be healthy, though. No more pies, pastries, tins, crisps and chips. The scummy, fatty low cost crap my old man bought and fed to me. Some tinned stuff he gave me looked and tasted like dog food. Probably was. That would have been his idea of a laugh.

I love steaming, fragrant curries, bowls of pasta, hearty soups, casseroles, fish stews, and big piles of vegetables. I fill up in restaurants on my own when I want to treat myself and think. That's when I plan, when I've eaten well of good food and feel snug inside. Then I've got energy and my mind starts ticking, thinking of the best games to play.

Time to play a new card. Gabe will understand. He must have some inkling already. But he won't know who. How long will he hold out for? He thinks his money has bought him peace of mind.

Wrong.

CHAPTER 5

Swift was in the garden with Cedric, who was strimming the edges of the tiny lawn. He was telling Swift that the pigeons had kept him awake the previous night.

'It sounded as if they were tap dancing on the roof, dear boy. Still, I suppose they have to have their fun.'

They both looked up at a plump bird perched on the chimney pot. It shifted from one foot to the other, glanced downwards and then soared away. Cedric pushed his straw hat back and laughed.

Swift shaded his eyes. 'I wonder if I could climb up there and erect a bird scarer?'

'I'm not sure pigeons are that easily put off. They like human company, you know. I read a while ago that they mate for life and they're very intelligent. They can identify themselves in a mirror and a researcher trained one to differentiate between a Monet and a Picasso. Then of course, there is the amazing heroism of carrier pigeons in the world wars . . .'

'Now you're making me feel guilty. The pigeons tormenting us just want to be our friends?'

Cedric smiled. 'I'm not suggesting you invite them for dinner.'

They sat for a while on the old cushioned swing seat, rocking gently. The sky was cloudless, a perfect azure. Cedric used his hat as a fan. He was wearing lilac Bermuda shorts and a blue and red T-shirt patterned with yellow bees. The flower borders looked dusty but Cedric weeded regularly and kept them watered. Lily had planted most of the shrubs, roses and perennials. This year Cedric, who loved bold colours, had grown bright pink salvias that reminded Swift of lipstick, butterscotch and orange dahlias, yellow, white and blue daisies and claret penstemons.

'I really should make jam but it's hard, finding the energy to do much in this heat,' Cedric said. 'Milo is coming round later and he's bringing damsons so I will have to crank myself up.'

'One of my favourite jams so if you need a taster . . .'

Milo was one of Cedric's oldest friends, a small bent man who walked like a tortoise, with two sticks. Swift was always amazed that he managed to make it up to Cedric's flat. They often listened to jazz and played dominoes late into the night, the sound of their laughter drifting down the stairs. Sometimes, if his mood was low, they made Swift feel as if he was the older man, listening to the juveniles having fun above.

'Have you seen anything of Nora since she was here last?' Cedric asked lightly.

'No, but I have heard from her. She's in Dublin for a while, looking after her mother.'

'Ah. She will be coming back, though?'

'That's her plan.'

'Well, good. Such a smart, warm woman. Now, I must get on and make sure my jam jars are clean. Then I must tidy Lily's roses or she'll return and haunt me, prod me with her secateurs in my dreams. I do love that pink tea rose. It's so delicate.'

Swift made a cheese sandwich and coffee and brought them into the garden. Nigel, next door's cat appeared immediately, lured by the smell of food. He was indulged and fat and sat near Swift's foot, blinking.

'You're not getting any of this. It's calorific and you're too plump,' Swift told him.

Nigel gave his light grey fur a cursory lick, and then fixed his gaze once again on the food. Swift's phone rang and he saw that it was Ruth.

'I just thought I'd let you know that Emlyn's trial finished yesterday. He got a heavy fine and he's been disbarred.' She sounded exhausted, terse.

Swift felt satisfaction and pain. The pleasure, if it could be called that, was strongest. He would have preferred it if Taylor had been sent to prison. He deserved it for the suffering he had caused. But being disbarred would be a heavy blow to his professional pride, even if his illness meant that practising law was now effectively over for him anyway. 'I'm glad for you that it's finished.'

'Yes.'

'How are you and Branna?'

'Okay.'

'You don't sound it.'

Her voice cracked and he heard her swallow. 'I'm so tired all the time. Branna's getting on well with her hearing aids, though. They don't seem to bother her.'

'That's good. I've looked into an online British Sign Language course in baby signing. It teaches key signs for babies and recommends starting them around Branna's age. There's useful advice about how to proceed. I thought I could send you a link, and then we can both learn the same signs. It says to do them one at a time so we can reinforce them.'

'Oh, hmm. Look, I'm too tired to do any of that stuff at the moment.'

'It's important to start it soon, Ruth, and we need to work together to help her. You can do it a couple of minutes at a time whenever you can. It's no big deal. Baby steps, almost.'

His attempt at humour fell flat. 'Don't hassle me, Ty. I'm not up to it. You do what you want.'

He was taken aback by her irritability and listlessness. He waited a beat. 'Is it okay to send you the link?'

'If you want. Listen, Olwen, Emlyn's mother is coming to stay for a while from tomorrow, to help me out. I just wanted to let you know. Emlyn had another chest infection and I've been feeling down. She offered to come and help so I said yes. I can't wait for her to get here now.'

'Okay. You get on well with her?'

'She's all right. Likes everything shipshape. Her medical knowledge comes in handy — she used to be a GP. I'd have preferred my own mum but she's still working so you know . . .'

'And does Olwen like babies?'

'I haven't bloody interviewed her and taken up references,' Ruth snapped. 'She made an offer and I was glad to accept it. See you Friday.'

He threw the phone down. Yet another member of the Taylor family having care of his daughter. He could feel his connection to Ruth weakening and didn't know what to do. It was important that they worked as a team for Branna, yet Ruth seemed far away and disengaged. The half-eaten sandwich lay on a plate on his lap. He had no appetite now. He tore a piece off and put it on the ground. Nigel approached, sniffed and licked it, then leaped back over the fence. Swift chucked it into the flower border for the birds or foxes to find.

* * *

Swift was now the official owner of the Mini Cooper. He drove to Tunbridge Wells with the roof open, making the most of the hot breeze, listening to Lou Reed singing about a perfect day. He found a parking space near the common and made his way to the prosperous town along the cobbled streets. Sonia Gath's address was in a road of tall Georgian houses, some of which had seen better days. Her basement flat had chipped wrought iron railings at pavement level, with a bike padlocked to them. Steep steps led down past a barred window to a scarred wooden door. Arching above it was a canopied porch with wind chimes suspended from it. The paving slabs were cracked and sprouting weeds.

A barefoot, thin man with a narrow face, wild hair and a wispy moustache answered the door. He gestured with a thumb for Swift to enter, calling, 'It's Maddox's lackey to see you.'

Swift went down a dingy, quarry-tiled hallway, past a huge poster of the earth photographed from space with the message, *Be the Change You Want to See.* He entered a small living room, which was dim and painted a pale green below ornate, cracked cornices and a ceiling with interesting bulges. It was lined with shelves and cupboards full of pieces of driftwood and metal, stacks of shells, stones, pebbles, broken pots, coins, fossils, jewellery, shards of glass, clumps of seaweed and strange looking sponges. A huge old farmhouse style table and dining chairs occupied the centre of the room on bare, tar coloured floorboards. At the end of the table, facing the room stood a tall ship's masthead. A tarnished, bronze and silver carved face and torso of a bearded man wearing a horned helmet. There was no other furniture. In the filtered, greenish light, the place resembled an underwater cavern. A woman sat at the table, sorting through a bowl of objects, a crab shell in her hand.

'Hallo. You're the private investigator?'

'That's right. Tyrone Swift.'

'Have a chair. Want some tea? We have mint or rosehip.' Her voice was smooth and resonant.

'Just water, thanks.'

'This is Jed Clifford. Jed, could you get our investigator a glass of water and I'll have a rosehip?'

Jed stood in the doorway, hitching low-slung jeans over his slender hips.

'Investigator! Maddox's snooper more like.' He vanished back through the door.

'Your friend doesn't seem to like me,' Swift said.

'Jed? He's not that keen on anyone except me. He's suspicious by nature. That can be useful although sometimes it's a drag.'

She smiled. She was striking, with long, cinnamon brown hair rippling down to her waist. Her eyebrows were dark and thick against her pale, luminous skin and her eyes were silvery grey. She was tall and big boned but lean and wearing an ivory sleeveless dress with glittering threads. A necklace made of sharks' teeth and shells was strung around her long neck. Swift thought of a mermaid beneath the waves, examining her ocean treasures. She bore little resemblance to her mother.

'Have you been beachcombing?' Swift examined a large, snail-shaped ammonite lying near him.

'That's right. We trawl the Kent coast, reclaiming what the sea has thrown up. We turn all this stuff into jewellery, sculptures and collages and sell them for ridiculous prices to well-heeled tourists who visit "*Royal* Tunbridge Wells" to soak up a bit of gentility. They're dying to be parted from their cash so we oblige them. All money for the cause.'

'The cause?'

'Saving the planet. Our label is the Sentinel Studio, if you want to buy any of our things in town. So, what brings you calling on us?'

'Gabe and Thomas Maddox have received some anonymous, unpleasant emails. They've asked me to look into it. I'm interested in anyone who might have had differences with them.'

Jed had brought in a tray of drinks and stood behind Sonia. 'You saying it's us?'

'No.'

'Sounds like it to me. Typical of slimy Maddox to send a flunky instead of fronting it out himself.'

Swift gave him a long, level look and he blushed a fiery, mottled red.

'It's okay, Jed, like I've told you before, save your energy for important battles. Sit down.' Sonia passed a chipped glass of water to Swift and took her tea, which was in a beautiful china cup with a broken handle. His chair had a loose strut and rocked when he moved. He wondered if they made a virtue of living with damaged things.

Jed sniffed, pulled a chair out and sat sideways on it, arms folded, a foot swinging. Despite the intense heat of the day, the room felt damp and there was a smell of mould and glue.

'I wondered if you could tell me about your protest against Gabe Maddox a while ago. I understand you lost that battle.'

Sonia gave him a quick, keen glance and picked a pink and cream shell out of the bowl, turning it over. 'Our group is called The Sentinels. We organised a protest and a petition. Maddox had bought a field adjoining his shitty holiday camp. He had browbeaten the old guy who owned it to sell it to him so he could cover it with sham Native American wigwams or whatever. He wanted to remove some hedgerows and he needed permission from the council to do that. We monitor planning applications and when we saw what he wanted to do, we mobilised.'

'The hedgerow was the important issue?'

Jed had been fingering his moustache. It reminded Swift of sprouting seeds. He sat up as if electrified. 'Important? Critical!' he said. 'Have you any idea how absolutely crucial hedgerows are to the environment?'

'I have some idea, yes.'

Jed continued as if Swift hadn't spoken. 'The hedgerows around that field contained hazel, ash and oak, honeysuckle and dog roses and were several centuries old.

Maddox wanted to rip them up for his theme park. He doesn't give a toss for biodiversity or the need to conserve and protect the soil. He's all about lining his own pocket.'

'Also, the hedgerows were home to all kinds of wildlife: butterflies, hedgehogs, dormice, birds including blue tits and whitethroats and a vital resource for honeybees,' Sonia added.

'I understand. But the council didn't?'

Sonia shrugged and threw her hair back over her shoulders. Her necklace shifted and settled in the hollow of her throat. 'Gabe Maddox had some of the councillors in his pocket. Enough of them to swing it his way.'

'How do you know that? It's a serious allegation.'

'We have our intelligence about the old boys' network,' Jed said. 'We couldn't prove it, though. The bastards closed ranks. Typical bureaucrats and fat cats, dodging and weaving, having their little meetings behind closed doors. They might hold all the cards for now but one day we'll have them.'

Sonia smiled again. She had a complacent expression, as if something amused her. 'We occupied the field when the diggers moved in. We were arrested and cautioned. I hope the people polluting that land now in their yurts and tipis are ashamed that they've helped destroy another part of our precious planet.'

Swift doubted that the holidaymakers would be aware of their crime. He looked at the posters on the wall opposite him, all with images of the earth and *Join The Sentinels* above the messages: *Stop Consuming, Start Sustaining*; *Forget Yourself and Share*; *One Life. One Planet. Make it Matter.*

'I haven't heard of The Sentinels. Are you part of a national organisation?'

Sonia shook her head vigorously, her hair swaying. 'No, we're local, just a small group, non-hierarchical. I started it a while ago. We prefer that focus. Start in your own backyard, that's our motto.'

'How many of you are there?'

'A new member just joined, making twenty-seven.'

'Kent is the garden of England but if bastards like Maddox and his cronies get their way, it will become a dustbin.' Jed rapped the table hard, making it shudder. 'He calls that holiday camp "Smell the Roses" but he's got to be joking. There won't be any roses left when people like him have finished. Those greedy parasites need to be taught respect for the land. Everything is about money for them. Money and profit. Everything has to have a value. They're predators, sucking our lifeblood. They want to paralyse us and make us powerless and they do it with their deals, their whispers behind closed doors. There are more of them than of us but we know we'll win in the end.'

Sonia ran her long fingers through the bowl and picked out a black and white shard of marble, which she set to one side. She exuded an unruffled self-possession while Jed was all heat and fervour. Yet Swift recalled Maura describing Sonia's shouting and aggression in the street. She had a switch that could be flicked. He thought he would try pressing it.

'The protest against Gabe Maddox can't have been easy for you, Sonia, given that your mother is his partner.'

'Nothing worth fighting for is easy,' she said coolly.

'But your mother must have been upset. She would feel mixed emotions. So would you, surely. It would be divisive.' He watched her carefully as she blew sand from a shell.

'My mother lives her own life and I live mine. She decided to start a relationship with a man she knew I would despise. If she chooses to be a handmaiden and a doormat for Gabe Maddox, that's up to her. I guess she likes social climbing, playing lady bountiful and brown-nosing the Freemasons and Rotarians, inviting them round for pre-dinner drinkies and her efforts at haute cuisine. Pathetic and sad. She embarrasses herself. It's all a pose. As you can tell, I don't have mixed emotions, they're quite clear. I don't see much of her so no, there was no big drama. Sorry to disappoint you.'

Jed sniggered and gave her a thumbs up. 'Your mum needs her head examined, shacking up with that old goat, running his errands. And he's revolting, trying to look young and cool, backcombing his thinning hair. Who'd want to sleep with that?'

Swift thought Sonia looked irritated by those comments but she said nothing and carried on with her sifting in the bowl. Despite her self-possession, he thought that she was embarrassed about her mother. Stella was living with the enemy and apparently in it for the long haul.

'Have you had any further run-ins with Maddox or his grandson?' Swift finished his water and leaned on the table. His chair groaned dangerously.

'No. We've been working on other important projects in the area: threatened woodland and a plan for a new supermarket so that more greed and consumption can be encouraged. If you're interested, I can give you pamphlets and you can sign the petitions. You could make a donation.'

Sonia sounded playful. She opened her eyes wide, challenging him. He ignored her.

'Do you both work as well as being Sentinels and selling your beach art?'

'We work part time, just to make enough to live on while we do our real job, protecting the environment. I work in a wholefoods shop and Jed's in IT.'

'You're pretty expert with computers then?' Swift asked him.

'Yep. I know my stuff.' He cracked his knuckles. 'I run our website and all our online petitions and calls to arms on social media. I could probably hack government websites if I wanted, see what crimes they're planning against our land, our water and our air, get the drop on them. I monitor some of the big agribusiness and biotech corporations with their intensive lobbying and spin. The ruling class, the carbon barons and the big corporations think they've got the little people on the run but they're mistaken. We can explode their secrets and conspiracies. We're going to show them. We're coming after them and they won't see us until it's too late.'

Jed became more truculent and boastful as he talked, pointing a finger, shifting on his chair. If either of them realised the possible relevance of Jed's IT skills, they showed no sign. Sonia looked a little bored and Swift wondered what their relationship was like. It seemed to him that Sonia was much more sophisticated than her partner. He was a callow and raw young man, the kind who would have found something else to preach about if he hadn't joined The Sentinels. Anger clearly bubbled very close to the surface with him.

'Do you both know about Oscar Maddox?' he asked.

'Of course,' Sonia said. 'Sad. Very sad. Why do you ask?'

'He was abducted not long before your protest against Gabe.'

'So?' Jed asked belligerently. 'What's that got to do with us?'

'The person emailing the Maddoxes seems to refer to Oscar.'

Sonia shrugged and Jed looked at the floor.

'Are either of you responsible for these emails?'

They glanced at each other. Sonia sipped her tea, tapping a finger against the base of the cup.

'No, we're not,' she said. 'Not our style at all.'

'We're too busy with our work to bother with that creep Maddox now,' Jed added. 'We put in long hours, we have to focus.'

Swift didn't think he was going to get any further with them so he took his leave. Jed showed him to the door, his reedy, insistent voice carrying in the silence.

'This burning heat, it's all to do with global warming, you know. We've messed with nature and now nature's messing with us. You have to respect, not exploit. That's the message we're trying to get across to people. If we abuse our atmosphere, we'll be repaid with harmful cosmic radiation. I bet you drove here today, didn't you?'

Swift turned. 'I did.'

'An electric car?'

'No, petrol.'

Jed bounced on the balls of his feet. 'You see! I bet you never thought of what you were doing to the planet, the toxic emissions from your engine polluting the air, the carbon dioxide, the use of resources like oil. Your choices matter, that's what you have to realise. At least if you'd taken the train you'd have—'

Swift put his hands up, palms forward. 'You make some good points but sadly, your delivery isn't selling it to me. You say a lot that I agree with but berating people is counterproductive. You know the saying: *You catch more flies with honey than with vinegar.*'

He took the steps up two at a time and made his way back into the town. Being harangued was tiring. He passed a shop selling paintings and crafts and noticed a label, *Sentinel Studio* on a large amateurish collage of birds in flight made from shells. It was priced at £150. He laughed and carried on. He stopped at a café for a tuna salad and a coffee and sat at a window table, watching shoppers plod past. As he ate, he thought about Sonia, Jed, and the dynamic between them. She wound him up and set him going, used him as an attack dog. She struck him as a woman who would be capable of doing anything she put her mind to, including sending anonymous emails. But she might well get Jed to do it and she would have had access to the background information about the Maddox men. There was something about that little smile she indulged in, as if she had an edge and was enjoying the power. Those emails also expressed pleasure in having the upper hand. And Jed. He was bright, articulate, a lover of conspiracy theory and very angry. If his bragging was true, he was skilled with computers. And yet . . . they seemed unlikely child abductors. Maybe he was wrong in his gut feeling that the Watcher and the abduction were linked. He needed to keep an open mind.

Swift took out his phone and found The Sentinels website. It was attractive and cleanly designed. There were clear links to follow about conservation, pollution, energy, green living and climate change. Jed Clifford ran a blog on it with daily posts. That day's was headlined *Stop Making Excuses* and pointed out the ways in which energy was wasted. It was forceful and well written.

His phone rang and he saw that it was Stella Gath.

'Hallo, Mr Swift. I wondered . . . have you got a minute?' Her voice was quiet and nervous.

'Yes. Are you okay?'

'Oh, yes, it's just that . . . well, this is going to sound very odd but I think we've had a break-in.'

'Have you called the police?'

'No. You see, there's no sign of an actual intruder and nothing has been taken. Gabe said to leave well alone.'

'I don't understand.'

'Nothing was stolen. Quite the opposite. Something has been left here. Gabe said I'm worrying unnecessarily but it seems so odd . . .'

Swift thought he could do with talking to Stella again anyway. 'Is Gabe there?'

'No. He had to go to Cardiff for a meeting.'

That worked for him. 'Look, I'm in Tunbridge at the moment. I can be with you in about twenty minutes.'

'Oh, I see. Yes, thank you that would be a relief.'

* * *

She was in a cream and apricot belted dress today, with little sprigs of orange flowers bordering the neck and hem. He wondered if she always wore these full-skirted dresses and if so, where she bought them. He knew more about women's outfits since his time with Kris Jelen. Kris had run her own business, making and selling fifties type clothes and had explained the different styles, cuts and materials to him. That was how he knew that Stella's dress had a swing skirt and shawl collar.

He smelled coffee as she opened the door and watched as she went through her steady routine with mugs, tray and biscuits in the kitchen. He imagined that whatever drama might occur, Stella would have a calm hand on the cafetiere. Her only sign of tension was an occasional tug of her right ear lobe. One of the worktops was crowded with food in various stages of preparation. A large duck was sitting in a roasting tray, surrounded by onions and there were tomatoes on a chopping board. The whisks of a food processor were covered with a glistening white foam. The oven was humming gently. He could see meringues cooking through the glass door.

'Tell me what's made you anxious.' He took his coffee.

She poured milk into her cup, catching the drip from the jug on her finger. 'It's most peculiar. I was up first this morning, about 7 a.m. I came down to make tea. When I went to raise the blinds, I saw these on the kitchen table. They weren't there late last night. I've no idea where they came from but someone has put them there.'

She led him to the table. On it lay half a dozen large green ferns. Their undersides had been spray painted silver. They had been fanned out on a white serving dish, their stems crossed.

'Have you moved them at all?'

'No. The dish is ours. It was on the kitchen counter. I called Gabe. I thought maybe he'd placed them there although it seemed unlikely because he went to bed before me last night. He was as baffled as I was. We checked all the doors and windows. There was no sign of anyone breaking in and as far as we can see, nothing has been taken.'

'You don't have an alarm?'

'We've never thought it was necessary. It's so quiet and safe around here. Gabe asked me to get the locks changed. I've called a locksmith, it will be done today.'

'Who has keys to the property?'

'Myself, Gabe and Thomas. We keep a spare set in a drawer in Gabe's office and they're still there. I phoned Thomas and he confirmed that he has his keys so there are none missing.'

Swift took a photograph of the ferns with his phone. 'Do ferns have any significance for you or Gabe?'

She shook her head. 'They mean nothing. There are plenty growing near the river. I wanted to call the police but Gabe said it would be wasting their time. He said it must be some kind of practical joke. He had to rush off to his meeting and he told me to throw them away. But . . . I don't know, I find it unsettling. A person has been in here without our knowledge, joker or not. They could get in again. I decided to call you.'

She pulled out a chair, her skirt billowing, and he sat with her. She had a tiny brooch in the shape of a seahorse on the bodice of her dress.

'Is your brooch from the Sentinel Studio?'

She touched it. Her tone became distant. 'Yes. I bought it in town. Is that why you're down here, because you were seeing Sonia?'

'Yes. I met her and Jed Clifford this morning. You didn't tell me that your daughter led the protest about the field Gabe bought.'

Her discomfort was palpable. He felt for her but he didn't like being misled.

'It's difficult, Mr Swift. Sonia is a strong-minded person. She had already taken against Gabe before the protest. Apparently, she detests him. She has certain values and beliefs and she disapproves of my relationship.' She looked upwards and shook her head. 'She has always refused to come here or participate in any way with our life. When I got together with Gabe, she moved out of my house and rented that horrible flat. I'm sure the damp is bad for her health. I suppose I didn't want to admit that my own child has taken against me. Rejects me. Cares nothing for me.'

For the first time, he heard bitterness in her voice. She took a tissue from her pocket and rubbed at a speck of grease on the table. He watched the graceful turn of her head and the supple movement of her bare shoulder and arm. The soft, dimpled skin above her elbow was the colour of almonds. He recalled the way she had caught the drip of milk from the jug on her finger. Time seemed to slow and for a moment, he was mesmerised. A ping from his phone brought him back to reality. He looked at the ferns again, thinking that Sonia might be able to access her mother's keys or copy them.

'How often do you see Sonia? Does she visit you at your house?'

'Very rarely and not for a long time now. I used to call at her flat but not anymore. I never felt welcome and I don't see why I should make the effort. One-way traffic. She makes me feel surplus to requirements.' She gave an odd laugh. 'Since she met Jed, he's always hanging around her. He's a peculiar young man, moody and irritable. Quite troubled, I think. I find him hard to talk to. I gather that he had a difficult childhood and was in juvenile court once. Mind you, even if I saw Sonia I don't suppose there would be much for us to talk about. Not now, certainly. No, not now. It's hard, being estranged but maybe it's for the best. I have a son but he lives with his wife in Italy and I don't see much of him. When I look back, I see that Sonia was always critical of me, even when she was quite young. My ex-husband was a critic. I could do nothing right for him. I suppose she picked it up from him. She has always been closer to him. He lives in Chichester now and she sees him regularly.' Her tone was sharp suddenly, her gaze distant. 'Sonia has said such appalling things about Gabe. I know that some people think that he uses me. He's always told me that he appreciates what I do. He is unfailingly kind and praises me to the skies. After years of unhappiness and loneliness, it was lovely to be called someone's star.' She spoke haltingly, as if struggling to express her thoughts. 'We all forgive people things if we love them. Try to understand their actions. I read recently about a woman who took her husband back even though he'd cheated on her with her best friend and stolen from her. I suppose she preferred the devil she knew to being alone. We all want to be cherished, don't we?'

She seemed to be appealing for his validation of her life with Gabe Maddox. He hardly knew her, yet what he did know suggested that Maddox might well be trading on her generosity and if Maura was correct, cheating on her. Her vulnerability got under his skin. He drew back in his chair.

'It's good to be cherished, yes.'

She gave a little nod, noting his unwillingness to comment. 'I don't know why I want your good opinion.'

'You don't need it. You know yourself and what you need in life.'

'Oh, sometimes I wonder about that.'

He thought she was about to say more but she pressed her lips together. He drew the plate with the ferns towards him and studied it again. 'There are interesting echoes here. Thomas had a break-in at his home after Oscar was born but nothing was taken. Thomas also left Oscar in the porch on the day he was abducted because the street was quiet and safe, just as you believed your home here is. Whoever left these is making you feel uncertain and worried. The emails seek to have the same impact. All of these acts are alarming intrusions.'

'You think the person who is sending the emails left these?'

'Probably.'

She moved around the table, stroking the edge with her fingertips, then crossed to the oven, checked the meringues and turned the cooker off, leaving the oven door slightly open. As she came back, she gestured at the duck.

'We're having a dinner party tonight for some business colleagues. I'm making duck ragout and raspberry and mango Pavlova.'

'You enjoy cooking?'

'Oh yes, it's a real pleasure. I went on a weeklong course on classic cuisine a couple of years ago and I had such a good time. Gabe bought it for me as a Christmas present. I lose myself in cooking, forget about everything else. Gabe loves my meals.'

'He's a lucky man. I hope he knows it.'

She looked pensive and tugged at her ear lobe. 'I wonder. He says he does but words are easy, aren't they? Words and actions have to match. I don't understand why Gabe isn't more worried by this break-in. He was so dismissive. Just as he was about the mugging in the lane. Do you think I should call the police?'

'I think it would be advisable, given everything that's happened. But it's Gabe's decision. The police would check for fingerprints but my guess is they wouldn't find any except yours and Gabe's. They'd tell you to get an alarm system, which would be sound advice.' It was a good question, though — why was Gabe Maddox so unworried by the mugging and the apparent break-in.

'I'll talk to Gabe later about an alarm. Do you think I should tell him I've spoken to you? I don't want him to feel that I'm fussing.'

She was standing in front of the window, the sunlight casting a peach glow on her face and neck. Again, he felt as if she was making some kind of appeal to him.

'Of course you should tell him. And tell him my thoughts. I think you should keep the ferns. Put them in a plastic bag, seal it, and wear rubber gloves. Just in case they might be evidence at any time.' He stood and regarded her. The more he got to know her and Gabe Maddox, the more he thought she deserved better. She was making do with crumbs from Gabe's table for the lack of anything else. 'Stella, sometimes you seem a little sad. As if something is burdening you.'

She swallowed and shook her head. 'Oh, you know, things have been tense for a while, what with Oscar's abduction, the emails and now this. It's a lot to think about. A lot to deal with.' She saw him to the door. 'Thank you for coming. I don't feel so anxious now.'

Halfway out, he turned to her. 'Have you ever met Gabe's father?'

She held the doorframe. 'No. They're even more estranged than Sonia and me, if that's possible. Gabe never refers to him. I've tried asking about him but Gabe's silence is as unyielding as this timber.' She tapped the robust door with her knuckles.

Leaving the windmill, he drove a little way along the road, wondering why someone had gone to the bother of entering their home to leave a strange gift. He stopped the car in a patch of shade and googled green and silver ferns. He saw immediately that they were a native fern of New Zealand, a much-loved symbol of the country and appeared on many icons. The silver underside glowed at night and was used to track forest paths. Maori people had often used them for bedding. He rang Thomas Maddox and asked if the family had any New Zealand connections.

'No. Not as far as I know. Why? Is this to do with the break-in at the windmill?'

He explained about the ferns and their significance in New Zealand. 'I'll check with your grandfather.'

He read an email from Abby Cheng, who had attached an age progressed image of a two-and-a-half-year-old Oscar Maddox. The image showed a boy with wide caramel eyes and his mother's curving mouth. He wondered if Thomas and Maura would like copies or if the sight of their lost son would be too much to bear.

CHAPTER 6

Swift and Cedric had taken Branna for a stroll along Brighton seafront and up and down the pier, and were now having lunch in a café, where Ruth would come to pick her up. Swift could tell Cedric had been shocked by Ruth's appearance when she dropped Branna off. She was hollow eyed and skinny, her face drawn. Swift was even more worried by the fact that she avoided his eye. She seemed closed off and in a hurry to leave them. He tried to focus on his daughter but Ruth's haggard expression nagged at him.

He sat, holding Branna while Cedric placed their order. The tiny hearing aids looked surprisingly jolly and he was sure that she was more alert and responsive as he chatted to her. Her hands waved and she pursed her lips, grabbing at his hair when he bent to kiss her. He had been practising his first attempts at the sign language he was learning. The advice was to start with everyday signs one at a time. He had decided on milk, more, eat and drink. He brought out her bottle and made the sign for milk, maintaining eye contact, shaking the bottle and saying the word. Branna blinked at him and he took this as meaning that she understood. He gave her the bottle and she glugged away happily.

'She's gorgeous,' Cedric said. 'She has your observant eyes.'

'I was told recently that I have a policeman's eyes so I'm not sure how she's going to turn out.'

Swift could tell that Cedric was dying to hold her,." so he handed her over with her bottle and sipped his coffee. It was good to be in the relief of the shade after the powerful sun. He thought about the winter and the complications of taking his daughter out in cold weather. Imagined having to sit in the car with her and watch the sea. He would be like those part time fathers he noticed loitering in museums, cafés and parks at weekends with their children, finding things to do to fill the time. He wondered if Ruth was depressed and if so, if she was getting any medical help. It was difficult to talk to her because she was so withdrawn and tetchy. She had made no comment about the sign language link he had sent her and he didn't like to broach the subject again so soon. Cedric was rubbing Branna's back and he forced himself to concentrate on her. This time was precious. He shouldn't be wasting it worrying. He took her bare feet and nibbled her toes, telling her they tasted delicious.

Half an hour before Ruth was due, a lean, stringy woman with a brisk manner and short grey hair like a helmet appeared at their table.

'Good afternoon. I am Olwen Taylor. I've come to collect Branna.' She clinked the keys she was carrying.

Swift stood up. 'I was expecting Ruth.'

'Yes, that was the plan but Ruth is asleep and I didn't want to wake her. She needs to rest when she can.' She was wearing olive coloured trousers with a short-sleeved white shirt tucked in to the waistband. The shirt's crisp collar, her upright bearing and snappy diction gave her a military air.

'You're rather early.' Swift drew out a chair for her. 'Can I get you a coffee?'

'I don't want coffee, thank you. I do need to get back so if you can give me Branna's things . . .' She started to pick up the bag of Branna's belongings.

'Hold on,' Swift said firmly. 'I've been waiting to see my daughter, looking forward to it. As it is, I have her for just three hours. I'm sure you can give me my full time with her.'

Olwen Taylor folded her arms, her chin raised. 'Well, I'm sorry about that but I have a very sick son and an exhausted daughter-in-law to take care of so I'm afraid putting you out a little bit isn't my chief concern.'

She grabbed the bag. Swift took Branna from a startled looking Cedric and sat down with her. A cold fury had seized him.

'I'll have my time with Branna. I can bring her to the house afterwards. Don't worry, I don't want to come in. You can get back to your criminal sick son.'

Olwen Taylor made a clicking sound with her tongue and sat, tapping her keys on the table. Cedric coughed, said he would get more coffee and went to the counter where he pretended to study the pastries.

'There's no need to be difficult.' Olwen's impatience was palpable. 'You'll no doubt see Branna again soon. I have a lot on my plate, you know.'

'I realise that.'

'I wonder if you do. Ruth has postnatal depression. Quite bad. I've treated a few cases in my time. She's on anti-depressants now and they make her even more tired in the short term. Has she told you?'

'Not in so many words. I don't get much chance to talk to her. I gathered that she's depressed.'

The woman squared her shoulders and leaned towards him. 'Oh, you "gathered." It's fine for you to swan down here to see your daughter as the mood takes you and then disappear again to London. This whole situation is such a terrible mess. My son is ill, frail and demoralised. His wife presents him with a child by another man, a child who turns out to have a disability and then she sinks into apathy . . . it's no way to carry on. I think he was unwise to take Ruth back and I told him so. But he loves her, you see and now he dotes on Branna. It seems to me that you've got the best of this chaos with your visitor privileges.'

Swift glanced down at Branna. She was asleep. He moved his chair back quietly. He could feel his heart pumping and knew that he was ready for fight, not flight. He had done his best to negotiate this situation but he could only take so much. His mouth was dry and ashy with fury. 'Can you keep your voice down, please? I'm sure you have many opinions but they don't concern me. You do know what your son did to me and an innocent woman, and why he was on trial?'

'Oh yes, I know all right. A good career thrown down the drain. I'm not excusing him but after all, his wife cheated on him with you. He's terribly ill and it seems to me that he has been punished enough. Many men wouldn't accept another man's child in the way Emlyn has. You have to hand it to him that he's trying to do the right thing now.'

'Do you have much to do with Branna?' Swift asked her icily.

She looked puzzled. 'No . . . I mean Ruth looks after her most of the time. Luckily, she's a good little sleeper, a very easy baby, considering everything that's going on. Ruth is lucky she's not a fretful child. I'm helping with Emlyn's care and the household in general. I do the laundry and cooking, most of the shopping. *Not* quite the retirement I envisaged but there we are.'

He was glad to hear that she didn't have care of his daughter. He doubted that she would be callous but she would be efficient and nothing more. He stroked Branna's head and fought his temper down, thinking about what he would say next. There was no point in antagonising the woman further. He was always at his most frostily polite when angry.

'I agree with you that Ruth shouldn't have gone back to her husband although not for the same reasons. I think she has put herself in an impossible situation and it's making her ill. I'm glad that you're able to support your son and Ruth, especially given your medical experience. I'm sure they appreciate it. But you have no say over how or when I see my daughter. You don't know me and I don't want to listen to your views on Ruth or me. You need to understand that.'

A mottled, beetroot flush swept up her neck and she gripped her keys. 'Oh, I really haven't got time for this nonsense. Emlyn will be wondering where I am.'

'Then you head back. You've eaten into my time with Branna so I'll return her in the next hour or so.'

She glared at him, clicked her tongue again and left. He watched her rigid back and thought she must have made a daunting GP. He wondered what it was like for Ruth, living with this disapproving woman. Branna gave a little satisfied grunt and filled her nappy.

'I think that's a good comment on what's just taken place,' Swift told her.

Cedric came back with coffees and apple cakes. 'I thought we might need a sweetener. You won the skirmish with the sergeant major, then?'

'I suppose. I just hope there aren't any more battles. I said I'll take Branna back in a while.'

'How does Ruth get on with her mother-in-law?'

'I don't know. I've only really heard about her recently. Ruth said she likes things shipshape, which may be a polite way of saying she's a menace. I need to talk to Ruth, a proper conversation. She seems far away. I wish she'd never gone back to that bastard.'

Cedric pushed a cake towards him. 'What's done is done. Ruth makes her own decisions. Always has, you know, and often without paying much heed to other people's feelings. Maybe she could come to London, have a few days away and some space to talk. Eat your cake, dear boy. Enjoy your time with the little one now. My nose tells me that we need a clean nappy.'

* * *

That evening Swift was surprised to receive a new email, direct from the Watcher. An attempt at engagement, setting up a battle of wits. He opened it as he was getting ready to go out.

Mr Swift, private investigator. Any significant clues? Any leads yet? I heard about those ferns. Interesting. What do they mean? Google might suggest something to you but of course, they could be a deliberate red herring. You might have the wrong scent in your nostrils. Oh boy, this is fun. I do hope Gabe ups his security. You don't want someone just being able to creep into your home when you're asleep. Bad things can happen while you're asleep. I know that from personal experience. I do hope nobody thinks I put the ferns there, by the way. Now that would make me lose sleep and then I might get really cross. Anyway, let me know how it's going.

Swift rated it as an attempt to mislead and confuse. It told him nothing new except he should continue to ignore and thwart the man. He changed his shirt, ran his fingers through his hair and caught a bus to Putney, where he had agreed to meet Tilda Harrison for a drink. She had called him after their meeting at Louis's naming ceremony. She said she hoped he didn't mind her looking him up. He recalled her as funny, attractive and light-hearted so arranged to see her in a wine bar near the bridge. She was waiting when he arrived, looking fresh in a sleeveless dress, a bottle of wine standing in an ice bucket on the table.

'I'm so glad you could come. I've been thinking about you.' She poured him a glass of wine.

'Well, it's always good to know I've been in someone's thoughts. Cheers!'

After an hour in her company he was clock-watching. She was witty and bubbly, true, but also terribly needy and lacking in self-confidence. As she downed a skinful of wine, she grew maudlin and tearful. Swift sensed an air of desperation about her as she described her ex-husband in long and boring detail, naming his sins and faults.

'I mean, once we were married he never bought me flowers or chocs or treated me. Other women get all that stuff, don't they? Trips abroad, to the theatre. I used to get him nice things. I had to remind him it was my birthday. All he wanted to do was watch bloody sport on the telly and go to Judo competitions. I might as well have stayed single. That's not a life, is it?'

'I can see it might get tedious.'

'I'll say! Sometimes I wondered if he'd notice if he came home and I'd moved out.'

Then she launched into stories of the primary school she taught at. 'They don't appreciate me at all. The head and the rest of them are so stuck up, you know? They didn't even bother to send me a card when I had appendicitis. I had a classroom assistant who was a right prig. I can't stand prigs, can you?'

'No,' he agreed, his heart sinking as she emptied another glass.

'I knew you'd understand. You're a nice bloke. I got passed over for promotion. One of the head's cronies got the job, natch. All the cards were stacked against me. It's horrible when you're not appreciated. Makes you feel small. People shouldn't behave like that. I bet you wouldn't. Why d'you think people treat me that way?'

'I don't know. Other people's motives can be hard to fathom. Maybe you should look for another job, make a fresh start.'

'Maybe. I'll think about that advice.' She leaned drunkenly into him, running a hand down his arm and across his chest. 'Gosh, you've got impressive muscles.'

He felt embarrassed and annoyed. He disengaged himself, saying that he had to get home.

She pulled a face. 'But it's early! I want to know all about you and your work.'

'Sorry, I have things to do.'

'Oh, that's just my luck! Let's do this again soon, huh?'

He saw her into a cab, saying he was going to be very busy for a while. He was relieved as he watched her being driven away. She pressed her face to the window, blowing kisses.

He sighed and walked home along the river path. He checked his phone and listened to a response from Philip Asher. The slow tones were deep and ponderous. Asher agreed to meet him for no more than half an hour and said that his advocate would be present to take minutes and ensure his welfare at all times. This was so that Swift '*needn't try to trick me and get me to say things I don't mean. If you do I'll have the law on you.*'

* * *

Swift had found a Suzy Mulligan who seemed the right age for the woman the police had interviewed. She was living at an address in Forest Gate. He had no idea if she worked, so headed there in the car in the evening. As he parked, he read an email from Gabe Maddox, responding to his query about the ferns placed in the kitchen. It was short and elusive.

No, don't know of any NZ relevance to family. Haven't got time to be worried about ferns. Good pointer to up security though. Don't know why Stella had to be a fusspot and call you. Women!

The street was full of multiple occupancy houses and dismal looking. There was a run-down billiard hall on one corner and a ladies' hairdresser called Curly Locks with sun-bleached stickers advertising 'OAP Specials' in the window. A handful of supermarket trolleys littered the pavement and further up the road, children were using one for joyriding. It veered wildly across the tarmac, narrowly missing parked cars. Swift left his car well away from them and walked along the cracked, uneven pavements.

There were several bells on the front door of the tall terraced house but none of them indicated a name. Swift pressed the bottom one and waited to see what happened. A woman in a pink and green sari opened the door. She seemed not to speak English and frowned when he asked for Suzy. He repeated the name and she called out to someone in her own language. Another woman shouted back from the depths of the house and she gestured up the stairs with a thumb and then vanished back through her own door.

The hall smelled of butter and spices. Swift went up the bare wooden stairs. The banister rail had deep gouges, exposing the light pine under dark green paint. He knocked on the first door he came to. It had been battered and damaged. A piece of board with nails protruding was hammered over the bottom half. A small, skinny woman, no bigger than a twelve-year-old, opened the door. Faded was the word that came into his head as he looked at her blanched complexion, ragged bleached blonde hair and dull eyes. She had the kind of shiny, transparent skin that revealed the purple threads of veins beneath.

'You here about the fuckin' mice?'

'No.'

'From the landlord? We'll pay the rent next week, honest.' Her voice was squeaky. He thought of Minnie Mouse.

'No, I'm nothing to do with the landlord.' He introduced himself and showed his ID. 'You're Suzy Mulligan?'

'Yeah. Why?'

'I'm sorry to turn up unannounced. I've been employed to look into Oscar Maddox's disappearance.

You remember baby Oscar? You visited Maura Haskin, his mother.'

She rubbed her forehead. Her hand was wrinkled, a tiny monkey paw. 'Yeah, I remember. That was nothin' to do with me.'

'Okay. I'm just trying to talk to anyone who was involved in any way. Could I come in for a minute?'

She looked him up and down, and then let him in to a narrow living room. It was painted purple and furnished with worn armchairs. The floor had torn lino. Posters of pop stars, the Twilight films, Harry Potter and fantasy figures — Wolverine, Captain America, Iron Man, Black Widow and Thor — lined the walls. At least a dozen patchwork dolls of various sizes and dressed in different national costumes were seated on a window ledge and on one of the chairs. Suzy sat opposite him looking wary. The padded sofa swallowed her and her feet didn't touch the floor. Her body was boyish, flat and angular, her cropped T-shirt riding above a concave stomach with a silver ring through the navel. The T-shirt was covered in a ladybird motif, accentuating her childlike look. She'd have blended in on a playground. She didn't look as if she had the stamina to bear a child. He chose his words carefully.

'I know that the police spoke to you back when Oscar was taken.'

'Yeah. Cos I had like a record. I did a bad thing once. I took a baby.'

'So I understand. I know that was because you'd lost a child yourself.'

'Yeah. My Crystal. She was beautiful. I cuddled her for two days. They let me. I wanted to bring her home for a bit but they said no. I read the other day that they do let you do that now in some places. Some woman had her baby for like two weeks. Pretended to feed it and everything. Maybe it was in America. They do things different there.'

'I'm sorry for your loss.'

'Yeah. Crystal had a lovely little coffin. White, with rosebuds. I went a bit crazy. I had, you know, treatment after that. The court said I needed help. They wasn't too bad to me really. I was like, mental.' She had tucked her hands below her legs and was swinging them back and forth.

He thought there was a remoteness about her, an odd disconnection. 'Tell me why you went to see Maura Haskin.'

'I dunno, really. I like just wanted her to know I didn't have nothin' to do with her baby. I saw her photo in the paper and she looked really nice. I knew how she was feeling cos I lost my baby. That's all. I took a photo of Crystal to show her. I didn't do nothin' wrong. She made me a cup of tea. She had a nice flat. Lovely things.' She sounded wistful and looked around her.

'Did you meet Thomas Maddox? He was Maura's partner.'

'Hmm, yeah. He, like, came in while I was visiting. He was really nice to her, putting his arms round her and everything.'

'Have you seen him since or been in touch with him?'

There was a curling plaster on her left forearm. She focused on it, picking at it and then attempting to reseal it. 'Nah. That was it.'

A key turned in the front door and a man hurried in, carrying a white plastic bag.

'Hey, I got us a Chinese. Who the fuck are you?' He stopped, swinging the bag. He could have been Suzy's twin. A little taller but just as skinny and with the same insipid look and fragile skin. His shaven head made him resemble a thinly covered skeleton.

'He's a detective,' Suzy said.

'What, a copper?'

'No. I'm a private detective. I'm making enquiries on behalf of the Maddox family.'

The young man flung himself down beside Suzy. His pupils were huge and his fingers moved around the carrier bag in an agitated circle.

'Who are they?'

Suzy responded. 'Remember that baby what went missing? Oscar. It's, like, his family.'

'Oh, right. What you bothering us for? Suzy didn't have nothin' to do with that. She was interviewed and everything. Fuckin' cops crawling all over her. It upset her. Reminding her of Crystal, that wasn't fair.'

Swift could see he wasn't going to be introduced. 'Are you Suzy's brother?'

'Yeah. I'm Billy. Why?'

'I just wondered. So, were you living together here when Oscar went missing?'

'Yeah.' Billy sniffed. He sat very close to Suzy, his scrawny arm touching hers.

They looked like two little anaemic sprites, side by side. Or, Swift thought, like, children who were playing at being grown-ups. Billy delved into the carrier bag and took out two foil cartons, handing one to Suzy. He ripped the lid off his and started eating voraciously with his fingers and a plastic fork. Sticky spare ribs and noodles with fried rice. He made little noises of contentment in his throat as he munched. Suzy uncovered hers and held it near her face, shovelling the food in and licking the spare ribs before chewing. Swift might as well not be in the room. He watched them and waited. Abby Cheng had said they were petty criminals and if they were, they didn't make much from their efforts, judging by the state of the flat. He observed Billy's jerky movements as food fell to the floor and decided that their income fed a drug habit. Amphetamines, he guessed. A mouse, quickly followed by another, darted across the floor, attracted by the pickings on the lino. Neither of them reacted and the mice vanished somewhere along the skirting board. Swift recalled the shop in Walthamstow selling mousetraps and wondered if he should mention it.

He broke into the sounds of slurping. 'Do either of you have any connection to New Zealand?'

Suzy looked at him. 'Nah. Our aunty emigrated to Oz a long time ago.' She nudged Billy. 'Do you remember? She sent us a fuckin' boomerang thing.'

Billy shrugged and tipped his carton up to his mouth to drain the juices. Then he dumped the empty carton on the floor, sighed, sat back and closed his eyes. The pale lids quivered. His breathing was fast, his chest rising and falling rapidly under his vest but he appeared to have fallen asleep.

'Suzy, are you sure you've never been in touch with Thomas Maddox?'

The sudden return to the subject unsettled her. She twisted her fork around in her food, spilling some on her lap.

'Nah, I like told you,' she said.

'I know, but I'm not sure you're telling me the truth. Did you see him somewhere?'

'Leave off, I said.'

'If you have, you might not have done anything wrong.'

She gave him a weasel look. 'I don't know why you're, like, going on about him. I never touched his stuff.'

'What stuff would that be?'

She glanced at her brother but he looked comatose. 'The stuff you meant.'

Swift watched as she forked the spilled food back into the carton with quick movements. Her little hands worked fast. Faster than her brain. 'I didn't mention any stuff, Suzy. Did you steal something from Thomas Maddox?'

'I thought you said you're not a cop?'

'I'm not. I'm trying to help the Maddoxes. I don't think you've done anything very bad. Not to Maura or Thomas, anyway. Maybe you stole from Thomas?'

She looked at Billy again. 'I only took a fuckin' rucksack. He was in a café. I recognised that Thomas. He, like, put the rucksack down. Stupid, or what? He was fuckin' asking for it. They've got a comfy life, nice things.'

'Comfy life? Suzy, their child was abducted and they've split up.'

She wriggled in her seat. 'Yeah, well. That's like nothin' to do with me. There wasn't much in the rucksack anyway. No fuckin' money. Just some books and music or somethin'. I needn't have bothered. If you tell anyone, I'll say you're lying. You can't prove nothin'.' Her squeak reached a higher register as she scored her point. She pulled the plaster off her arm and threw it into the remains of the congealing food.

'And that's it, is it? You haven't done anything else to that family?'

'Like what?'

'You haven't sent emails or stolen anything else of theirs?'

Her face crumpled suddenly. She drummed her heels against the sofa and started crying loudly. 'I gave that baby back, the one I took. I wasn't right. I was, like, ill. I never touched that fuckin' Oscar. Why you coming here saying I did? It's not fair. Billy, tell him, it's not fair!'

She was shaking, curling up against her brother and hitting his arm. He woke and shot up, agitated again.

'What is it? What you done to her?'

'He's saying I took Oscar!' Suzy wailed.

'What you doing, bastard cop? Leave her alone. Why you here?'

Billy's pupils were even huger. He got up and circled the room, muttering. He stared out of the window, then pulled the curtains closed, shaking himself. Suzy was rocking from side to side, scratching at her arms and moaning.

'Get him to go away! I want him to go away! Get him out!'

Billy rushed over and stood in front of Swift, his hands and legs trembling.

'Bastard cop. Leave us alone. You shouldn't have come here. I don't like you.' His eyes glittered, his breathing laboured.

Swift got up and moved towards the door. Although he was a good foot taller than Billy, the man looked frenzied. Suzy continued to howl, beating at her own head with her fists. Billy whipped a flick knife from his pocket, opened the blade and danced with it, curving it through the air. He was laughing, jittering from side to side, coming closer.

'Want some of this? You can fuckin' have it! You can have some! Come on!'

When Swift had been stabbed in the thigh he hadn't seen the knife coming. This time he sidestepped, grabbed Billy by the right arm and struck him in the elbow joint. His arm buckled and he yelped, losing balance. The knife dropped to the floor and Swift kicked it away before throwing the door open and running down the stairs. He took the last four in one jump. Billy didn't follow but carried on yelling that if Swift ever came back he could have some.

Swift dashed to his car, then sat for a few moments while his breathing calmed. The scar on his thigh tightened as he thought of the knife glancing towards him. He pressed down on his leg and opened a window, then started the engine and drove slowly. He played Diana Krall, his heartbeat slowing as he listened to her singing softly.

He stopped at a pub and ordered half a lager. It was cold and blissful. He stared into its amber depths. His head felt heavy, his nose blocked. He swallowed a decongestant with his first sip. The Mulligans had depressed him. They were the kind of sad creatures he had spent a lot of his time arresting when he first joined the Met. He thought that all he had established was the explanation for one of the thefts carried out on Thomas Maddox. He wouldn't bother telling Thomas, couldn't see the point when the young man had so much else to concern him. He was sure that the pathetic siblings wouldn't have the ability to orchestrate any other acts against the family. Random, low-level thieving would occupy their dreary days. He felt bad that he'd reminded Suzy of her dead baby, but on the other hand, she had displayed an ugly callousness.

* * *

The bus and train to Wimbledon took a couple of hours, due to congestion and a passenger on the railway track. Swift listened to Michael Jackson, thinking that the tedious journey would at least affirm his eco credentials with Jed Clifford.

Philip Asher's flat was on the ground floor of a large and handsome square property near the common. A plaque above the front door stated that it had once been a hospital for foundling children. A majestic purple wisteria covered the building and landscaped gardens curved around it. Huge stone pots filled with trailing lobelia and fuchsias stood on pediments on either side of the paved drive.

Asher opened the door and leaned on his walking stick, staring at Swift. He told him in his flat tones to follow him. His right foot was twisted inwards and dragged as he walked. He had been a dancer, Swift recalled, and he could see some grace in the man's head and hand movements but he was very overweight. His body looked lumpy in navy jogging trousers beneath a large tent-like blue shirt. He wore white leather ballet pumps. He lowered himself into a chair, groaned and waved at a young woman seated beside him.

'This is Libby. My advocate.'

Libby nodded and said hallo. She was elfin and young, with dull skin, a shy smile and solemn manner.

'Thank you for seeing me,' Swift said.

Asher looked at him with a resentful expression. His sand coloured hair was long and swept back in a side parting from his high forehead. He was wearing clusters of earrings and lots of chunky gold jewellery. He had planted his walking stick between his legs and leaned on it with both hands. 'Libby will tell you the conditions of the meeting and take notes,' he said in his slow monotone.

Libby sat forward, knees tucked neatly to one side, consulting a notepad. 'Philip faces challenges in his life. He speaks slowly and must be allowed time to express his views. He will see you for no more than twenty minutes because he gets tired. If he feels upset at any time, he will end the meeting.'

'Fine,' Swift said.

'Are you all right to start then, Philip? Would you like some water?' Libby asked solicitously.

Asher closed his eyes and moved his head from side to side. He appeared to be counting silently. On a table beside him was an open box of half eaten nougat. Above him hung a large photograph of a slim, lithe man in a white singlet and leggings, his feet bare, his hair flowing as he leaped across a stage. It was clearly Asher before his accident. The juxtaposition of the picture and the damaged man beneath was stark and presumably deliberate. Swift decided that Asher had a penchant for the melodramatic, which possibly predated his accident.

'Philip is just gathering himself, organising his thoughts,' Libby explained to him in a hushed voice.

He nodded, wondering how long this would take, and looked around. The room was furnished with beautiful Scandinavian chairs, upholstered in lemon and white. He clocked a desk with a computer and laptop standing by the double doors that led on to a patio. Files and paperwork covered a white table. On the wall opposite was another group of half a dozen photos, showing Asher in dance poses, some with a partner, some on his own.

'Just start.' Asher squinted at him.

'Could you tell me about the problems you had with Thomas Maddox last year?'

He clasped his hands more firmly on his stick. His skin bulged tightly over the rings on his fingers. 'He was no good at his job. Spent his time telling me about his personal life. Should have been helping me. I had a dreadful accident, you see. Ruined my career, my life.'

Libby was jotting notes in large, rounded letters. Swift nodded understandingly.

'I'm very sorry. When did you have the accident?'

'Four years ago. I was a professional dancer. Danced in lots of countries. I was in demand, respected. My career was ended tragically. I was crushed by heavy scenery on stage. It was during rehearsal. Spent months in hospital. Since then I've struggled to find any help. No one has time for the injured and sick. My days are spent fighting for compensation. The theatre said I had been told not to go on stage while scenery was being moved. Liars. Liars. I have to look for crumbs of charity.'

There was no emotion in his voice and Swift thought that the words sounded rehearsed. Libby looked at him, nodding agreement.

'So, regarding Thomas Maddox. You made a complaint about him.'

'He didn't understand at all. He was self-absorbed. Selfish. He was supposed to be there for me to help me with my battles.' He stopped and Swift went to speak but he held up a hand and did his eye closing and head moving again, then resumed. 'I have so many battles with bureaucrats who have no compassion. I needed someone to be my champion. Thomas took advantage of me. Telling me all about his son and how awful his life was. Making me feel terrible and worried about him. He sucked my energy. I'm very vulnerable. I'm a sick man.'

'I understand you alleged he made sexual advances to you.'

He gave a dramatic shudder and picked up a small battery powered fan. He turned it on and waved it in front of his face. 'Yes. I was talking to someone in the support group I go to. Told him all about Thomas. I said that he'd traded on my sympathy. On my caring nature. This person was very worried about me. He understood my concerns. Said Thomas had exploited me. Disrespected my sexuality. Urged me to complain.'

'But then you withdrew the complaint.'

'Yes.'

'Why was that?'

He squeezed his lips together, raised his stick and tapped it on the floor. 'I have so many battles. I didn't have time for all the questions. So many questions they started asking me. They gave me headaches. I have no strength. It felt like harassment. They were bombarding me. I was the victim but it felt like I was being accused. I had to focus on my priorities. Have you any idea what it's like to be a casualty of the system? I'm not well. I had a tragic accident. I'm a defenceless man. I have to fight day in, day out . . .'

Libby put a hand on his arm. 'Don't upset yourself, Philip.'

He patted the hand. 'Thank you. Don't know what I'd do without you. My angel Libby. My guardian angel. It is upsetting, talking about it. I trusted Thomas. I was kind to him. Shared his sorrow. Empathy was always my downfall. Too much empathy for this cruel world. Then he abused my trust. I know I should have stuck to my guns. Carried on with my complaint. But I didn't have the stamina.'

From what he had seen of Thomas Maddox, Swift didn't believe a word of it. 'And you haven't contacted Thomas since?'

'Certainly not. Now I have Libby. My angel who understands me. Helps me in the right ways. I'd be lost without her. Every day is a fresh battle. Fighting with the faceless ones who torment people like me.' He gestured at the files on the table. 'Look at those hundreds of letters. We have to write to lawyers, councillors, bureaucrats. I may have to go to the European court.'

Swift nodded. 'Thomas Maddox has had some unpleasant emails. So has his grandfather. That's why I'm talking to people who know him. You did send Thomas emails when this was going on?'

Asher pulled a sour face and fanned himself some more. 'You taking notes, Libby? You keeping up?'

'Yes, I've recorded everything.'

'You're trying to make me say things now,' Asher told Swift. 'Pretending to be nice. Sympathetic. Now you want to trip me up.'

'It's not in my interest to trip you up,' he lied. 'I just ask questions and try to get answers. Do you have any connection to New Zealand?'

Asher stared at him with cold, dull eyes. 'I went there once with a dance troupe. Some time ago.'

'Whereabouts did you go and do you know anything about the silver tree fern—'

Asher put a hand behind his ear and shushed him. 'Wait, wait, I can hear them,' he whispered. He dropped the fan in his lap and closed his eyes, a look of fierce concentration on his face.

Libby rose silently and crossed to Swift on tiptoe, crouching beside him and whispering. 'Philip hears the spirits of the foundling children sometimes. They're crying and calling for his help. It's amazing, how perceptive he is.'

Swift looked down into Libby's gullible face and wondered how long she would last before Asher made another complaint. He sat back and studied the man as his eyelids flickered. Libby watched him too, with a look of adulation.

'I'm sensitive, you know.' Asher opened his eyes. 'Hard being open to the pain and joy of others. I've always been like this. Even more so since my accident. Suffering makes you so aware. I tried to hear little Oscar Maddox but I never did. I told Thomas that must mean he's alive. I gave him hope. Look how he repaid me. I can hear those poor little foundling children who lived here. Sometimes I wonder if I should move. The sadness is so overwhelming. I lie awake at night worrying about them. I worry more about them than about myself. But if I moved . . . no. I would feel I had let them down, wouldn't I, Libby?'

'I know you would, Philip, and I'm sure they would miss you.'

'Yes. I am their friend. Their only friend. I know what it is to need help. A friend in this world.' He stared at Swift. 'Maybe you have lost someone? Do you have someone who has passed? I could listen out for them and let you know if they have something to say to you.'

Swift thought immediately of Kris and took a breath. This man knew how to find tender spots. He looked at him, a clear, searching gaze. 'You didn't answer my question about emails to Thomas Maddox. Have you sent any recently?'

Asher slumped back, a hand to his head. 'Exhausted now. No more. Can't take any more. I'm a helpless man. My head is splitting. Libby . . . can you . . . please.'

Libby stood and said that Mr Asher needed to rest. Swift let himself out as she fetched water and medication, Asher faintly calling her an angel. He walked to Wimbledon Common, feeling frustrated and irritated by the narcissism and selfishness he had witnessed. He was angry as well. Philip Asher had added to Thomas's suffering with his nonsense about Oscar. He was poison and self-obsessed.

The sun beat down remorselessly. It was hard to think straight in this incessant heat. The days were slipping past in a drowsy haze. His eyes were cloudy and itchy. He rubbed at them and blinked hard. He was finding it hard to make connections. Asher had a history of sending nasty emails and tormenting others and had been to New Zealand. He was clearly used to using computers. But his apparent involvement with Thomas Maddox post-dated Thomas's various unlucky accidents and Oscar's abduction. Asher had been injured four years ago and wouldn't have been physically capable of causing Thomas's misfortunes or breaking into homes or of mugging Gabe Maddox. Unless Asher was working with someone in a malicious partnership.

Swift longed for clouds and a breeze. He walked among the shade of the oaks and aspens and saw a windmill in the distance. He recalled reading that it housed a museum with a diorama about its construction and that it had a Victorian room. He wondered if Gabe Maddox and Stella had visited it and got some ideas for their conversion there. He stretched high, standing on tiptoes, and touched an oak branch. Despite his aching back, the river beckoned.

* * *

When I was a child, I was powerless. My old man held all the aces. Made sure I got a plate of misery every day and ate every last mouthful. Goaded me that I hadn't been wanted. He'd been landed with me. A resented burden for him to carry.

I did a pretty good job of bringing myself up. Got myself educated. Bright, I was bright. People told me that. Not that they took much interest.

Now, though. Now I've got loads of power. Buckets of it. It tastes good.

A teacher in a care centre once told me that I could be on the stage. I had the talent to transform myself, she said. I could become whoever I wanted and it was a real skill. She gave me a lead part in a play. How right she was. It's my biggest advantage in life. Being whoever someone thinks they want, need. Telling a good story. It's great, being a chameleon. Name changes for starters. Then shaping and practising my act, my turn treading the boards. Coming on and off as different characters. It's a drama, all right. And the curtain will fall with a flourish.

There might even be blood. Real, not stage.

And I can decide.

CHAPTER 7

Mark Gill's modern, sparsely furnished flat was hot, thronged and noisy, with Prince playing full blast. Swift and Mark had worked together in the Met and had stayed in touch. They shared an interest in pulp fiction magazines and when he was passing through Soho, Swift had visited a specialist shop and bought Mark a 1937 copy of *Dead Guys, Live Broads* for his birthday. He knew that Mark had been looking for it. It had the usual lurid cover: a man in a suit lying splayed on a floor in a pool of blood and a woman wearing a blue fox fur and a veiled hat standing over him, smiling and holding a smoking gun. Swift had enjoyed the opening paragraph:

A flash of flame and smoke erupted from Marylou's slim black thirty-eight revolver. Curtis Kines slumped to the floor, bright red blood gushing from the hole in his chest. He was a big man but death made him kind of smaller. Marylou had butterflies in her stomach. She liked them. 'Sucker,' she said sweetly, tucking the gun in her bag and blowing Curtis a last kiss.

Mark sat in a chair, bottle in hand, ignoring his guests as he read the magazine. Swift had downed several cold beers and leaned against a wall while a woman who was growing merry on champagne described kidney stones to him. She was a renal specialist, she told him as she finished one glass and reached for a refill.

'Some of them can be the size of a ping pong ball. The most common ones are mainly calcium oxalate and they can look quite pretty, despite the awful pain they cause. I hope I never get them, I can tell you. I've seen big blokes like you writhing in agony on the floor. I wouldn't wish them on my worst enemy.'

Swift's lower back winced and a trickle of sweat warmed his forehead. He took a deep draught of beer. She was an attractive woman with violet eyes and he was wondering if he would be able to get her off medical subjects when his phone rang. He saw that the caller was Stella Gath and excused himself, pushing his way to the hallway, where it was a little less noisy.

'I'm so sorry to bother you this late. Gabe asked me to ring you. Thomas had an accident on the tube, a couple of hours ago. He's okay but he's in hospital with some injuries. Gabe is in Hereford on business and can't get back until tomorrow. He asked if you could go to see Thomas. He's worried about him. Apparently, he almost fell on to the track as a train was coming in. A woman managed to catch his sleeve and pull him back.'

'Do you know how it happened?'

'No details, no. Thomas rang Gabe from the ambulance. It happened at Green Park in rush hour. He told Gabe he felt someone push him. I think the police are involved.' Her voice faltered. 'What on earth is going on, Mr Swift?'

'It might have been an accident. Those tube platforms are often heaving in the evenings and people surge forwards when they hear a train. Don't jump to conclusions.'

He knew it wasn't accidental, could feel it in his bones. He took the hospital details, said a quick goodbye to Mark and called a cab. He thought briefly of the woman with violet eyes, and then shrugged. The way his luck with women was running, she would turn out to be married with a brood of children. The late-night streets were busy, the pavements outside cafés and pubs crammed with languorous, scantily clad people who didn't want to go home because they knew they wouldn't sleep in the smothering heat.

At the hospital A and E department, he was asked to wait. He bought water and a black coffee from a small kiosk and watched the walking wounded come and go. There was a succession of people wearing plasters and bandages, hobbling on sticks and crutches. A young boy wearing a piratical looking eye patch, a rake thin man with a terrible cough, a woman with a cut hand and blood seeping through the towel wrapped around it and an elderly couple, both in wheelchairs parked side by side, holding hands. It was close and sticky in the waiting area and the vinyl chairs felt slimy. Thomas was in an assessment unit and no one could tell him how long it would be before he could have a visitor.

Swift flicked through a copy of the evening paper, which was filled with weather related stories. He read that road surfaces in the capital were melting, train rails buckling, the mortality rate had increased, heath and farmland fires were raging, hospitals were inundated with cases of dehydration and exhaustion, the products in a chocolate factory had melted, a waxwork knight in a castle museum had dissolved into a puddle and there had been a spate of drownings with people trying to cool down in the sea and rivers. The heatwave was forecast to continue for several more weeks, when it would break, with thunderstorms and torrential rain.

Swift finished his water and checked his phone. He had sent Ruth two emails, asking if he could talk to her. There was no reply. He stared into space for a while, then texted her.

I'm worried that you haven't been in touch. I'll ring you soon. We need to talk and I'd like to make another date to see Branna x

The heat and the beers he had drunk were making him sleepy. He went to the toilets and splashed his face and hair with water, then bought another coffee and lingered outside in the oppressive night among flower tubs littered with cigarette butts. An ambulance crew was taking a break and smoking while taxis came and went. A night bus trundled to a halt, disgorging an army of nurses, porters and cleaners arriving for their twilight shift.

Back inside, he had a text from Gabe Maddox, asking if he had seen Thomas yet. He replied, saying he was still waiting. He thought about the hot, dusty, crowded confines of the tube. He knew that gritty, scorching breeze that announced a train arriving and the way people moved forwards in anticipation. When the platform was teeming, the crowd could be like one large moving mass. Seasoned travellers on the older lines knew where the doors would open and positioned themselves. He had once seen a girl carried out of a train when the doors opened, forced from it by the sheer weight of passengers swarming from the carriage. She had turned and tried to get back on, falling as she faced the tide of impatient humanity. He avoided the tube when possible, taking buses around the city. It was slower, but he could breathe and get off and walk if traffic was heavy. Londoners spent hours grumbling about their broken transport system with its delays and frustrations. It was a twenty-first-century city with a Victorian infrastructure, gasping beneath the demands placed on its crumbling foundations.

Half an hour later, a nurse beckoned to him and took him through to a wide corridor with bays leading off it.

'Mr Maddox has asked to see you now. He had a concussion so just a few minutes, please.'

'Are you keeping him overnight?'

'Yes, for observation. He can go home tomorrow if we're happy with his progress.'

Thomas was propped up in a bed, wearing a green hospital gown, a large dressing on his chin. His left arm and elbow were badly grazed. His face was the colour of candle wax, his eyes heavy.

'Thanks for coming,' he said.

'That's okay.' Swift pulled up a chair. 'Have the police talked to you?'

'Briefly. Said they'd see me again once I'm well enough.'

'What happened?'

'I'm not sure but I know I was pushed. Not a nudge, a real shove in the back. It was heaving on the platform, there were delays so the crowds had built up. I was at the front, by the platform edge. There was that gust of wind when the train is coming and then I was falling forward. If that woman hadn't grabbed me . . .' He swallowed and shivered. 'I fell backwards, lost my balance, and bashed my head as I went down. I passed out for a few moments, I think. Everything was echoing.'

'You think someone did it deliberately?'

'I know it. I just know it. I felt that . . . that presence I've been aware of before.' He looked at Swift. 'Someone wanted me dead.'

'Did you tell the police that?'

'Yeah, but I don't know if I was making much sense.'

'Did anyone know you were making that journey? Was it a regular one?'

'No. I was on my way back from a client and I walked through Green Park to get some air. It was a one-off visit, not a regular client so not a route I travel often.'

'Did anyone see anything?'

'I don't know. The woman who caught me said she hadn't. She was so nice, stayed with me and made people move away.' He moved his head, wincing. 'I know everyone will think it was an accident.'

'I'm not sure it was, if that's any consolation. How are you feeling?'

'Bashed. Achy. Terrified. I don't understand what's happening. There was a split second when I thought I was going to die down there. I didn't want to.' He moved restlessly, plucking at the top of his gown. 'I feel cold, then hot. The nurse said it's shock.' He looked at Swift, an appealing glance, then away. 'I feel really frightened.'

The nurse parted the curtains and looked in.

'I'd better go. Rest up. You need to recover from the shock. I'll contact your grandfather to tell him what's happening.'

He took a taxi home, and rang Gabe Maddox. His phone went to voicemail so he tried Stella. She sounded terse and said that she would speak to the hospital and make sure that she or Gabe fetched Thomas when he was discharged. He could come back to High Hawksford to recuperate.

Swift's stomach reminded him that he hadn't eaten since having a prawn sandwich at lunchtime. He stopped the taxi near the Thames at Hammersmith and bought fish and chips. He sat on a bench by the river. The tide was rising and the dark water seemed to merge with the velvet night sky. A party boat glided in a passing pool of light, raised voices at full volume, then slowly fading.

He thought about the angry, taunting emails, the violence of an attempted murder, someone breaking into homes and causing injuries, always keeping under the radar. A man who had possibly stolen not just security and peace of mind from the Maddox family, but a child. He was making little headway with this investigation. No one fitted into the frame and he had no focus. The only thing to do was to plough on, keep asking questions and hope for some luck.

* * *

Swift rang Maura Haskin's doorbell just after seven in the evening. She had said she would like a copy of the updated picture of Oscar and he thought it would be kinder to hand it to her in person. He rubbed his lower back with his knuckles as he waited for her to answer. He had been to see Jerry Cheng in his clinic above an art supplies shop in Pimlico. Cheng had made him lie flat on his stomach while he manipulated Swift's muscles and inserted needles that had only stung slightly when he twisted them. It had helped. The pain was ebbing. He looked up — the sky was now a pinkish grey, the worn out day dragging itself to an end. The air was thick with dust, fumes and cooking aromas.

Maura invited him in and explained that they were just having dinner. A well-built but slim man with dark brown hair was sitting at the small gateleg table by the kitchen.

'I didn't mean to interrupt your meal.'

'No problem, we've almost finished. This is my partner, Ross Walker. Ross, this is Mr Swift, the investigator.'

Walker stood and held out a hand. The skin was dry, the grip firm. He was of medium height and his sleeveless vest showed off his well-honed biceps. 'Pleased to meet you,' he said warmly.

'Have a glass of wine,' Maura urged.

She seemed more cheerful than she had been on his last visit and he guessed that was to do with Walker's presence. He accepted and sat down with them. The remains of salad and roast chicken lay on the table with a bottle of mayonnaise and a French stick. Walker took another piece of chicken breast and sliced it into small portions. His skin was clear and matt, his dark, thick eyebrows perfect arches.

'You've heard about Thomas?' Swift asked Maura.

'Yes, he rang yesterday. He told me he refused to go to High Hawksford. The hospital said he should be with someone who could keep an eye on him but he insisted on going home. He thinks someone tried to push him onto the track. What's your view?'

'It's a difficult one and hard to prove.'

Maura sighed. 'Like all the other things that have happened to him.'

'Sometimes it sounds like he has a bit of a persecution complex,' Walker said. 'I mean, some people are just accident-prone. I hope he doesn't expect you to go round and look after him, babe. He does tend to rely on your good nature.'

'Well . . . he's been through a lot,' Maura said.

Swift drank some wine and placed an envelope by Maura's plate. 'I've brought the age progressed image of Oscar from the police.'

'Oh, yes.' She looked at the envelope nervously, her fingers edging near it and then drawing back.

'Let me open it for you.' Walker reached across and took the envelope, lifting the flap. He studied the photo and then passed it to Maura. 'Steady now, babe, you know this is hard for you.'

She had the kind of face that showed every fleeting thought and emotion. She gazed at the boy, her eyes filling. 'Yes, I can see it. I can see how they've done it. My Oscar.' She traced the outline of the face with her fingertips and then looked at Swift. 'I wonder if my Oscar is alive and looking like this or if he's still my baby and buried where we'll never find him? You know, sometimes I feel guilty because I struggle to remember him and how he looked. He was with me for such a short time.'

Walker laid a hand gently on her shoulder. 'Now come on, keep your courage up. It was always going to be hard, seeing this.' He looked at Swift, his eyes concerned. 'I wasn't sure this was a good idea. Maura said you'd suggested it.'

'I asked Maura if she would like a copy. I wanted one for the purposes of my investigation.'

'Well . . .' He rose in his chair, stroked Maura's neck and kissed the top of her head. 'Don't dwell on it now. We'll look at it later and talk it over. I know how rough it is but you know it probably is a good thing to think of Oscar as he might be now. It helps you to hope.' He refilled her wine glass, slid the photo back into the envelope and placed it beside him. 'How is your investigation progressing?' he asked Swift.

'It's ongoing.'

Walker took a piece of bread. 'Do you think the bastard who took Oscar is sending the emails?'

'I don't know yet.'

Maura was drinking her wine and staring at the table. Her knife and fork lay in a tangle of half-eaten salad.

'Maura, do you have any connection to New Zealand, or do you know of the Maddox family having any connection?'

She looked at him, puzzled. 'New Zealand? No.'

'Funny question,' Walker observed.

'Yes, it must sound odd. There's an indication that New Zealand has some reference to Gabriel Maddox.'

'Have you asked Gabe?' Maura rested her chin in her hands. She looked tired.

'Yes. He says there is none.'

'Come on, babe, eat a bit more,' Walker said. 'You've had a long day. Have some more salad, at least.'

Maura gazed fondly at him. 'Sometimes you're more mumsy than my mum was.'

'Well, someone has to look after you, get your vitamins down you or you'll fade away.' He forked salad on to her plate.

'Have you given Thomas a copy of the picture?' Maura asked.

'Not yet. He said to leave it a while. I don't think he could face it at the moment.'

Swift had visited him that morning. The caravan door was locked and Maddox had looked out of the window before letting him in. It was baking inside, with all the windows closed. Maddox was dressed only in boxer shorts and sat at the piano, playing drifting riffs of notes. An open tin of soup stood by the tiny cooker and there was a packet of bread on the table. Maddox had said he felt better and was going to take it easy. His eyes were still full of fear. Swift had pointed out that he might feel more secure if he stayed at High Hawksford or with a friend. He thought that if someone was trying to assault Maddox, the caravan was a flimsy home and offered little protection, even with locked doors and windows. Maddox had said listlessly that he wanted to stay in his own place, stay quiet and think. He didn't feel up to Gabe bustling about and telling him what to do.

'I hope that doesn't mean Thomas will want to start talking to you about this picture. I hope he's not going to ring and upset you.' Walker put a hand on Maura's. 'Let's leave the answer phone on tonight. I know you worry about him but he's such a drain on you. He needs to try and deal with his own stuff.' He glanced at Swift. 'I don't mean to sound unkind, I know Thomas has had his own sorrow. It's just too much for Maura sometimes. Thomas needs to move on instead of latching on to her energy.'

'Have you met him?' Swift asked.

Walker said no, he hadn't, but he had heard all about him. 'You eat up now, babe, try not to worry.'

Maura responded to him, apparently reassured, obediently forking up tomato and lettuce. The doorbell rang and she went to get up. Ross moved his chair back.

'You stay put, I'll let him in. It's my dad,' he explained to Swift. 'I forgot to give him a card and present I bought for my cousin's engagement so he's just dropping in to pick it up on his way there.'

He ran downstairs and reappeared quickly with a balding, paunchy middle-aged man in crisply pressed jeans and a white T-shirt. 'This is my dad, Victor,' he said.

Swift stood and shook hands with him. He had the stained teeth of a heavy smoker and was wearing a pungent aftershave. He smiled and blew a kiss to Maura.

'I hear you're looking out for our Maura,' he said to Swift.

'Sort of.'

'Good, that's good. Look, I have to dash. I'm late as it is. Have you got the pressie, Ross?'

'Won't you have a drink?' Maura came over and kissed him on the cheek.

'I'd love to. It'll have to be another time. Soon, okay?'

Ross handed him a small carrier bag. 'Thanks for doing this, Dad. Give Ann my love. Tell her I'll ring her soon for a proper chat.'

Victor laughed, saying Ann wouldn't hold her breath. He prodded Ross's arm, reminding him to fix the washer in the bathroom tap next time he was back, waved cheerily and said he would see himself out.

'The bathroom tap!' Ross sat back down. 'He's a slave driver. I get back knackered and he gives me jobs to do. Mind you, he always has a meal ready for when I turn up so I can't grumble.'

'What do you work at?' Swift asked him, finishing his wine.

'I sell solar heating in the southeast.' Walker pointed skywards. 'This heatwave has been good for business, reminding people that those rays can reduce their fuel bills. Is there ice cream in the freezer, babe?'

'Yes, I got some of that honeycomb, your favourite.'

'Terrific, you're a wonder.' Walker took a tiny radish, crunched it, and then nodded at Swift. 'So, what's it like, being a private eye? Do you get lots of fascinating cases?'

'I've had a few. It varies.'

'I suppose it must be pretty satisfying, investigating, getting answers.' He leaned forward, arms folded on the table, shoulders hunched.

Swift glanced at Maura, who was fetching the ice cream from the freezer. 'Yes, that's true, although it's often distressing for the people involved.'

'I suppose. I can see it must be tough work at times.' Walker held his pudding bowl out to Maura, asking for three scoops. 'So, you look pretty fit, good muscle tone. How do you manage that with the job you do?'

'I have a boat. I row on the river.'

Walker nodded. 'I work out, do a bit of running.'

'A bit!' Maura turned to Swift. 'Ross runs every day, no matter the weather. Would you like some ice cream, cool you down?'

'I won't, thanks. I'd better be going.'

'Good to meet you,' Walker said. 'I appreciate what you're doing. It certainly helps Maura.'

Maura saw him to the door. 'Thanks for the picture. It was a bit of a shock, seeing it. I'll look at it properly later on, when I've had time to take it in.'

* * *

It was too hot to think about cooking but the roast chicken had stimulated his appetite. On the way home Swift stopped in at his local pub, the Silver Mermaid. He ordered tomato and basil pasta and a salad, took his glass of wine into the garden, and sat at a table. He had contacted Abby Cheng about the incident at Green Park and saw that he had a missed call from her. He returned it, watching a boy go higher and higher on the swing at the end of the garden.

'Hi,' she said wearily. 'Hot enough for you?'

'Don't. At least I've got a nice cold wine.'

She groaned. 'Oh, don't tempt me, I'm on duty. Anyway, I looked at the recent record about Thomas Maddox and the tube incident. Nothing clear on CCTV. There were massive delays that evening and to be honest, the platform at Green Park looked like a hive of worker bees. The woman who pulled him back, Laila Silva didn't see anything. Luckily for him, she had quick reactions.'

'Did you see the more recent anonymous emails that I forwarded to you?'

'Yep. But you know, they're still vague. Nasty but vague. I've passed them to my techie contact. She's working on it but she says not to expect any results soon. What's the reference to ferns about?'

Swift explained, adding that the family claimed there was no New Zealand connection.

'Strange. If Gabe Maddox doesn't want to report it, there's nothing to be done. Again, could be someone with a grudge. I'll call Thomas Maddox soon. You haven't found a likely suspect?'

'No, still working on it.'

'Good luck, then. Enjoy your wine.'

His phone rang as soon as he finished speaking to Abby. Simone on the warpath.

'Tilda Harrison,' she said peremptorily. 'What are you playing at?'

'Hallo, Simone. Nice to hear from you. I've no idea what you're talking about.'

'She's very upset. Said you two met up and got on really well but you've been blanking her.'

'We did meet. I didn't enjoy it much. I didn't want to see her again so I've tried to indicate that politely.' Tilda had left him half a dozen voicemail messages, each one more imploring and desperate, asking if they could meet again. He had eventually left a message for her, saying that he was busy and unable to see her.

'What's wrong with her? She's a lovely person.'

'I'm sure she is. Just not someone I want to spend time with.'

'You know, she was messed around enough by her ex. I didn't think you would upset her like this. She's vulnerable and you're the first man she's gone out with. She was in tears . . .'

'Simone. Simone. Please. We didn't "go out". We had a drink. One off. It happens. I don't want to meet the woman as a charity case. That would be insulting to her.'

'Look, Ty, you can't keep moping around after Ruth for ever like a devoted puppy, you know. She's married. She just plays you, keeps you hanging around because it suits her. You indulge her too much. Everyone thinks so. You need to move on and get over Kris, too. You spend far too much time on your own. Tilda is so kind and understanding. I don't know a nicer person.'

It was the 'everyone thinks so' that did it. He wanted to yell at her, tell her to back off. But . . . but . . . she was married to his dear cousin and if he fell out with her every time she crossed a line, the relationship would be impossible. He took a drink as she rattled on, then left a silence. 'I don't want you butting into my life so let's not pursue this topic,' he said flatly. 'How are Louis and Mary?'

'Oh, fine. Mary is at a conference. Louis is terrific. Honestly, Ty, I'm only thinking of you, you know. You need to get out there, break away from your old life, try to—'

'I don't want to fall out with you, Simone so I'm going to ring off. Give my love to Mary.'

Cedric was approaching with a gin and tonic as he ended the call and his food was served. He took a deep breath and lifted his shoulders up and down. Cedric wore a panama hat and one of his more colourful Hawaiian style shirts with a busy pattern of passionflowers and grapes. Swift drifted parmesan over his meal and then forked up pasta as Cedric squeezed his slice of lemon into his gin.

'Thought I might find you here, Ty. Looks good. The chef here understands the concept of *al dente*.' He removed his hat and rubbed his brow. 'I know this weather is going to break soon and I can't wait. I think I'm starting to go mad from the heat. The air tastes dirty.'

Swift hooked a juicy basil leaf and looked up at him. He seemed distracted, his eyes weary.

'You okay, Cedric? Following all the advice and keeping cool and hydrated?'

'Hmm? Oh yes, all of that. And if in doubt, I have another gin with lots of tonic. Quinine is good for you, isn't it?'

'I know it treats malaria. Not sure about its uses for heat stroke.'

They fell silent as Swift finished his meal and mopped up vinaigrette with his bread. He was still feeling angry about Simone's intrusion and the doubts she had raised. Was Ruth playing him? He didn't think so, or at least not deliberately. Sometimes he thought he had lost all sense of perspective about her. The boy on the swing was laughing wildly as he soared through the air. Cedric pushed his ice cubes around with a finger, and then cleared his throat.

'I've had a bit of trouble with a credit card,' he said.

'In what way?'

'Well, I must have mislaid one. Someone used it so I've got a bit of a bill.'

Swift put his cutlery on his plate and wiped his fingers with a napkin. 'Your credit card company should repay you if it's theft. Have they contacted you?'

'Yes, a couple of days back. They said they had noticed unusual spending. I looked for the card and couldn't find it.'

'How much?'

'Three thousand, more or less.'

Cedric was busy with his ice cubes, poking at them and focusing on them as if they might reveal a secret. His eyesight was weaker these days but he refused to wear glasses in public. Swift's heart sank as he guessed what the problem might be.

'So they told you where the money was spent?'

'Yes. Two thousand on flights and the rest on a laptop.'

'What's happening? Are they contacting the police?'

Cedric sighed. 'No. I rang them back and said I remembered using the card for those items.'

Swift sipped his wine, watching the flying boy as he pointed his legs like arrows and arched his back. Swift had loved to soar on a swing in childhood. That feeling of giddiness and recklessness, that illusion of weightlessness.

'I think it's Oliver, you see,' Cedric said dully. 'I think he took the card. He knew it was in the drawer. I keep it there because I use it so rarely. I've phoned him several times but there's no answer and he hasn't replied to my messages.'

'So you think he's probably having a holiday somewhere with his new laptop?'

A rueful smile. 'Yes. That about sums it up. I don't want him to get into trouble, dear boy.'

'What are you going to do when he reappears?'

'I'll talk to him.'

He'll deny it, Swift thought and you'll let him lie. 'You have cancelled the card?'

'Oh yes. They offered me another but I refused. I don't need it.'

'I'm sorry, Cedric. Oliver shouldn't treat you like this.'

'No. Of course it might not have been him but . . .'

The dusk deepened and amber lights strung through the tree branches came on in the garden. More people arrived as a band came and set up equipment. A man sat at the next table, his dog at his feet, gazing up at him with adoration. The man dipped his finger in his beer and held it out to the dog who licked it enthusiastically. Swift turned away, Simone's words, *devoted puppy* echoing in his ears. The swinging boy and other children vanished home to bed. As Swift brought back another round of drinks, the band were launching into *Lay Down Sally* and Cedric was tapping the table, his troubles momentarily forgotten.

CHAPTER 8

A kestrel hovered in the still air, its pointed wings and long tail clearly outlined in the pearly morning light. Swift sat still and watched it, oars trailing in the water. It plunged, diving down to the riverbank and grabbing its prey in its curved beak. He edged the boat in by the bank, took a drink of water and read the latest email sent to Gabe and Thomas Maddox.

Here's a riddle for you, Gabe. You don't know me, you wouldn't recognise me but you've met me. Was I in one of your business meetings maybe? Or did I have a holiday in your luxurious accommodation? I might reveal all one day.

Have you heard of 'ambiguous grieving'? I read about it on the internet. The idea comes from the USA, like a lot of other touchy feely jargon. It's accurate, though. It means that state you're in when you don't know whether to grieve or live in hope. You must both be in that state most of the time. Especially you, Thomas. I'm not so sure about Gabe. Have you got a heart, Gabe? Sometimes I wonder. How would I make sure you have?

I heard you almost had a run in with a tube train, Thomas. You should be more careful. The world is a hostile place. Hope you're feeling better.

I emailed your investigator but he's very rude. No reply. Maybe he's asleep. Hope you get your money's worth there.

He ate a cereal bar, tracking the kestrel, clearing his mind of the Watcher's noise for a while. His phone rang and he was pleased to see that it was Nora Morrow.

'You're up early. I'm on the river.'

'Lovely. I couldn't sleep and my mum's awake so I'm making breakfast. Tea and toast but we're almost out of marmalade. I've had a look at those emails you sent.'

'I've just had another. What did you think?'

There was a clatter of crockery. 'I agree that the emailer is male. There's a lot of goading and malice. Leaving those ferns is saying that the Watcher can enter any part of their lives. Most strange.'

'He's intelligent, a planner, willing to bide his time but he's angry, too. The anger bubbles constantly under the surface.' He pictured Jed Clifford, his wild hair waving as he denounced Gabe Maddox. The Watcher had referred to his childhood several times and Stella had said that Jed had a troubled past. He needed to speak to him again.

'Are you going to reply to the Watcher?'

'No. I reckon that is what he's after so I'm withholding. Trying to make him feel less in control.'

'Yes, that's the best tactic. It might annoy him enough to push him into revealing something. There's something grandiose about his personality. He thinks he's better than the rest of humanity.'

'Yes, that comes across strongly. I'm hoping he'll get impatient with me and it will draw him out.'

They talked for a while. He could hear the rasp of a knife on toast. The connection faded now and again. He thought it made the conversation sound artificial and wished he could speak to her in person. She asked after

Yana Ayo, the young Syrian woman. Swift had helped Yana find accommodation with Malory Meredith, a woman he had met during his last investigation.

'I called in to see them a couple of weeks ago,' he said. 'They're getting along well and it looks as if Yana will stay there for a while. She's enrolled at the local college. Cedric meets up with them regularly.'

It was good to hear Nora but the fractured communication was frustrating. He steered away from the subject of Ruth and Branna. He simply didn't know what to say and she wasn't a woman for small talk. She said she'd better take her mother's breakfast to her before the tea got cold.

It was only 7 a.m. but given that Gabe Maddox had forwarded the email to him at five thirty, Swift reckoned he was up and about. He rang him, watching the kestrel resume its hovering. The Watcher was somewhat like the bird, lingering and observing, choosing his moment to pounce.

'You've read it then?' Maddox sounded vigorous, sparky.

'Yes. It's more personal this time, a little more content about the sender. I'm sure it's a man. There have been a couple of mentions of his childhood and that seems to be where this bad feeling started. Does that mean anything to you?'

'Nothing.'

'You didn't have any siblings who drifted away?'

'I had one sister. She died of polio when I was a child. So unless she's come back to haunt me . . . I spoke to Thomas last night. He's holed up in his caravan, licking his wounds. He said the police told him they didn't think they could go anywhere with what happened in the tube. Too many people, too much heaving and shoving and nothing useful on CCTV.'

'They might change their minds when they see the latest email although it's still vague. I'm going to visit your father later.'

'Good luck with that. How did you get on with the eco warriors?'

'I think they would know how to send you anonymous emails.'

'What did you make of Sonia?'

'She's sure of herself. She likes to pick a fight and bear a grudge but as I said, I believe it's a man behind this. Jed Clifford seemed full of righteous anger.'

'That waste of space! He's hardly a mastermind. You've had more direct contact from this emailer, right?'

'Yes. More of the same kind of stuff. I'm not responding because that's what he wants.'

'Right, I see where you're coming from. I've got to go, having an alarm system installed this morning. Keep me posted.'

Swift took his oars and continued upriver, taking it easy, not wanting to pull any muscles. A group of early morning runners pounded along the path to his right, their heels kicking up dust. The Watcher was becoming more violent. Presumably, the ultimate reckoning, whatever it was, wouldn't be postponed indefinitely. He had no clue who this man was, yet he sensed that he was circling, inching nearer.

* * *

Jed Clifford's blog announced that more than nine thousand people in London died prematurely each year because of air pollution. He would be taking part in a protest about it and particularly about the effects of diesel on the environment. He encouraged anyone who could, to come along and join in. The protest was taking place at the junction of Tottenham Court Road and Oxford Street, one of the most polluted parts of the city.

Clifford had to be a possible candidate for the Watcher. Swift wanted to speak to him again without Sonia present. He set off for the West End, hoping that she wouldn't be there. Oxford Street was the usual crush of tourists, harassed shoppers, buskers and nose to tail traffic. The hot, stagnant city air tasted soiled and sulphurous. A group of about thirty mainly young people were gathered on the pavement. Most wore nose plugs and black smog masks and held banners: Stop Ecocide, Fight for Clean Air, Big Business = Big Poison, Airpocalypse Now! A young woman played a set of bongo drums and chanted *breath is life!* Swift saw Clifford holding a placard with The Sentinels logo. He was talking animatedly to a couple holding shopping bags, his jeans hanging droopily on his scrawny hips. His hair was wilder than ever, as if he had been plugged in to the mains. There was no sign of Sonia. Swift put a pound in the collection box, accepted a leaflet and stepped into a doorway to read it.

That Toxic Taste

Can you taste it? It's what you're breathing. It's in your lungs and your blood right now.

England has the UK's dirtiest air.

Air pollution in London kills almost one in ten people.

Our cities are never far from a smog crisis because of all the pollutants pumped into our air.

Air pollution causes and exacerbates heart and lung problems, strokes, skin conditions and cancer.

Right now, you're taking in particles of sulphur dioxide and nitrogen oxide. Diesel is one of the worst pollutants and it's pouring from cars and lorries all around you.

In the worst affected areas, it can wipe more than ten years off a life.

Join us to fight for the clean air we need to live.

Breath is life.

There were details of organisations to contact, with email addresses and phone numbers. The Sentinels was listed. When he saw that Clifford was on his own, Swift worked his way around the pavement.

'Hi.' He raised his voice over the din of the street, the bongos and the chanting. 'Are you pleased with the turn out?'

Clifford lowered his mask, his eyes hard. 'What are you doing here?'

'I'm concerned about air quality,' Swift shouted truthfully. 'I row my boat on the Thames and sometimes my lungs ache when pollution levels are high.'

'Right. What are you doing about it?'

'Not enough, like most other people. I place my vote where I think it will do most good.'

'Yeah. And you drive your car.'

Swift hadn't come for a discussion about the environment but he couldn't resist. 'And how did you get here from Tunbridge Wells? Did you walk or cycle?'

'I got the train, of course.'

'More diesel fumes then. I came on a hybrid electric bus so maybe I have brownie points today. Still, we won't get into an argument about who's more worthy. While I'm here, I wondered if you've got a minute.'

'Why?'

Sweet talk him, he decided, looking at Clifford's obstinate mouth. 'I know you're skilled at IT. I wanted to pick your brain about the internet. I could really do with some help. I've donated to the group and I could buy you a coffee.'

Clifford pointed to his rucksack. 'I have a flask of rosehip tea with me. I don't need capitalist poisons produced by exploited third world labour in my body.'

'Okay. Well, could we talk for five minutes? It's too noisy here. I'll meet you in Soho Square. It's just nearby.'

Clifford adjusted his mask strap and glanced at his watch. 'How much did you donate?'

'A pound.'

'Put another twenty in and I'll meet you in half an hour,' he said dismissively.

Swift reluctantly parted with a twenty-pound note under Clifford's watchful eye, then crossed the road and went up Oxford Street. He turned down a side street and was soon in the peaceful oasis of Soho Square. He bought a coffee and a newspaper and sat on a bench near the mock-Tudor gardener's hut. A plane tree threw a small patch of dappled shade. A group of girls sat on the far side of the grass, chatting, eating crisps and comparing purchases. One of them held up a shirt, dancing it through the air. He leaned his head back for a moment, glad of the comparative silence.

He was halfway through the newspaper when Clifford arrived. The young man sat beside him, took a food flask from his rucksack and unscrewed it, releasing the savoury aroma of soup. He uncorked another flask and poured a cup of pale pink tea. His sleeveless T-shirt exposed his skinny arms and the bony hollow of his neck. There was a wiriness about him, despite his lanky body and a sense of feverish enthusiasm.

'I haven't got long.' He spooned up thick chunks of vegetable. 'What do you want to know?'

'Is it very hard to send anonymous emails? If I put my mind to it, could I do it, for example?'

Clifford caught carrot on his finger and slurped at it. 'I should think so. You'd have to read it up but it's not rocket science if you work on it, take some time to understand the tech speak.'

'I looked at The Sentinels website and your blog. They're good. Did you teach yourself how to set them up?'

'I studied computer sciences at school.'

'What does that involve? It wasn't available when I was a student, or was in its infancy.'

'My course concentrated on computational thinking, problem solving, designing systems, understanding human and machine intelligence.' He smirked. 'I know what you're up to. If you're still trying to pin those emails to the Maddoxes on me, you've got it wrong. I wouldn't waste any more time on Maddox. I'm done with him. Yes, I finished my business with him.'

Swift watched the girls pick up their bags and drift away, heads close together. 'When did you get interested in the environment? Before you met Sonia?'

'Yep, when I was in my teens. I saw which way corporate greed was driving humanity.' He had gobbled up the soup and was licking his fingers slowly and methodically, like a cat. He burped softly and patted his stomach. 'That was good.'

'You seem pretty angry a lot of the time. Stella Gath told me you had a difficult childhood.'

Clifford darted a quick look at him, then laughed. 'Who doesn't? Old Stella. What a sucker she is for a sob story. What a total sucker. She's always worrying about people and wanting to mother them. Pity she doesn't worry about Gabe a bit more. He doesn't need mothering, he needs sorting out. He says *jump* and she says *how high*? Pity she doesn't worry more about herself.'

'Maybe Stella understands more than you think. Tolerance isn't a bad quality. So, were you in care at all or have you got a police record? For assault or stealing? Troubled kids often end up with criminal records.'

'Fuck off! Who do you think you are, asking me stuff like that? Arrogant git.'

'Yes, I can annoy people. Do you have any connection with New Zealand?'

'You what? Hardly. Other side of the world. It would be great to go there some day but I won't be doing that until they build planes that don't pollute the atmosphere.'

'Right, of course. Have you ever met Gabe or Thomas Maddox on a personal basis?'

Swift thought that the question had thrown him. For a moment, he looked away. Then he finished his tea and wiped his mouth with the back of his hand.

'No. I dealt with Gabe Maddox because of the protest. He's not the type I mix with socially. Boring bourgeois old farts. I don't know the grandson. I don't envy him having Gabe for a grandad.'

'Did you know that Thomas had an accident on the tube?'

'No and I'm not interested, to be honest. I don't know why you're wasting your breath with pointless questions. The Maddoxes aren't on my radar these days.' He brushed his hands on his jeans. 'Like I said, my business with Gabe is done.'

There was a false lightness in his tone. Swift felt flat and discouraged. It seemed that he could make no progress, that he was leafing through pages and they were all blank. He scrutinised Clifford and thought over what he had just said. He had an idea and thought it was worth a punt.

'It was you who attacked Gabe Maddox a couple of weeks ago, wasn't it?'

'Don't know what you're talking about.'

But he was blushing. Clifford had no subtlety.

'I think it was you. And I think Gabe knew it. But why leave it so long after you lost your protest? Was it just a general warning not to mess with the environment?'

Clifford looked furious. He clenched his right fist and punched it into his left hand. Then he leapt up and busied himself packing up his rucksack. He shook his hair back and stood close to Swift, breathing hard. Savoury fumes filled the air. 'You're an interfering bastard. I've had enough of you and your insinuations. You'd better be careful if you think I attack people. I might creep up on you when you're not expecting it. Fuck off with your questions and your weird ideas. You're wasting my valuable time. I have to get back to my work.'

Swift stayed there with his coffee after Clifford departed. He was sure that the young man had attacked Gabe Maddox but couldn't understand why. He was full of angry tension but it was hard to see why he would carry out the kind of campaign the Watcher was waging. He mulled over the different strands of the case until his brain felt crowded and weary. He had an appointment later in the day to see Wilfrid Maddox. He suspected it would lead him up another blind alley.

* * *

'Can you make yourself useful and put a light bulb in for me? Bloody carers say they can't do it. Against health and safety or something. What about my health and safety? I can't see to do it.'

Swift took the light bulb from Wilfrid Maddox, stood on a chair in the living room and fitted it.

'Let there be light!' Maddox flicked the switch and left it on despite the strong sunshine flooding the room.

He lived on the ground floor of sheltered housing. A bland, functional one bedroomed flat. The door to the tiny bedroom was open, showing a narrow single bed, an old mahogany chest of drawers and a row of shoes on the floor with shoetrees in.

'Welcome to my cupboard,' he had said at the door. 'You're supposed to shrink as you get older. Then you can be tidied away.'

'It's functional,' Swift said. It was one of the smallest living rooms he had been in. An old, scarred piano stood under the window.

'Hah! Well, I suppose I don't need a palace, the way I creep about. And I was lucky that this place was built around the corner from where I used to live. Born in Bermondsey, die in Bermondsey!'

His voice was reedy but he seemed keen to talk. He was slightly built, with a cloud of white woolly hair and crooked, stained teeth. His glasses had thick, smudged lenses that magnified his rheumy eyes and one of the arms was secured with an orange sticking plaster. His white trainers and gaily-striped T-shirt gave him a deceptively youthful air. There were only two chairs so Swift took the one facing the window. It was upholstered in a faded velour and sagged beneath him. The room was airless, with no windows open and there was a lingering smell of fried food.

'You've always lived in this area, then? Swift asked.

'That's right. And my parents before me. I worked in the docks, like my old man. That was before the posh cafés and art galleries arrived here. And what do they call them? Hipsters, that's it. In the sixties, hipsters were trousers. No docks left now. I miss the sound of ships' engines and the whiff of diesel. And the lovely malty smell from the biscuit factory and a pint in The Cock and Monkey. But I've had my time. You have to make way. Anyway, what makes you come visiting a decrepit old fogey like me on a fine day?'

'I know Thomas comes to see you. He says he's told you about the emails he and his grandfather have been getting.'

'He said something about it. I don't do email. All double Dutch to me. I don't know why anyone would be nasty to Thomas. He's a well-meaning lad. Nothing like his grandfather, thank goodness. He rang and told me about the accident on the tube. Dangerous place, the underground. I knew a bloke got stabbed there back in the fifties. Someone came up behind him with a knife and did for him, quick as a flash. They never got who done it. Too many people about, too much commotion. I've often thought someone might stick a knife in Gabe's back.' He scratched at a patch of dry skin on his forehead and flakes floated around him.

'Why do you think that? I know you and Gabe don't talk.'

'No. We never got on once he grew up. Even as a little kid, he was cocky and full of himself. Then he got big ideas once he left school. Making an ordinary, decent living wasn't enough for him. He started wheeling and dealing, cutting corners. He thinks he can buy his way through life. That's all very well as long as you don't cross the wrong person. Sounds like he has now.' He moved his glasses down his nose and rubbed his eyes.

'And you had a daughter?'

'That's right. Little Vera. Sweet little thing she was. Lovely singing voice. She died in the early fifties. She got polio and didn't make it. I'd have had her to look after me now, wouldn't I?'

'Possibly. I'm sorry about her death.'

'Well, a long time ago. A lot of water under the bridge since then.' He removed his glasses, rubbed them on the end of his shirt and put them back on.

'Do you mind if I ask what you and Gabe fell out over?'

'I do, funnily enough. Don't see why it's any of your business.' He tapped the side of his nose.

Swift nodded. 'Fair enough. The reason I ask is that I think that Oscar's abduction and these emails are connected. I also think that the answer to what is going on lies somewhere in the Maddox family, but I don't know where.'

Wilfrid Maddox crossed his skinny legs. 'Poor little Oscar. I only met him once. Thomas brought him. Had him in a sling type thing across his chest. Funny looking way to carry a kiddie. He doted on that baby. Now he comes here and he sits where you're sitting and cries. I don't know what to say to him. Nothing I can say. I give him a cuppa and a biscuit. Seems to comfort him. I don't really remember Gabe when he was a baby. Children were women's work back then.' There was a silence. Maddox coughed and rubbed his throat. 'Tell you what, get me a stout from the kitchen and I'll have a think. Have one yourself if you want. Pour it carefully, mind, I don't want it all foam.'

Swift went to the tiny kitchen. There was a frying pan on the cooker with two burnt sausages in it. He saw that the electric ring was still on low and turned it off. A dozen bottles of stout were lined up by the draining board. He found a bottle opener and a tall glass. His grandfather in Connemara had loved his stout, believing that it kept him fit and healthy with its quota of iron. Swift had watched him pour it, holding it up to the light, admiring its dark caramel tones. He tilted the glass and poured slowly, achieving a small head on the drink, ran himself a glass of water and took it through to the old man.

'Not bad at all, you might make a barman yet.' Maddox took a deep draught and licked foam from his lips. 'You not having one?'

'No thanks. Water's fine for now and I'm not a stout drinker.'

'Suppose you go for poncy wines. All the young blokes do now. Give me a stout any day. A proper drink with a bit of body to it.'

Swift sipped his water. There was the faint drone of a television from upstairs and occasional bursts of applause. Maddox sat his glass on his knee, holding it with one veiny hand and put his head back.

'You've wasted your time coming here. I fell out with Gabe because he sold his grandmother's ring. She'd left it to him to give to the girl he married. That ring was special to her. Her dad was in India with the British army and had it made for her, gave it to her on her twenty-first birthday. It was sapphire and diamond. I found out that when Gabe's wife died he flogged it. What kind of man does that? Money and more money, that's all he cared about. We had a big bust up over it and I haven't seen him from that day to this. Good riddance to bad rubbish.'

Swift felt disappointed. 'When was this?'

'Can't remember exactly. Thomas was little. Julie, my granddaughter, used to come and see me for a while and bring Thomas but then she stopped. I suppose she got ill. Gabe didn't even tell me she died. Karen, a friend of hers let me know. She still comes in regular to see me. So there you are. Sometimes I reckon I stay alive to annoy Gabe. I know the thought of me hanging about gets on his nerves.'

'Well, it was good to meet you anyway. I see you play the piano. That's where Thomas gets it from.'

'My mum was musical. I taught myself, didn't have lessons like Thomas. The piano's out of tune. I used to play two nights a week at The Cock and Monkey for free beer.' He rose unsteadily and sat at the piano, cracking his fingers and running them up and down the keys. A tinny, flat sound came out as he launched into playing and singing:

What a wonderful fish the sole is,
What wonderful fish are soles.
Though I'm glad to relate,
I'm partial to skate,
When served on a plate with rissoles.

He coughed, laughed and turned to Swift. 'Still got it, eh?'

'You have.'

'That's an old music hall song. Ah well, no free beer anymore!'

The front door opened and a woman called a greeting as she rushed in, carrying a bag of shopping. 'Ooh sorry,' she said, 'didn't mean to interrupt.'

'This is Karen,' Maddox said. 'Kaz, this is a detective. He's looking for Oscar. Can't remember your name, young sir.'

'Tyrone Swift. I'm a private investigator.'

'Blimey. Isn't it a bit late to be looking for Oscar?' Karen was small and rounded, in a bright cherry skirt and white top. Her afro hair was coloured auburn and plaited at the front, then rolled into two buns at the sides of her head.

'Gabe Maddox has asked me to.'

She pulled a face. 'Oh, him.'

'You were a friend of Julie Maddox?'

'That's right. We were at school together. I've got fish fingers and oven chips in here for you, Wilf. I'll stick them in the freezer in case they start defrosting. Don't want to kill you off just yet!' She cackled loudly.

'You just try. There's life left in the old dog for a while, I reckon.'

Swift said goodbye to Maddox as Karen took the bag to the kitchen. The old man raised his glass and turned the radio on loud for a news bulletin, leaning in. Swift paused and put his head through the kitchen door.

'I gathered from your expression that you don't like Gabe Maddox.'

'I don't, no.'

'Any particular reason?'

She was bending at the freezer and glanced up at him. 'Well, he's a racist to start with, or used to be anyways, and I'd guess he hasn't changed. He never liked me going to the house. And he used to upset Julie, trying to run her life. She was always crying on my shoulder. Mind you, she cried easily. She was a right softie. I've seen Thomas here now and again and he's ever so like her.'

'In what way did her father run Julie's life?' He could hardly hear her over the noise of the radio. He pushed the kitchen door to and stood with his back to it.

She closed the freezer and straightened, pulling her top down. 'Telling her various boyfriends weren't good enough for her, that kind of thing. He was a bossy bloke and she couldn't stand up to him. He could be a real charmer when he wanted but he was a bully as well. Always wanted things done his way. Julie's mum used to stick up for her but once she'd gone her dad ruled the roost. She was raped, you know and then she found she was expecting. He wanted her to get rid of the baby. But she managed to stand her ground that time.'

'Yes, the family told me about that. Julie must have been terribly upset after the rape, finding out that she was pregnant.'

'Yeah. But then she really wanted the baby so, in a way, it worked out okay. I have to admit, her dad gave way and stood by her then. I suppose nobody's all bad.'

'When did you last see Gabe Maddox?'

'At Julie's funeral. I didn't see that much of her after Thomas was born because they moved to Highgate. Her dad had made a pile of money buying and selling property so they went to a more upmarket area. She rang me now and again and she told me when she got cancer. I did meet her once, in a café at Hampstead Heath. Thomas was just walking and we had a coffee and fed the ducks. She seemed pretty upset that day, looked as if she'd been crying. She said her dad didn't like some bloke she was keen on. The usual stuff. I hear her dad's in Kent now. Poor Thomas. Lost his mum when he was little and then lost his baby. How much sadness can someone take? Life's not fair, is it?'

'No, it isn't. Did Julie tell you anything more about this man she'd met?'

'No. Thomas fell over and cut his knee and she had to take him home. She did mention some bloke who was involved with her dad's business who was nice to her. Oh, what was his name? Hang on a minute, it was the same as someone famous.' She tapped her forehead and her foot simultaneously. 'Gary Cooper, that was it! Just like the actor. Don't know if he was as handsome, though. He was an accountant, that's right. She said he was an accountant, dealt with her dad's taxes. Fiddled them, knowing her dad.'

'Did the family ever know anyone in New Zealand?'

'Shouldn't think so, never heard it mentioned. They were all from round here. Julie's mum was a local girl too.'

She looked at the pan. 'Those sausages have died a death, think I'll chuck them.'

'Mr Maddox had left the cooker on.'

'Not again! I tell him he'll have a terrible accident and burn this place down one day but he won't listen. He could have those ready meals but he insists on doing his own.'

'Independence. We all want it and want to keep it.'

'Not much good to you in a coffin,' Karen muttered, seizing the frying pan and ditching the charred contents in the bin.

* * *

Poor old Thomas. So accident-prone. Such bad luck. You have to be careful in places like the tube. Very crowded. Anything can happen. It was interesting to see what would happen. It was all chance and the spin of a coin. He was saved this time. It wouldn't last though. The cat would run out of lives.

I went to a restaurant and ate steak with spinach, followed by apricot and pear tart afterwards. A brandy to round things off. A little reward.

It was good to think about what I'd achieved. Each little win. Those ferns had been a good touch, meaningful to someone but mysterious to the rest.

The detective is thought-provoking. Playing his own games. I know what he's up to, trying to draw me out. But I'm always ahead of him. He's getting bogged down in lots of detail and complications. And yet, in a way, it's all so simple. That's the beauty of it.

Up the snakes with them all and down the ladders.

Roll the dice.

Fun for me. They'll lose.

CHAPTER 9

Ruth sounded faint and drowsy.

'I was worried. I haven't heard from you.' Swift was on his way to see how Thomas Maddox was and give him a picture of Oscar. The bus was almost empty. Swift was on the top deck and tree branches swiped the window now and again.

'Sorry, I know. Emlyn's been in and out of hospital with an infection and Branna's had colic. A bit full on here.'

'Did Emlyn's mother mention that she saw me the last time I had Branna?'

'She was tight-lipped about it but said she thought you were full of your own importance.'

'I see. I didn't take to her either.'

'No. She can be standoffish. She means well. Obviously, she worries about Emlyn.'

'How is Branna? Can you give her something for colic?'

'Yes, she has medicine. She's better now although it still comes and goes. It makes her a bit grumpy and wakes her up.' She gave a huge yawn.

'Olwen said you're being treated for postnatal depression.'

'Yes. I'm okay, just a bit tired. The medication helps.'

'You didn't tell me.' He hadn't meant it to sound like an accusation but realised that was how it seemed.

'There's nothing you can do. I don't see any point in going on about it. You know I've never liked people who bore on about illness.'

'Well, look after yourself. I would like to see Branna soon. Can we arrange that now?'

A long pause. 'Look, Ty, things are busy here right now, life is complicated. Emlyn is on different drugs that need monitoring. Can we leave it a few weeks? Give Branna time to settle from this colic, get back into a routine.'

He knew he was being held at arm's length and there was little he could do.

'Okay, Ruth. You will let me know if I can help you in any way, won't you? I miss Branna, you know. It's hard.'

'Hard? Tell me about it.' Her voice lowered, stumbling. 'Sometimes . . . sometimes I have these terrible thoughts and I feel so bad. I lie awake and imagine that I'm free of Emlyn and I wish . . . I wish him gone. There, I've said it. I wonder what kind of person I've become. Sometimes I hope that next time . . . that next time I go into Emlyn's room I'll find him dead. Then he'll be at peace and so will I. I picture his funeral and I know that I'll feel sad and relieved. It is awful, dreadful, but I can't stop the thoughts and images coming. I see Olwen looking at me and I worry that she knows.'

More than once, he had imagined the same scenario himself, wondered how long Taylor could live. 'Ruth, you're exhausted. I think a lot of people in your position would have those thoughts. Don't beat yourself up.'

'Easy to say. Branna is crying. I'd better go. I'll ring you soon.'

She was gone. He looked out at the urban sprawl of south London. The bus stopped and loitered at a parade of small shops: a fast food chicken outlet, a launderette, a betting shop, a mini supermarket, a boutique selling saris and a chemist. They were all grimy and down at heel. The sun magnified every flaw in paintwork, every crack in plaster. He felt the surge of anxiety that often spilled through him these days when he thought of Ruth or spoke to her. She had changed from the woman he had known and lived with, and become unpredictable, moody, acting on impulse. This is how it's going to be, so you had better get used to it, he told himself. You are always going to be gauging the weather with Ruth and her husband and asking if you can have time with your daughter. He looked at the photos he had taken of Branna on his phone, thinking that she would already have changed by now, some weeks on.

The caravan park was silent in the late morning. The grass had just been cut and the pungent, new mown smell filled the air. The sun still beat down brutally, with no sign of the clouds that had been forecast to arrive soon. The curtains were pulled across Thomas's caravan windows. There was no answer to Swift's knock. He tried the door handle and it opened. Swift knocked again and called Thomas's name but all was silent. A couple of fat flies were circling inside the door. His instincts told him something was wrong. He went inside, closing the door. The heat was intense. The living area was much the same as on his last visit, the small table littered with a smeared soup bowl, an open crisp packet and a handful of chocolate biscuits. A bluebottle was patrolling half a chicken sandwich. The air was rancid. A couple of pairs of shorts were hanging on the clothes airer. He touched one and it was bone dry. The sink was stacked with unwashed crockery and a half empty soup pan sat on the small electric ring with a wasp's corpse floating on the surface.

The louvered door to the sleeping area beyond the kitchen was closed. Swift knocked on it. There was no response. He took a tissue from his pocket and used it to open the door slowly. A heavy, sour smell hit him. The room was dim. He could see a shape as he stepped into the thick atmosphere. Thomas lay on his back on the bed, dressed only in denim shorts. His eyes were closed, his face greyish white and waxy. He looked crumpled and worn. Death had aged him. Swift noted that his bare feet were blueish. His hands lay at his sides, palms down. The fingers of each hand had been severed just behind the knuckles and laid out a few inches from the stubs left on the hands. A small pool of pinkish fluid surrounded them. The chewed fingernails seemed shrunken. Swift looked closely at what remained of this sad young man. He could see no other injury or sign of damage. He touched an arm. Thomas was cold, his skin flaccid. Rigor mortis had left the body.

There seemed to be no oxygen, just the cloying stench of decay. Swift felt as if he was going to be sick. A wave of heat and cold washed through him and the room turned shadowy. He hurried from the bedroom and opened the caravan door. He sucked in the scorching air, bending forward with his eyes closed until he felt the nausea subside. He unbent slowly, lights flashing beneath his eyelids. He wiped his forehead with his arm and swallowed, then stepped outside, found his phone and rang the police.

He went into the caravan again and closed the bedroom door using the same tissue. Back outside, he found a small patch of shade at the rear of the caravan and sat on the grass. He rang Gabe Maddox and left a message, saying that he had serious news about Thomas and he had called the police. He tried Stella Gath but got voicemail for her as well and left the same message. He closed his eyes and pictured Thomas's body. There was no obvious cause of death. He thought that the fingers must have been cut off after death because there was so little blood. The way they had been displayed seemed like a horrible mockery. He was sure that it was the Watcher's work. He had either killed Thomas and cut off his fingers or found him lying dead and then desecrated his body. Why would he wish to do that and why were Thomas's fingers significant? Because he played the piano? None of the emails had referred to Thomas's musicianship. Sheet music had been stolen from Thomas but Suzy Mulligan was responsible for that theft. Swift's head felt heavy. Nausea swelled again and this time he retched into the grass. He found a bottle of water in his rucksack, drank and sprinkled some on his face.

The police arrived and a slightly built man with floppy hair and busy eyes introduced himself as DI Colman. Swift showed him his ID and explained who he was and how he had found Thomas Maddox's body. Colman wiped his brow and asked Swift to wait while he took a look inside.

'You can sit in the car if you want. I've left the engine running with the air con on.'

Swift slipped gratefully into the back of the car. It was littered with cigarette butts, food wrappers and empty drink cans but the cold air felt like heaven. A detective was busy securing the area and laying barrier tape on the grass. Colman slid into the back with him after a while.

'Can't do much more until the forensics and pathologist arrive. Nasty bit of surgery on the fingers. Looks like they were chopped off after death. Maybe we have a murderer who likes a bit of mutilation.'

'I wondered about that. Rigor has gone as well so he must have died a couple of days ago. He had an accident recently and suffered concussion. The police spoke to him about it. You need to contact a DI Abby Cheng who has been involved with Thomas Maddox. His son was abducted two years ago.'

'Got her number? I'll ring her now.'

Swift gave him the number. He left the car and went to the shade at the back of the caravan. Swift knew he was being checked out. He watched Colman pushing his hair back and pulling his shirt away from his body as he talked on his phone. There was a huge circle of sweat like a dark stain on the back of the shirt. A couple of children had noticed the activity and approached over the grass. One of Colman's colleagues sent them packing. Colman returned, twirling his sunglasses in one hand.

'Okay, DI Cheng verified what you've said. You been in the police?'

'In the Met, yes.'

'Right. Well, that's handy.' He gestured to a woman officer standing guard by the caravan door. 'Tell my sergeant what you know about Maddox. He lived here, presumably?'

'Yes. He borrowed the caravan from a friend after he split up from his partner.'

DI Colman pulled a face. 'I hate bloody caravans. Boiling in the summer and freezing in the winter. When it rains, you can't hear yourself think. My dad owned one in Weymouth. He used to drag us there for all our holidays. It always pissed it down. Nightmare. Any family?'

'His next of kin would be his grandfather. I phoned him and left a message saying something serious had happened. And there's his ex.'

'Any idea who might have done this?'

'I'm not sure. Thomas and his grandfather have been getting anonymous emails and there have been some other unexplained attacks and break-ins. I don't know if those are related to Thomas's death. The accident he had was on the tube and he might have been pushed.'

'Sounds like a murky old soup. Okay, talk to my sergeant. Leave your details. You'll know the ropes on this but if you're talking to any of his family, don't tell them about the fingers. Leave that to us. It's a horrible detail but they'll have to know. I'll be in touch.'

The sergeant, Davida Ramen, joined Swift in the car and took down the details. He had another drink of water and looked at the envelope with pictures of Oscar in his rucksack. He thought of Maura and wondered how this new loss would affect her.

As he went back towards the bus stop, he rang Maura but she didn't pick up the call and he didn't want to leave a message. He tried Gabe Maddox again with no success. He spotted a café near the bus stop. It looked invitingly dim. Despite the heat of the day, he felt in need of a warm drink. He ordered a large coffee and a slice of fruitcake and sat in the slipstream of a tall fan, feeling the sweat dry on his neck. The sugary cake restored him. As he sipped his coffee, he looked out of the window and saw that there was a funeral parlour across the road. Two men were lifting a covered shape from a plain van and placing it carefully on a wheeled trolley. They pushed it slowly down a small alley at the side of the shop. The scene reminded him of the words spoken at funerals: In the midst of life, we are in death. He savoured the last of his coffee, wondering how Thomas Maddox had died. His phone rang and he saw that Stella Gath was calling.

'I got your message and Gabe has just left me one saying that the police have contacted him and Thomas is dead,' she said. 'Thomas. Poor Thomas. That poor man.' She sounded as if she had been crying.

'I'm so sorry.'

'What happened?'

'I don't know. The police are there now. They'll give you the details when they can. Is Gabe around? I've been trying to reach him.'

'No. I'm at home, in my own home.'

'Oh, I see. Do you know where he is?'

She sniffed. 'No. I don't care, either. He can go to hell.'

'I'm sorry. Has something happened?'

'Yes. You could say that.' She breathed in on a sob. 'I can't believe what is happening today. It's all too much. I had some mail of my own this morning. I won't be going back to the windmill or working there.' She started to cry, quietly but uncontrollably.

Swift listened. 'Stella, I'm sorry. You're clearly very upset. When you say mail, do you mean one of the anonymous emails? Take your time, take your time.'

She gulped and he heard her blowing her nose. 'No. Some post. I can't . . . I can't talk now.'

She rang off. Swift paid his bill. His phone buzzed and he saw he had an email. From the Watcher:

Frankly, I'm not impressed with you, Mr Swift. Your website makes such good reading but you don't live up to your own publicity. There you are, running about like a headless chicken, getting sweaty and exhausted. Trotting around London, down to Kent, asking your questions. All leading you exactly nowhere. You really haven't a clue. I can tell. You're not adding enough to my fun, although I am enjoying myself. Come on, buck up, show a bit more effort. It's all getting too easy.

Good, the silence was needling the Watcher. He was right, though. The investigation was sluggish. If he had made more progress by now, Thomas might not be lying dead and disfigured. He was irritated with himself and felt that he had failed the young man. He put his phone away. He needed to know what had been sent to Stella Gath. Whatever was happening and whoever was behind it, he felt that there was a gathering and malicious momentum. He saw a taxi with its light on and hailed it, deciding to get the car and head to Tunbridge Wells straight away.

* * *

Swift found Stella's address on Google. She lived on the outskirts of Tunbridge Wells. On the motorway, he switched on the radio and listened to the cheery voice of a weather forecaster.

Tomorrow, London and the southeast will be hotter that Rio de Janeiro, courtesy of this ongoing tropical air mass and its heat plumes. The Met office has issued a level three health alert until midnight tomorrow. Pollen and UV levels continue to be very high. In the meantime, spare a thought for the people of Grimsby, who had a mini tornado yesterday. It is still likely that there will be thunderstorms soon.

He got lost in a maze of cul-de-sacs after heading down a slip road to the town. Eventually he found Stella's address in a road of modern semi-detached houses near the hospital. The blood orange sun was sliding down the western sky, the horizon aflame. He was momentarily blinded and had to lower his sun visor as he drove towards it. There was a short drive at the side of the house with a Volkswagen Polo parked on it. A neat, clipped lawn fronted the house and a pair of bay trees in terracotta pots flanked the white front door.

Swift left his car at the kerb and rang the bell. He saw a figure approach through the panes of frosted glass. Stella was wearing a white cotton dressing gown and carrying a whisky glass. Her face was blotched, but pale as bleached bone beneath the redness. Her eyes looked huge and puffy. Her hair was loose and wet, straggling down her back.

'Oh, it's you.' Her voice was thick with tears.

'I'm sorry to disturb you.'

'Hmm. I just had a shower. Trying to wash my cares away. It didn't work so I took to strong drink.'

'Can I come in? I won't stay long.'

She stood back without speaking, closing the door after him and leading him into an open plan sitting and dining room. Fresh from the shower, she smelled of apples and honey. He was aware of his own griminess and sweaty T-shirt, the clammy dampness of his hair. He imagined the smell from the caravan, the reek of death, shrouded him.

She gestured to a chair and he sat as she took a tissue from a box beside her and blew her nose. She stood for a moment, lost in thought, then sat on a small sofa.

'You found Thomas . . . I'm sorry . . . sorry that happened. What a day, what a bloody day this has been.' She leaned towards him and touched his hand fleetingly. 'You okay?'

'I'm okay.'

'You look pale.'

'I have found dead people before. I'll be fine.' An image of Kris Jelen lying on the floor, her face blue from strangulation, flashed before his eyes.

'How did Thomas die? Did he suffer? Please say he didn't.'

'I'm not sure, Stella. I wish I could tell you that he didn't. I went to see him and found him dead on his bed. There'll be an autopsy and that should determine cause of death.'

'My poor Thomas. I really liked him. A sweet boy. He was just a spotty teenager when I first knew him. Very affectionate. Very welcoming to me. I appreciated that, especially after the disaster of my divorce and the way Sonia behaved. He was nicer to me than my own daughter was. He once told me he was glad his grandad had found someone kind. There had been various girlfriends over the years. No one who lived in. Always younger. I was the most mature woman Gabe had taken up with. I suppose I did become a bit of a mother figure for Thomas. He played the piano so well . . . used to serenade me after dinner. Sometimes we'd sing together, although I haven't got much of a voice. Never again, now. That young man wouldn't have harmed a fly. It's just not fair.' She pressed the backs of her hands against her eyes. 'I hate crying, makes me feel so ill and block headed. Do you ever cry?'

'Sometimes. I cried when my mother died and when my fiancée left me for someone else.'

She nodded and pinched the bridge of her nose. 'How old were you when your mother died?'

'Fifteen.'

'Too young. Have you ever got over them, your mother and your fiancée?'

'No. I would like to get over my fiancée. Now and again I think I've succeeded but . . . the emotions are all there.'

She lifted her hair over the back of the sofa. 'Emotions. So many emotions. So much loss and so many gaps left in our lives. I'd say you're an honest man. Loyal. I'll find it hard to get over Gabe. He's turned out to be a bastard. Another bastard. I make a speciality of them. Shame I never met someone like you. Someone constant. I bet when you leave the house a woman would know you weren't lying about where you were going.'

Swift said nothing for a while. Then he leaned forward. 'Could you tell me what's happened?'

She finished her whisky. 'I'm going to get another of these first. Want one?'

'Not whisky. I'll have a white wine if you have any.'

'Oh yes, got lots of that. Gabe gets it from a special supplier. To keep me happy. Hah!'

He watched her glide away in her pink pumps, her hair rippling as it dried. Now that it was freed, it looked like her daughter's. The room was exactly as he would have expected, furnished carefully and modestly in pale colours with a matching pattern of cornflowers on the chairs and curtains. The carpet was cream, the walls off white. There were a few china ornaments and two pallid paintings of quiet seascapes. A little bland but comfortable, ordered. Two large, stuffed toy cats, a ginger and a smoky black, lay in front of the wall mounted electric fire. From the corner of his eye, they looked lifelike. He preferred them to Gabe's eerie collection of dead things.

She brought a tray with bottles of wine and whisky. She had tied her hair back with an elastic band. It was hard to look at her raw face. Something had undone Stella, broken her.

'Was your post about Gabe?'

'Oh, not just about Gabe. Oh no. I'm almost too embarrassed to show you.' She took a deep breath, reached for her bag, took out some photographs and passed them to him.

There were two printed photographs. They were good quality but slightly unfocused, as if taken through a window, but the naked figures sprawled on the bed were clear enough. Gabe Maddox and Sonia Gath lying side by side, entwined. The second photo was of Gabe lying on his back and Sonia sitting astride him, head thrown back, and her hair falling like a curtain.

'Charming, aren't they?' Stella mumbled.

Swift sat back. 'I'm sorry. This is very hard for you. Do you know who sent you these?'

She put her head in her hands. 'There was no note.'

'Did you keep the envelope?'

'No. I chucked it in the bin. My name was typed. It came through the letterbox, not posted. I suppose you think they're from the emailer.'

'Don't you?'

'How would I know? I don't seem to know anything, do I?' She gulped whisky. 'Good double bluff though, don't you think? Sonia pretending she couldn't stand Gabe and him never having a good word for her. Like the plot of a trashy romance.'

'Have you spoken to Sonia or Gabe about this?'

She looked at him and her eyes were suddenly burning behind the grief. 'I never want to speak to my daughter again. I wouldn't give her the satisfaction of seeing me upset. She is so . . . so *heartless*. If only my son had been the one to stay at home and she had gone to live in another country. My son *is* kind. I've put up with so much coldness from Sonia. Gabe left early this morning for some meeting. Possibly with Sonia, for all I know. I don't care anymore. I photocopied the photos and left him a note. I packed my things and brought them here. He can go hang. I'm sorry for him about Thomas. I know it will tear him apart but I don't think I can help him now. I wish he hadn't had to go through so much grief in his life but I'm fed up with being used and walked over. I never want to see him again either. What they've done is unforgiveable.' She looked at the photos again and shuddered. 'Would you forgive someone if they did this to you?'

'I don't think so.'

'No. No. My God, he's disgusting, look at him. Look at them. He is forty years older than she is. He's doing that while he's telling me I'm his bright star, his shining star, his twinkling diamond of a star. My God, how could he do that?'

'I'm sorry to ask you this but do you know where this bedroom is, in the photos?'

'Sonia's flat. Her bedroom. I suppose she was carrying on while Jed was at work. He's a reliable mug, like me. They picked us well.' She was still gazing at the images.

He thought back to Gabe strolling in the dusk near the windmill, then recalled his last meeting with Jed. The strange look on the young man's face and the hint of satisfaction in his voice. He realised why Jed had said that his business with Gabe was finished. Ah, he thought, Jed knew about Sonia and Gabe. Somehow, he had found out, either by seeing them or picking up on some other clue. That was why he thought Stella was pitiable. That was why he attacked Gabe. Gabe had surely recognised his attacker but had good reason not to divulge that knowledge. He touched the corner of a photo. 'Maybe it would be best to destroy those. Looking at them is only going to make you unhappy.'

She shook her head. 'Oh no. I'm keeping them. Just in case I'm ever tempted to trust someone again. A reminder of how very very stupid I can be.' She drained her whisky and poured another, splashing some on the carpet. 'I put so much into that business, into our home. Put money into it too. Slaved away. Loved it though, I did love it. And him. I really loved him. Would have done anything for him. See, even though I knew he had a roving eye, probably had affairs, I really believed he loved me. Even if I heard bad things about him . . . I thought we had something special. He was never tetchy or pushy with me, not the way I saw him sometimes with other people, with Thomas. He treated me so well, you know . . . as if I was royalty. I thought I had finally struck lucky after my rotten marriage. *Nothing's too good for my star*. My own daughter . . . my own daughter. They must have been laughing.' She put her hands to her face and stared at him. 'All those years, being part of a family. Things coming together, gelling. Building up memories. I worked my fingers to the bone in the windmill, you know.'

'Yes, I do know.' He wanted to leave, go to High Hawksford and see if he could find Gabe Maddox but Stella was downing more whisky and reminiscing, tears glistening on her face again.

'That windmill . . . it frightened me at first. Always sounds . . . creaks and groans. Like things were moving. Ghosts of people who worked it. When the wind blew, the sails whistled and clinked. Then I got to love it. I could see all the weather coming from up the top. Saw thunderstorms moving, big cloud shapes. Saw lightning crashing over us once, saw it hit the village church. It felt so close, that lightning. I felt it go through me. And rainbows, saw beautiful rainbows and evening skies. The sun rising and setting. Heard the jackdaws chattering when they perched on the sails. Thomas loved all that too. The sights and sounds. Well . . . all gone now. All gone.' She put her glass down unsteadily and folded her arms around her body. 'The last time I spoke to Thomas on the phone, he sounded so tired and worried. He had no peace or joy in his life since Oscar. He said you had an updated photo of Oscar. He wanted a copy.'

'I have some copies in the car. I can leave one with you if you like. Stella, I had better go now. I think that this emailer is becoming very dangerous. Make sure you lock your doors and windows.'

'Okay. If you say so. I would like a picture of Oscar. I often think about him.'

He went to the car. When he returned with the picture, she was trying unsuccessfully to straighten one of the seascapes.

'I got this because it reminded me of a tune Thomas used to play by Ravel. It was about a ship on the ocean. I loved that tune. I could hear the waves and the wind. Don't usually go for classical music but that was lovely.'

She stumbled to the sofa and he handed her the picture. While she looked at it, he levelled the painting.

'Darling little boy. I can keep this?'

'Yes, it's yours.' He looked at her slumped on the cushions, bleary eyed, drunk and thought she might fall asleep where she was for the night. 'Do you mind if I go round the house and check your windows and doors?'

'Hah! Sir Galahad! Go on, then.'

He was pleased to find that there were locks on all the double-glazed windows and mortice locks on the front and back doors. He closed and locked the kitchen window and checked upstairs, securing the bathroom window. When he came down Stella was sipping more whisky.

'You'll have a terrible head in the morning,' he said gently.

'Who cares? No one to tell me off. Don't have to look nice for anyone. Gabe used to call me *my classy Star*, said I made all the other women look second rate.' She stumbled from the sofa and lurched towards him, threw her arms around him and pressed her face into his chest. 'Why couldn't I have met a man like you?' she whispered again. Her hair was sweetly damp. She felt soft and warm. Her tears soaked hotly into his T-shirt. He kissed the top of her head, held her close for a moment, and then stepped back.

'No more whisky for now,' he said. 'You know it will make you feel worse. I've locked up and I have to go but you need to secure the front door after me. I won't get in the car until I hear you turn the key. Okay?'

She wiped her eyes, nodding. He waited until he heard her lock the door, then hurried to the car and headed for High Hawksford.

CHAPTER 10

There were no lights in the lower storeys of the windmill but a lamp glowed in the top room. From a distance, it resembled a lighthouse. Bats flitted through the inky night and the eyes of some small creature glinted from the verge. Gabe Maddox buzzed him through the gates and opened the door. He was wearing a crumpled light blue suit and looked tired and distracted, his tie knot half undone.

'I was just about to ring you,' he said.

'I've been trying to get hold of you.'

'I know. I've been busy in the West Country since early morning and there was a poor phone signal. The police managed to reach me earlier. You'd better come in.'

He led the way to his Victorian den at the top. His energetic bounce had been replaced with a weary tread. Dean Martin was playing low, crooning about memories. A crystal decanter of whisky was beside his wing back chair and a half full glass.

'I'm sorry about Thomas. It's terrible news for you,' Swift said. 'I've just been at Stella's. She's on the whisky too. Hearing about you and Thomas in the same day is a lot to take in.'

'Yep. I got the photos and her note. Dramatic, the note. Not like Star to be dramatic.'

Swift took the chair with its back to the stuffed animals, forever frozen in death. 'She's suffering.'

'Want a drink?'

'No. Better not, I'm driving and I've had a glass of wine with Stella.'

'I bet you're always a boy scout, law abiding. Don't you ever want to be naughty, push the boundaries?'

He thought of his personal life. 'There are different ways of doing that.'

'Right. Anyway, I suppose once a copper, always a copper. So Star's in a state.'

'Yes. I left her to sleep it off, hopefully. I told her to be careful about security, given your emailer's latest moves. You should, too.'

Maddox kicked his soft leather shoes off, undid his tie and let it hang loose.

'You found him, did you? You found Thomas?'

'Yes.'

'I rang the police from the car. I wanted more detail. I got some plod who said I'd be contacted tomorrow. I tore a strip off her, insisted a top guy speak to me. My grandson's dead and I get a plod. A DI Colman rang me back. Very smooth, lots of "sir" this and "sir" that. He obviously pressed some buttons because I had a visit from a couple of local police just before you arrived. They said they didn't know the cause of death yet. I told them I wanted to know if my grandson had been murdered and they'd better be quick finding out. They told me about Thomas's fingers, said they thought they'd been cut off after he died. You saw that, did you?'

'Yes.'

'My God. What kind of sick bastard uses a knife on a dead man?'

'Someone violent and vicious. But if that mutilation was done by your emailer you know that already. Cutting

Thomas's fingers off is significant. It might indicate resentment of his musical talents.'

Maddox stood and went to the window, looking out. 'They said I'll need to go and identify Thomas. I know I'll have to bear it. I buried his mother and now I'll have to bury him. I want to get my hands on whoever did this to him.' His phone rang and he grabbed it from his pocket, listening and nodding. When the brief conversation finished, he leaned his forehead against the window, then sat down again. 'That was DI Colman. He said initial findings show that Thomas died from something called Second Impact Syndrome. His brain swelled suddenly and rapidly. It can happen after concussion. He probably felt ill and had a blinding headache, lay down and never woke up.'

'So if your emailer was responsible for pushing him in the tube, and I believe he was, he has ultimately caused Thomas's death.'

Maddox swirled his whisky and sipped. 'Is that what the police will think?'

'I don't know. They'll probably be more interested in the finger mutilation than the tube incident. But I think they'll look again at the history of Thomas's bad luck and the emails now, once they have time to consider the whole picture. You need to make sure you go over all the details with them and tell them about the break-in here.'

Maddox threw back his whisky, then leaped from his chair and started pacing the room. His anger surged out and his voice rose. 'I'll be suing that bloody hospital, that's for sure. Discharging Thomas when he was still ill. Bastards. They should have kept him under observation. This might never have happened. He would be alive now. The boy would be alive.' He tugged off his jacket and flung it on the floor, then stopped at the window, threw it open, leaned out and spat into the air. 'I'll be onto my solicitor first thing in the morning. Negligence, that's what it was. They probably needed the bed for some saddo druggie or health tourist from the third world. I'll skin them. I rang Maura to let her know about Thomas. I'll phone her again to tell her I'll rip up those medics who failed him.'

He doubted that would offer Maura much comfort. 'Was she okay?'

'Yeah. She said her neighbour from downstairs was with her.'

'Did you see Thomas after he left hospital?'

Maddox gazed out again at his land. His hair looked glossy and thicker in the lamp light. Swift thought he'd had a new dye job.

'No. I've been so busy, rushed off my feet. I'm negotiating a deal for land in Herefordshire to establish another Smell the Roses. I phoned him, tried to persuade him to come here. Star would have fetched him. He wouldn't come. Always obstinate for the wrong reasons, that boy. Those doctors will be sorry they were ever born when I've finished with them.' His fists were balled tight. 'How did Thomas look? Did he look peaceful?'

'He was lying on his bed with his eyes closed. He looked at peace.'

'Well, some would believe he's with his mother now. I wish I could. I might go to that bloody hospital myself. Demand to see the director or whatever they call themselves these days.'

'I can't comment on the hospital's decision but I think Thomas would be dead now even if he hadn't had the brain trauma.'

'What do you mean?'

'I mean that I think your emailer went there intending to finish off what he hadn't achieved on the tube, but found him already dead.'

Maddox sat down again, leaning forward, eyes glittering. He looked his age tonight, mouth drooping, mauve bags under his eyes. 'You still have no idea who this is, or where he is?'

'No.'

'What the hell am I paying you for if you can't stop all this happening?'

'It's a good question. What's happened to Thomas now is a game changer. The police will be investigating a crime, asking lots of questions. Do you still want me involved?'

He was half expecting that Maddox would say no. He was fiddling with his whisky glass, fingers agitated. He seemed to be conducting an inner battle. There was something tearing at him and Swift thought he was about to divulge it but he mastered his feelings. He looked at Swift, a veiled glance, suddenly impassive again.

'Yes, I want you to stay on the case. Are you anywhere near finding this bastard?'

'It's hard to say. There have been a number of dead ends. The thing is, Mr Maddox, I don't believe you are telling me everything you know. You concealed the fact that you were having a relationship with someone who might have been targeting you.'

'I told you not to bother with Sonia. She's irrelevant.'

'Not to her mother.'

Maddox flinched. 'That's between me and Stella. Sonia was just sex. Fun and sex. She felt the same way. You're a bloke. You know how it is. Irony is, I finished it a couple of weeks ago. I decided it was too awkward and risky. She understood. She's a cool customer. I'll talk to Star, get her back onside. She knows I'm mad about her. Once she's over the shock I'll make it up to her, take her on a nice holiday somewhere. She's always wanted to go to Bali.'

It was all just trade as far as Maddox was concerned, bargaining and repositioning, keeping the balls in the air. His comments about finishing with Sonia slotted into place as Swift thought about Jed Clifford again.

'You ended it with Sonia because Jed Clifford beat you up. He found out, didn't he? He jumped you when you were out walking.'

Maddox waved a hand. 'Oh, yes, all right. It was Clifford. He found out I was seeing Sonia. So yes, I ended it. Sonia was too much trouble by then. I suppose I should have told you but I just wanted to forget the nonsense and I didn't want anything getting back to Star.'

'It's not only about Sonia. I think you understand the relevance of those ferns that were left downstairs, the message they carried. You might have had an idea prior to that but I think the ferns were a definite marker. Maybe you have a better idea of who this man is than I do. He's extremely dangerous, you must know that.'

The shuttered look returned to Maddox's face. The bland, unreadable mask of the dealmaker and breaker. Swift felt thwarted. The man had a hidden agenda. Maybe he could tease it out.

'Have you been corresponding with the emailer?'

Maddox gave an exasperated sigh. 'I'd hardly spend my money on you if that was the case. Give me a break. I wouldn't talk to that scum.'

Swift couldn't tell if he was lying or not. He had been about to mention Gary Cooper but decided not to. Two could play the game of keeping their cards close to their chests.

'Did you talk to my dad?' Maddox demanded.

'Yes. He told me why you fell out.'

'You mean he told you his version of it.'

'That's the thing about stories, isn't it? There are always a number of versions. It depends on the point of view.'

'Whatever. Still going strong, is he?'

'He said he stays alive to spite you.'

Maddox glared, and then laughed. 'I like you, Swift. You irritate the hell out of me but I like your frankness. Right, as soon as you get a sniff of where this scumbag is, I want to know. Understand? Identity, address. Never mind the police. They can do their own work at their usual snail's pace. I'm still paying you.'

'Whoever this man is, you can't approach him on your own. He's full of resentment and he's sadistic. Do *you* understand? I'm not in the business of putting lives in danger. If I identify him, I will decide on how to manage the information. I can't ignore the police.'

Maddox looked down, calculating. He put the top on the decanter, smoothed his wrinkled tie. 'Okay,' he said mildly. 'I understand you have professional boundaries. Keep me updated though, I must insist on that.'

Swift placed an envelope containing Oscar's picture on the table. 'This is a computer-generated image of what Oscar might look like now. I thought you would like to have it. I've given one to Maura and Stella.'

'Okay. I'll look at it but not tonight. I can't face it tonight.'

* * *

Swift turned to head back to London but changed his mind and drove to Sonia's flat. He was reflecting on the fact that Maddox had said Thomas might now be with his mother but he hadn't included Oscar in their company. Because of lingering hope or because he believed or knew that the child was alive?

There was a party in a house across the street from Sonia's. All the windows were flung wide and people spilled noisily into the tiny front garden. David Bowie and Mick Jagger were duetting on *Dancing in the Street.* The air was so still, every sound travelled, magnified. There was a light on in Sonia's basement but it took a couple of minutes for her to open the door. She had braided her hair and she wore a long gold and white kaftan with tiny mirrors stitched on the bodice. When she moved the mirrors glinted and glimmered.

'I had a feeling you might turn up,' she said. 'Gabe's told me about the latest events.'

'Can I speak to you?'

'Sure. I was out back, in the garden. Come through.'

It was a backyard rather than a garden. Small and rectangular, with a couple of old chairs, a green plastic table propped against the wall with a leg missing and tubs made from beer barrels, planted with white flowers that gleamed palely in the dark. Faint light spilled out from the back of the house and a citronella candle in a metal lantern stood on the ground, burning with a lemon flame. The music and noise from the party drifted over, surging and ebbing.

'Rules of engagement,' Sonia said. 'You can spare me any lectures.'

Swift sat, knowing the chair would wobble. 'Gabe told you about the photos?'

'Yep, when he phoned. Us in bed, Gabe said. Pervy. Not nice, being snooped on.' She pointed with a thumb behind them at a low sash window. 'That's my bedroom just there. The perv must have stood outside. Hope he enjoyed the free show.'

Her face was shadowed but she was speaking in her usual laconic style. She sat upright, knees raised, her bare feet propped on a chair seat.

Swift gestured at a sagging timber door in the back wall of the yard. 'Is that an alley running along the back?'

'Yeah. The door lock's broken so it would have been easy to sneak in while we were too occupied to notice.'

'Have you noticed anyone hanging around here or anything unusual?'

'No.'

'When did it start?'

She looked up at the sky, and then glanced at him. The bodice mirrors sparkled as she shifted her weight. 'Is that . . . what's the phrase . . . is that germane to your enquiries?'

'I suppose not. I'm just interested.'

'Oh well . . . Gabe came round here one day soon after we lost the protest against him. He brought chocolates, said he didn't like Stella being upset and could we agree to disagree, et cetera. Chocolates! Men have such limited imaginations. I was going to throw him out but then I decided I found him oddly attractive. He's mature and well . . . you know . . . skilful. Funny, too. Makes me laugh.'

'So your ideological differences and your mother didn't get in the way?'

He saw her teeth gleam as she smiled. 'Good sex is good sex. We suited each other in that way. Both predators. He wasn't faithful to my mother anyway. She has always chosen to be a sap where men are concerned. And I happen to like expensive chocolates.'

'What about Jed, when did he find out?'

'Just before he beat Gabe up. Except he didn't really find out. He came home early from work one day with a migraine and he saw Gabe leaving here. I told him Gabe had turned up and had tried it on with me but I'd sent him packing. So he stupidly went and attacked Gabe and then he sulked for a while. All very macho and old-fashioned. Gabe assumed Jed knew we had been having an affair and I couldn't be bothered to enlighten him. Anyway, it put an end to our little dalliance, which was probably for the best. It would have run its course soon enough.' She bent down and moved the candle, her hair swinging. 'That's bad news, about Thomas. Gabe's pretty cut up.'

'So is your mother. Did Jed have a difficult childhood?'

'He's never talked about it much. His mum abandoned him, I know that, and I think he was in care for a while. He doesn't mention his dad. Why?'

'Just filling in the blanks. Are you sure that Jed hasn't been emailing the Maddox family?'

She laughed, a light chuckle. 'I heard that you'd been grilling him in London. I doubt it although you never really know anyone else, do you? He tends to blunder around in the world. I haven't noticed that he has any talent for being devious.'

How he disliked this woman. 'Unlike you.'

'Rules of engagement, remember. No moralising.'

A whoop of laughter echoed from the party and Adele's voice boomed into the night.

'Where's Jed now?'

'Out with his mates. I packed him off after Gabe rang me. I told him not to come back tonight. I wanted to be on my own.'

'Have you considered that whoever took those photos might make them more widely available?'

'If the perv does . . . well, I'll cross that bridge then. What's the worst that's going to happen? It would hurt Gabe more than me. If Jed decided to piss off, it would be annoying but I wouldn't mourn for too long.' Sonia stood, stretching like a cat. 'I can't help you. I haven't seen any prowlers. I don't know who's been emailing or taking photos or who took Oscar and I'm invited to the party so I'm going to head over there.'

They left the flat together and he watched her drift across the road, holding a bottle of wine, waving to a friend, apparently without a care in the world. He thought that despite their opposing views, she and Gabe Maddox were in many ways a perfect match.

* * *

Clapham Common was teeming with sunbathers, joggers, mothers with pushchairs and toddlers, several huge bouncy castles, girls playing cricket, dogs on leads, a gospel choir singing spirituals, and a thin man with a sandwich board proclaiming that meat eating was the cause of all ills. The sun glared pitilessly on them all. Swift passed the bandstand and a child's paddling area. He was grateful for the cool spray from the dolphin-shaped water feature. Excited screams filled the air as a group of boys targeted one another with water pistols.

Gary Cooper had told him to come around eleven thirty when he had a space in his diary. His office was above a shop that sold perfumed candles, cushions, photo frames, personalised mugs and the kind of spindly white furniture that looked as if it would buckle if a man of six feet three attempted to sit in it. Swift pressed the bell on the intercom at the door with the sign, *Gary Cooper Associates. Personal and Business Accountants.* He announced himself and the door buzzed open. A flight of steep stairs led to another door of frosted glass. It opened into a small reception area with bright blue carpet and a grey-haired woman sitting at a computer. She smiled at him and asked him to take a seat, adding that Mr Cooper wouldn't be long. The place was basic with cheap furnishings but a shelf of healthy looking plants behind the administrator's desk cheered it up.

'Do help yourself to water.' She pointed to a cooler. 'I'm afraid it's stuffy in here, but I don't open the window too wide because of the traffic noise and the fumes.'

'Thanks.' Swift fetched a beaker of water. 'Would you like one?'

'No, I'm all right, thank you. I'll have a cup of tea soon. Is it my imagination or is it even hotter today?'

'It's building. It must break soon.'

'Oh, that's what they keep forecasting but I've stopped believing it. My poor garden is suffering terribly. My next-door neighbour, an old gentleman, was taken to hospital with heat stroke last weekend. Every lunchtime and after work, I go to the supermarket around the corner and loiter by the chill cabinets. Delicious. Mind you, sometimes there are so many of us doing it, the real shoppers can't get to the ice cream and frozen peas!'

She had a warm, infectious laugh and he smiled at her. The whole of London was talking about the weather. It was the only topic of conversation. He was reminded of a baking July when his mother, who was suffering menopausal hot flushes, took to standing in front of the fridge with the door open. His father had said she would confuse the thermostat. She had cheerfully replied that you only live once and confusing a thermostat was worth it for the thrill of the chill. She had died of a rapid cancer the following summer. He was glad that she had gone for the thrill of the chill when she could.

Gary Cooper came to greet him within a few minutes. Swift wondered if he ever found his name a burden as he failed in the tall and handsome stakes. He looked in his early fifties, a small portly man with thinning black hair and poor skin. His office was a mess of paperwork and files, his desk cluttered with coffee cups and the remains of a doughnut.

'You mentioned Gabe Maddox.' He rocked back in his chair. His voice was thin and light. 'That's a name I haven't come across in a long time. And fine with me that I haven't, if I may say so.'

'You don't have fond memories?'

'Hardly. He owed me a backlog of fees for work done. I got it in the end but I had to threaten him with legal action.' He had an ingratiating manner, lots of smiling and nodding.

Swift watched bright red jam ooze from the lump of doughnut on to the plate, then drip on the desk. Cooper would have been a bit older than Julie. Maybe he had been her lover and the falling out with Maddox had been about more than an unpaid bill? He tore his gaze from the jam and settled it on Cooper. 'Gabe Maddox engaged me because he and his grandson Thomas were receiving unpleasant emails. His grandson died recently and there was probably foul play. Gabe's great grandson was abducted a couple of years ago. I visited Gabe's father, Wilfrid Maddox, and met a woman called Karen. She told me you were friendly with Julie, Thomas's mother.'

'That's right, I knew Julie. Lovely girl, soft and sweet. Terrible that she died so young. I'm sorry to hear about Thomas, too. I met him a couple of times when he was a tot.'

'It would help if you could tell me about your involvement with the family.'

Cooper picked up a paper clip and fiddled with it. 'I knew Gabe for about three years. He was living in Bermondsey and was on the up. He started off with a market stall but he saw that property was the place to make money. He needed an accountant so he came to me. We got pally. He was good company, a real mover and shaker and a laugh. A calculating bastard, though. Hard as well, especially when he wanted his own way. He took no prisoners. One of those alpha males. If he thought you had crossed him, he iced you out. He had done that with his dad. He might have succeeded in business but his home life was sad. He had lost his wife by then and Thomas was just a baby. I was at the house now and again, sorting out his books. He doted on his daughter and Thomas, I will say that for him. He was never one to mope or let the grass grow. Just got on with life.' Cooper had opened out the paper clip and was using a pointed end to clean under his nails.

'I've heard that Gabe was controlling with Julie, kept her under his thumb.'

Cooper nodded and continued his grooming. 'Well, she was a mousy little thing, in awe of her dad. You know she was raped?'

'Yes, and Thomas was the outcome.'

'She was sort of naive and timid. I suppose Gabe worried about her and his way of protecting her was by ordering her about, keeping a close eye on her. Anyway, he moved them to Highgate. Nice house, lovely neighbourhood and garden. I think he reckoned that Julie would be tucked away and safe there. My wife didn't like

Gabe. She said he was a smiling tyrant. She was pleased when I stopped working with him.'

'And money was the only reason you stopped doing his accounts?'

Cooper threw the mangled paper clip in a waste bin. 'That's right.' There was a silence, and then he gave a little laugh. 'Well, okay . . . it's all a long time ago but Gabe tried it on with my wife one night. He had taken us out to dinner. There was dancing and he got fresh. She was livid, said she never wanted to see him again.'

'You weren't a bit too sweet on Julie? Her friend Karen said Julie liked you a lot.'

'Now you're adding two and two and making five. And I'm the figures man, I should know. I had, I still have a beautiful wife. God knows how I got her but I did and I've never strayed. I was fond of Julie but she was just a kid emotionally.'

'Okay. So, did Julie talk to you?'

'Now and again. I liked her. There was nothing to dislike about Julie. She was pretty, in a pale kind of way, and very good-natured. I suppose I played a big brother role. There was one day I remember, after they had moved to Highgate. I was there and Gabe was in the garden talking to a builder about an extension. I could see Julie had been crying. I asked her if she was okay. She made me a cup of tea and told me she had met some bloke. He was painting scenery at a local theatre. I think it was called The Spotlight. It had a café attached and she had gone in for a coffee. She was keen on him but she said Gabe had seen them outside a pub and warned her off.'

'Any particular reason?'

'Gabe didn't like foreigners, reckoned they began at Calais and too many of them had already slipped into the country. Out and out racist, in fact. Julie said this bloke was part Maori and he'd come to London from somewhere in New Zealand the year before. I got the impression he floated around, doing odd jobs wherever he could get them. Julie was very taken with the fact that he was working in the theatre, found it all a bit exotic. He had been telling her stuff about his Polynesian ancestry, spoke some Maori, and taught her the Haka dance. I suppose Gabe thought she had got involved with a waster but the Maori bit would have done it for him. It was bad enough that Julie had been raped and now she was taking up with some bloke with the wrong colour skin. I just said that in the end, who she loved was her choice. What else could I say? I parted company with Gabe soon after that so I don't know what happened. Julie died a while later.'

Swift felt that he was turning a corner at last. The silver and green ferns made sense now. Something else whispered at the back of his mind as well. 'Did Julie mention this man's name?'

'Sam, I think. She didn't say his surname.'

'Did you talk to Gabe about it?'

'No. There would have been no point. Gabe wouldn't brook any interference in his family affairs and things between us were already on the slide.'

The room was incredibly hot and still. The chairs were faux leather, black plastic, designed to stick to skin. Cooper was dealing with his cuticles now, pushing them back with his thumbnail. Swift wondered if he had much work or if he sat here most of the day, eating doughnuts and self-grooming. He certainly didn't think he would have the interest, motivation, or energy for a campaign of hate.

'Did you know of anyone else Gabe Maddox fell out with, in business or personally?'

Cooper shook his head. 'Can't help you. It's all a long time ago and I've never seen him since way back then. Is he still in Highgate?'

'No, in Kent.' Swift peeled himself off the chair. 'Thanks for your time.'

'Hope I've helped.' Cooper finally noticed the leaking doughnut and scooped it up with a ragged, greying hanky he produced from a pocket.

'You have, thanks. You've been a big help.'

Back in the street, he turned onto the pavement and bought a bottle of ice cold water in a newsagents. He stood under the canopy outside, rolled the bottle between his hands and then poured most of its contents down his throat. He sipped at the remainder, stopping to look at a display of information about the area while his mind turned over what he had just learned. He read that far below his feet lay a warren of deep level tunnels, dug to shelter the population during the air raids of World War II. They had housed dormitories and chemical toilets and given refuge to thousands. Most were now lying abandoned but some were being used to grow salad vegetables.

Reading about food, he realised that he was hungry. He moved on to a café called Tart and bought a slice of onion quiche and a coffee. Mostly, he thought best when alone — on the river, walking or sitting on the swing seat in his garden. Sometimes, though, the hum of conversation and everyday noises of rattling crockery, doors swinging and the hiss of steam were a useful background medium. He demolished the crisp pastry and stirred his coffee. Gabe Maddox and Sam from New Zealand must have fallen out over Julie. Maddox would certainly have understood the significance of the ferns and had possibly guessed the identity of the Watcher. Swift now appreciated that Gabe and Thomas had both wanted him to investigate but not for the same reasons. Gabe was hoping that he would lead the way to the Watcher. And then . . . what was he planning then? To wheel and deal, maybe. Yes, that would be Gabe's style, especially if he thought Oscar might be alive.

According to the Watcher, Gabe had mistreated him. Maybe Gabe thought he could barter and manoeuvre to resolve whatever he had done wrong in the past. It was how he dealt with life's difficulties and winning was crucial to him. He could ring Gabe Maddox now and tell him what he had discovered about Julie's Maori boyfriend. He could insist that Gabe tell him what he knew. And yet . . . he knew that Gabe wouldn't, that he would slip and slide, deny the story with bluff and bluster. Best to carry on, except he wasn't sure where to turn next.

He sipped his coffee, closed his eyes and realised what had been niggling at him. He took out his phone and scrolled to the folder of the Watcher's emails, finding the one he wanted:

Oh, Thomas, when your cherished one is no longer with you it will be icy cold inland and icy cold on the shore.

He typed a few words of it into Google and discovered that it was from a Karakia, a Maori prayer used for spiritual guidance. He felt himself notch up a gear. Okay. The Watcher had to be Sam from New Zealand or someone connected to Sam. He looked up The Spotlight theatre and was relieved to see it was still in business. He was about to ring the number when Stella Gath phoned him.

'How are you?' he asked.

'Oh, you know . . . I hope I didn't embarrass you the other night. I had a dreadful hangover the next day. My memory is a bit hit and miss. I suspect I embarrassed myself.' She sounded shaky but in control.

'There was no embarrassment, Stella. You'd had a terrible shock.'

'Yes. You were kind. So I wanted to say thanks. Kindness means a lot when your life is falling apart.' She swallowed and cleared her throat. 'But there's something else. I looked at that picture you left, the one of Oscar. I opened it after breakfast and I've been staring at it on and off all morning.'

'Yes?'

'It's just . . . well, I've been telling myself that I'm imagining it. Wishful thinking. You see, I'm sure I've seen this little boy somewhere. And in the recent past.'

His heart skipped. 'Have you any idea where?'

'No. That's what is so frustrating. He just looks a bit familiar but I can't say why. I've been telling myself it's all in my head and I'm remembering baby Oscar. I've been so upset and my brain feels creaky from lack of sleep. But the thought keeps coming back to me. I'm not a fanciful person and my recall is usually reliable.'

That was true, she was usually steady Stella. 'Do you think this was somewhere locally?'

'Well . . . I'm not sure but I think so. I haven't been away much in the last couple of years. Too busy working with Gabe, keeping the business shipshape. I'm sorry, I'm probably confusing you. I'm confusing myself.'

'Put the photo away for a while and look at it later. It might come to you. Even if you did see a child who looked like the picture, it doesn't mean it was Oscar. Age progressed images are a stab in the dark.'

'Yes, okay. Have you . . . have you spoken to Gabe at all?'

'I saw him after I left you. Has he contacted you?'

'He's left eight messages for me. All saying how sorry he is and how much he misses me. He told me how Thomas died and that someone removed his fingers! That's dreadful. I'm terribly sad about Thomas but I don't want to speak to Gabe. Not for a while, anyway.'

'That's your call. If you do speak to him, best not to mention what you said about the picture, in case it comes to nothing. I gave him a copy.'

'Okay. I've left a message for Sonia, asking her to come here later this week. I've decided I want to tell her to her face that I never want to see her again. I'm going to put this house on the market and move away.'

'Where to?'

She sighed. Her pain was audible. 'I'll stick a pin in the map. Or maybe go to Italy, see my boy.'

'Stella, don't make any hasty decisions. You need to recover from what's happened. Wait a little while, until the hurt eases.'

'You think it will?'

'Inevitably. Bit by bit.'

'Well . . . we'll see. I'll look at the picture again this evening.'

'Phone me if you remember anything. And take care.'

Her voice dropped. 'I meant what I said and I remember saying it. I wish I'd met a man like you.'

'You hardly know me. I might have terrible personal habits and a bad temper.'

She responded with a half laugh, half sigh and ended the call. Swift sat back, watching a waiter deftly balancing three plates. Stella was astute but her memory had been affected by trauma and loss. He would just have to wait and see if she dredged up anything useful.

He had emailed Maura to give her his condolences about Thomas. He saw that he had a reply from her:

Thanks for your message. I know you tried to call me. I'm so sad about Thomas. I can't really think straight at the moment. The police contacted me. They want to talk to me, go over all the stuff that has happened. Sometimes it feels as if this nightmare will never end.

* * *

My old man broke my fingers when I was nine. Off his head on some hallucinogen. Snuck in while I was asleep. Brought a lump of concrete down on both my hands. He told the hospital that the concrete had fallen on me and warned me my life would be hell if I said anything different.

After the surgery, I was in hospital for weeks. The fingers never regained full flexibility. Once they healed and I was back with him, I bought a padlock and locked my door at night.

My old man always toadied up to the social workers who floated in and out of my life. He wanted me with him. Funny that, when he told me all the time that I was a waste of space. Nobody had wanted me. I was rubbish, should have been shoved in the dustbin at birth. He told me my mother didn't want me, said he could have me. He only kept me for the state handouts. He got me back from social services because he needed someone to torment and punish. Someone to send out to meet a dealer when he wasn't able to get off his mattress. And he wanted the child allowance.

Strange, finding Thomas like that. Something had finished him off before I could. I almost felt as if I'd lost a friend. I'd built up a kind of relationship. You get to know someone when you find out so much about them. There had been a closeness. I stood and looked down at him, feeling just a tiny bit sad. What a way to end up, in that shitty caravan. It was almost as bad as some of the squats my old man dragged me around. Stinky and dirty. It just showed, you never knew what was coming your way. Thomas wasn't in good shape though. Pudgy, unfit. Looked a candidate for a heart attack. All that crap food lying about.

The fingers were spur of the moment, unusual for me. Satisfying. Exciting to work without a plan for once. A bit of a thrill. It's a shame that I had to chuck my Swiss army knife afterwards but that's how the cookie crumbles.

The police will be back on the case now but that's okay. They haven't been much good so far. And with Swift involved, floundering around, it might only muddy the waters.

It all adds to the pleasure. I'm on the bridge, hands on the wheel, steering the ship. Only I know the course.

CHAPTER 11

Swift arrived home late afternoon and threw open the windows and the back door. He changed into shorts and a clean T-shirt, splashed his face with water and bathed his stinging eyes. The evening river was calling, the scent of sedge and silt, the rhythmic pull of oars and chatter of birds heading for home. A chance to quieten his brain. Heaven. He was pouring fruit juice when he heard Cedric's familiar tap on his door.

'Ty, my dear, I wanted to phone you but she said not to.' Cedric was speaking softly as he came in. His reading glasses were perched on top of his head.

'Who said not to phone me?'

'Ruth.'

'Ruth? Is something wrong?'

'She's upstairs in my flat with Branna. They're both asleep on my bed.'

They stared at each other, and then Cedric patted Swift's arm.

'Sit down, dear boy. Can I get myself a glass of that juice?'

'Of course.' He didn't sit but followed Cedric into the kitchen. 'What's happened?'

'Let's go outside, breathe whatever air there is.'

They sat on the swing seat in the shade. The sun was on the flowerbeds, singeing the leaves of the fire red geraniums. Cedric's bright blue Bermuda shorts showed off his shapely, darkly freckled legs. A neighbour a couple of doors away was playing the piano, a light, waltzing tune. Swift had a sudden memory of Thomas's severed fingers.

Cedric rocked the seat gently. 'I came home about two hours ago and found Ruth sitting outside on the step with Branna. Her car is up the road. She looked done in. Branna was just waking up. I brought them in and up to my place. Ruth fed Branna, had a cup of tea, then I suggested they have a rest.'

'What has Ruth said?'

'Very little. I didn't want to ask because she seemed so . . . so edgy. I am glad you're back. We might as well leave it now until they wake up. Sleep seems best in the circumstances.'

'Thanks, Cedric. Something must have happened.'

'Yes, I'd imagine so. I have a feeling it might be to do with the martial mother-in-law.'

The pianist started playing *The Green Leaves of Summer*. Cedric hummed along.

'Such a lovely but melancholy tune. It brought tears to my eyes when I first heard it. It was the theme for that film *The Alamo*. I went to see it with Milo in Holloway Road. He was sniffling too. We've always been a sentimental pair. We cried buckets at *The Fault in our Stars*. Have you ever cried at a film?'

'Only *Casablanca*. The scene where they sing the Marseillaise in Rick's bar.'

'Ah yes. That's electrifying.'

'Have you heard from Oliver?'

'Nothing. I keep hoping he'll ring.'

When Ruth and Branna woke, Cedric brought them down and vanished. Ruth looked dazed, her hair sticking up, crusts of sleep in the corners of her eyes. Branna was full of beans, wriggling as Swift held her and kissed the top of her warm head. She was heavier, looked around more. Ruth drank two glasses of water, watching them, running a hand through her hair.

'Sorry.' She sank onto the sofa. 'I didn't know what else to do, where to go.' She was as pale as an invalid who has been confined to bed for weeks.

'What's happened, Ruth?'

It spilled out. She talked for a long time. He listened, saying nothing, giving Branna a teething ring to play with and suck. She described how Emlyn's anger had returned after his sentencing. Shouting, screaming, throwing things, upsetting Branna. New medication was prescribed but didn't help much. Olwen had taken over the house, imposing her rules. She was cold and critical of Ruth's past, her behaviour, her mothering skills, her attitude to her husband and countless other perceived faults. She took little notice of Branna and had left her crying one day when Ruth fell asleep.

'I couldn't stand it any longer, Ty. I just can't handle it. I began to feel like an interloper in my own home. I thought of going to my mum's, but Shropshire's so far away and she's still working. Emlyn was raging all this morning. Branna got so upset, she started screaming in a way I've never heard before. I can't put her through any more of it. I wasn't fitting her hearing aids so that she wouldn't be aware of him. That's not fair on her. Her development will suffer. I packed some things and left. Olwen didn't try to stop me.'

He held Branna close, holding one of her hands, stroking the pearly nails. He was appalled and outraged by what he had heard. All his misgivings about Emlyn Taylor and his mother had been confirmed. He would give no more leeway or benefit of the doubt. He sat beside Ruth.

'I'm glad you left. It was the right thing to do. You should have told me about all this before now, Ruth. It sounds like hell. I would have come and taken you both away from there. I won't allow Branna back in that house again. I won't negotiate on that.'

She looked straight at him. 'Yes. I know. I wouldn't go back.'

'Are you still on medication?'

'Yes, a lower dose.' She rubbed her eyes. 'I'd love a shower.'

'Go and have one. Clean towels in the airing cupboard. I'll get us something to eat. Branna can help me.' He lifted her up high, dancing her through the air, making her laugh. 'What shall we have, Ms Swift? Omelette and salad?'

He saw Ruth looking at them. Saw tears in her eyes. She turned away and rummaged in a bag for toiletries.

They ate after Ruth had fed Branna and put her in her travel cot. Ruth refused wine, saying it mixed badly with anti-depressants. She looked better after her rest and shower but she was still pallid.

'Is it okay if I stay for a couple of nights? I'll look for a place to rent although I'll have to go a bit out of London.'

'You're not going back to Brighton? It's where you have friends, networks.' He didn't want her to, hoped she would say no.

'Not as many as you might think. Emlyn has absorbed my time, I haven't had much opportunity to mingle and make friends. I have made my mind up. If I go back to Brighton, guilt and duty might tempt me to stay involved with Emlyn. I think anyway that his mother might move him to live with her and that would be for the best. Maybe that has been her agenda all along. She handles his moods and his illness better than I do. And you're right, I should have left before now. I can't expose Branna to any more distress. It's not fair to her and I have to make her my priority. She has a life ahead of her. Emlyn's is time limited now. I'm going to look for work lecturing, get my career back on track. In the meantime, I have savings and some money my grandfather left me. I might get some marking and moderating to do as well. Paid work, and I can do that from home.'

He finished his food and stacked the plates. Two distressed women in one day. Time to speak some words of advice and caution to the second.

'You must stay here for as long as you need, Ruth. You've been through a lot and you need time to think and plan. Branna needs some stability. I can sleep on the sofa and you and Branna can have my bedroom.' He held a hand up as she started to speak. 'Hang on, I thought it through while I was cooking. This is a no strings attached offer. I can get a sofa bed for my office downstairs and sleep there. I only use it occasionally for clients and it certainly won't matter for a while. That way, you have room to breathe, a calm environment to think things through. Please say yes.'

She let out a breath. 'If you're sure . . .'

'I'm sure. I can't lose — I get to see more of Branna.'

She nodded, swallowing hard. 'It's just . . . I don't want you to think I might . . . that we might . . .'

She looked at him, her eyes soft and regretful. He understood in that moment that she no longer loved him, that a door had closed. Too much had happened and something had to give. It felt as if an icy hand was gripping his heart. It hurt and it would go on hurting. He knew that life took its toll and love sometimes withered.

'Yes, I understand,' he managed to say. 'I'll get the rest of your things from the car and change the bed for you.'

He busied himself, fetching Ruth's bags, parking her car nearer to the house, sorting out sheets and duvets, remaking his bed and setting up a makeshift one for himself on the sofa. Ruth sat in the garden, talking softly to Branna, singing to her. When he took her out a cup of tea, she told him that the peace and quiet was blissful and more effective than medication. They sat side by side on the swing seat for a while, not talking.

Ruth was in bed by 10 p.m. Swift said he would keep Branna with him for the night so that Ruth could get some unbroken sleep. He took out his daughter's hearing aids and lay them in their case, then changed her and held her in his arms until she fell asleep. He lay on the sofa and watched the night fall, heard the hum of traffic die down and birds calling as they roosted. There was a faint lilting from Ella Fitzgerald up in Cedric's flat. He was resisting closing his eyes because he didn't want to recall the sadness in Ruth's. Then he gazed at his sleeping daughter, her cot on the floor beside him. He touched her warm, rounded cheek, stroked the back of her hand. He started to weep. All the emotions he had repressed and avoided for so long ambushed him. The tears blinded him. He cried at last for Kris Jelen and for the Ruth he had finally lost forever. He sobbed out his grief quietly until his chest ached so as not to disturb his sleeping child.

* * *

The Spotlight theatre was in a converted Baptist church and retained the panelled oak door and gothic windows. The frames had been painted pale pink and blue and a banner above the door informed Swift that the current play was *Death of a Salesman*. The box office was in a small glass fronted triangular space and the tiny man in there looked hopeful as Swift stepped from the glare outside.

'Are you here for the matinee? Front row tickets available.'

'No. I've come to see the manager, Dora Goldman. I have an appointment.'

'Oh. Trying out for a part?'

'No, not that.'

'Well, hang on. I'll see if she's back from lunch.' He had a peculiar, shifting voice. It seemed to hover between registers without ever settling in one.

Swift waited while the man vanished through a door with a key code. The place had a sleepy feeling, quiet and noiseless. He looked at posters for previous plays with actors he had never heard of. This season was devoted to American dramatists: Miller, Hellman, and O'Neill. A woman with enormous bright green glasses teamed with white and plum streaked hair drifted towards him. She was eating an apple.

'Hi.' He held out his ID. 'I rang yesterday. I'm Tyrone Swift. I'm trying to find information about a man who worked here about twenty to twenty-five years ago.' He thought she had probably just been born then.

She took another large bite of apple, speaking through it. 'Well before my time. Not sure I can help you but I have a broom cupboard of an office out back. Follow me.' She spun around, taking a final bite of her apple before lobbing it expertly into a waste bin. The tiny man darted past them, back into his box office.

'Sold any more tickets?' Dora asked him.

He shrugged. 'Three. It's too hot and people know we haven't got air con.'

Swift thought that *Death of a Salesman* might seem heavy going for a summer's afternoon. Dora's windowless office was crowded with them both in it. She sat on a stool and he elected to stand by a cabinet.

'Shoot.' She pushed her glasses up her nose.

'The man I'm interested in was from New Zealand. He was called Sam. I don't know his surname.'

'An actor?'

'No. A handyman of some kind. Painting scenery, that kind of thing.'

'Well. There won't be any written records. Theatres like ours use loads of people for stuff like that. They come and go. Back then, it was probably cash in hand. What's he done?'

'I don't know that he's done anything. I'm investigating a number of things including a missing child.'

She took more notice. 'Gosh. I see. The only person who might be able to help you is Roly. He's the guy at the box office. Basically, he does whatever is needed around here apart from acting. He's the only person working here who was with the theatre back then. It's a matter of pride to him that he came here in 1985 and has never missed a day's work.'

Swift nodded, thinking that the job probably wasn't too onerous. 'Could I have a word with him?'

'Sure. I'll take over the box office for five mins. You won't be long, will you?'

He was tempted to ask if she was expecting a rush but smiled and assured her he wouldn't.

Roly slipped in and sat on Dora's stool. He was like a little gnome, with wrinkled skin, wide spaced eyes and a snub nose.

'I hear you're a private detective,' he said brightly. 'That's exciting.'

'It can be. I hear that you've worked here a long time.'

'Over thirty years,' he said proudly. 'I've been told this place might fall down the day I leave. They say I'm like glue. Always there, holding things together.'

'I'm hoping you might remember someone I'm trying to find out about. He used to work here.'

'I've never forgotten anyone who's worked here.' He tapped the side of his head. 'Excellent filing system in the grey matter.'

'Good. This guy was from New Zealand. I don't know his age but he must have been youngish. His name was Sam. He painted scenery. This would have been in the early nineties.'

Roly crossed his legs and hugged a knee. Then he put an index finger to his temple, rotating it. 'Just flicking through the card index.' He was clearly enjoying his brief moment centre stage. 'Flick, flick, flick and voilà! You're talking about Sam Pitford. And believe me, he was the pits. He's easy to remember because he was the only Kiwi we've ever had working here and he was trouble.'

'Tell me more.'

'Well.' Roly wriggled on the stool, pleased to be chewing the fat and reminiscing instead of hanging about in the hope of customers. 'He was here for about five months. He painted well, I will give him that. But he was unreliable. Argumentative too. He picked fights.' Roly made a drinking motion. 'Always stank of booze. That's why the manager fired him in the end. He was reeling around back stage. That was a nasty scene, when he was fired. I thought he was going to get violent. He smashed a couple of props on the way out. They were needed for the opening of *The Tempest* that night so there was a right old panic on.'

'How old was he, would you say?'

'Late twenties. Full of himself. Full of wind and piss, more like. He was good looking and he knew it.'

'A ladies' man?'

'Oh, definitely. Dark hair, dark looks, handsome. Made a big deal of being part Maori. He used to do that Maori greeting, pressing his nose and forehead to someone. Well, it was always to a woman. Some of them fall for that stuff. I once saw him doing it to a new actress and telling her it meant they were exchanging the breath of life. She went all daft and fluttery. Why are you looking for him?'

'I can't divulge that. Did you ever see him with a woman called Julie Maddox? She lived near here and came to the café. That's probably how she met Sam. She had a little boy, Thomas.'

Roly wrinkled his nose and spun the stool from side to side. 'Can't say I recall a Julie. The café didn't last long and I never thought it was a good idea. It closed down after just a couple of months, didn't make any money. I didn't go in there much — it was in an annex next door and run by another company. This building has always been my focus, you see. Thing is, Sam was always sniffing after women. He had a couple on the go here and he would have others hanging around outside, waiting for him. I tried to stay away from him. I didn't like him. He was quite frightening sometimes, you know, physically. His manner. He could be ever so charming but you never knew what mood he would be in. That was the booze talking, I suppose. Doug, the manager at the time, only kept him as long as he did because he was having trouble getting stagehands then. Is he in trouble? It wouldn't surprise me.'

'Maybe. Do you know what he did after he was sacked?'

Roly shook his head. 'I think he stayed in the area for a bit. I saw him once or twice around the shops at Archway but I kept out of his way. Then after a couple of months I never saw him again.'

'You don't know where he lived?'

'No idea. From a couple of comments he made, I reckon on people's floors and in squats or wherever he got laid that night.'

'Is there anyone else around here who knew him?'

'Don't think so. Not that I know of. You could tell he was a drifter. According to him, he'd worked all over Europe and the UK, picking up bits of work here and there.'

Roly saw him out to the foyer. 'Now, are you sure I can't sell you a ticket? It's a terrific production, got good reviews.'

'I'm busy, I'm afraid. Maybe some other time. Thanks for your help.'

He walked a couple of streets, cutting through Waterlow Park and into the east section of Highgate cemetery. He knew he would find shade there. Despite the weeks of heat, the paths were still fringed by verdant growth, with tumbling ivy and overhanging trees. He stopped by a moss-covered mausoleum and rang Gabe Maddox. Opposite him, a life size stone angel was lying on her side on top of a grave, as if sleeping, her arms and wings neatly folded against her long, mildewed robes.

'Mr Swift. Yep?'

'Hallo, Mr Maddox. I'm in Highgate. I've just had an interesting conversation in The Spotlight theatre.'

'Oh yes. And you're telling me this because . . . ?'

'I was discussing Sam Pitford with a man who works there and knew him. Sam Pitford from New Zealand. Sam who knew Julie and went out with her. Sam who you disapproved of and told Julie not to see.'

'Where did you get all this garbage from?'

'Partly from Karen, a friend of Julie's, partly from Gary Cooper. The rest from a man in the theatre. I think that the emails and all the other events are connected to Sam Pitford and I think you have come to that conclusion too. You need to tell me what happened back then.'

'I don't need to tell you fuck all. Pitford was a waste of space who buggered off. End of. As for that Cooper, he was always a pain in the backside and a useless accountant. Stop bloody pestering me about pointless stuff.'

'You know, you're paying me to ask questions but you get annoyed when I do. What's eating you?'

'Yeah, I am paying you, so bloody well get on with the job and let me know when you do find out who this nutter is instead of coming up with this rubbish. It's not Sam Pitford doing this. I know that for a fact.'

'How do you know?'

'Because he's dead, that's how, Mr Smart-arse. Someone in New Zealand wrote to tell me. Well, wrote to Julie but she was long dead by then. Some bureaucrat sent it. They found our Highgate address in Pitford's belongings and thought Julie might be a relative.'

'When was this?'

'Fifteen years ago or thereabouts. Just before I moved from Highgate. I chucked the letter away. Nothing to do with me.'

'Why did you say that the family had no New Zealand connection?'

'Because I bloody haven't. None of us has. Pitford was nothing to me except a wastrel who made use of my gullible daughter until I told him where to go. So shove your daft theories where the sun don't shine, get your finger out and stop annoying me.'

The line went dead. Swift moved across to the angel and ran his hand down her smooth, warm flank. He was tempted to throw the towel in after that conversation. He had never had such an irascible, uncooperative client. A client who was hindering him, lying to him. He kicked a stone aside. It clattered against the base of the next grave, where there was a small, butterfly-shaped headstone. He read the epitaph:

Lucille Hanworth
Born 2 April, 1932
Died 15 June, 1936
Flights of angels sing thee to thy rest

He thought of Maura's haunted eyes, saw her tenderly handling Oscar's toys and clothing, sniffing the scent of her vanished boy. He reflected on Thomas's despair, his mutilated body and a small child who might be alive somewhere. Answers and some justice had to be found. Gabe Maddox could take his bad temper and sod off. He would continue with this enquiry until he established the truth.

Little Lucille, he said softly, *this doesn't add up*. He bent down and pulled a few weeds from her grave. There were those ferns and the Karakia. In some way, despite Maddox's denials, this was connected to Sam Pitford. He would have to find the Watcher despite his employer.

* * *

Mary had asked him if he could meet for lunch. He rarely managed to see her without Simone so he was pleased to make a date with her in the Silver Mermaid. The garden was packed and noisy. A huge barbecue glowed with steaks and sizzling sausages. The red-faced chef wiped his forehead with the hem of his apron and turned chicken legs with tongs.

'Madness, barbecuing in this weather. I don't fancy the chef's sweat mingling with my meat,' Mary said.

They agreed to sit in a small alcove inside and both ordered sweet-spiced fishcakes with beetroot salad from the specials chalked on the board by the bar. Mary was in her work uniform, a pale grey suit and white shirt, her wavy brunette hair brushed back from her face. She looked calm, composed, and efficient. Reassuring. Swift had never seen her look hot and bothered. The only time he had known her cry was when she was eighteen and her girlfriend dumped her. He had taken her rowing and she had lain back and sobbed before getting very drunk on the beer he had stashed behind him.

Now he drank a shandy while she sipped sparkling water because she had to keep a clear head for an afternoon meeting. He could tell she had something on her mind from the way she creased her napkin in tiny, exact folds. He thought he knew what it might be.

'Has Simone been complaining about me?'

She looked up, laughed, and pushed the napkin aside. 'You know me too well. She said you had a falling out over her friend Tilda. You haven't been in touch lately and I wanted to check if we're okay. If you're okay.'

'Of course we're okay. When have we ever not been okay? I have not fallen out with Simone. I can't speak for her. She's making a mountain out of a molehill. I agreed to have a drink with Tilda. When I met her at Louis's naming, I thought she was amusing, attractive. Once I spent an hour with her I realised I didn't care for her company.'

'Oh.' Mary sucked a sliver of lemon. 'Simone said Tilda was terribly upset and in tears.'

Swift threw his hands up. 'I didn't do anything to upset her. I said I didn't want to meet again. She kept leaving me messages. I have been polite, considering that she pestered me. She is desperate and thin-skinned. Simone is too, you know. Thin-skinned, I mean.'

Mary nodded. 'Yes, I know she can be. I know that sometimes she gets over-involved with people, takes on their concerns and thinks she can help them steer their lives. She means well.'

Like Joyce, he thought. 'That's up to Simone. It seems to me that she was making things worse for Tilda by interfering and prolonging things. I don't want her trying to steer my life or telling me what I need to do.'

There was a silence. Mary cleared her throat.

'Simone told me about the time she asked you to father our child. I need to tell you that I know because I think it's the elephant in the room.'

'Ah. When did she tell you?'

'A couple of weeks ago.'

'Right. I feel well and truly wrong-footed. I didn't tell you because I didn't want you to be upset. But you're right, it has been hanging there.'

When Mary and Simone were planning to start a family, Simone had visited him alone and suggested that he father their baby. He had been outraged. She had become very upset when he refused and had thrown a glass of wine over him. They had never spoken of it since and she had become pregnant through sperm donation soon after. As far as Swift was concerned, Mary would never know about the regrettable incident. It had shown him a manipulative side to Simone that he didn't like and had coloured his feelings towards her ever since.

'Listen Ty, it's okay. Really. I was a bit taken aback when Simone told me but I understand that she was feeling desperate at the time. I'm glad I know. It clears the decks.'

'Thanks.' He smiled, relieved. 'It's good to know I'm a magnet for desperate women.'

Mary nodded in mock sympathy. 'And by the way, thanks for saying no to Simone. That would have been far too complicated, even for you.'

'Ouch. I don't know why I love you.'

'Hmm. You know, you can be a bit sensitive and aloof. Simone meant well, about Tilda, I mean.'

'Perhaps, but it's interfering and unwanted.' He spoke more sharply than he had intended. 'Sorry, I don't mean to take it out on you.'

'Right. Just don't forget that people do worry about their friends and family, especially when they know they've had hard times. They might not always express it in the right way.'

He heard the mild reproof in Mary's voice. He had nothing more to say on the subject and didn't want to return to the topic of Simone. Their food arrived and they didn't speak until they had almost finished. The silence felt like a kind of truce.

'You mentioned on the phone that Ruth's staying with you. What's happened?' Mary put her knife and fork together and looked at him gravely, head to one side.

'She turned up with Branna. Things became unbearable in Brighton.' He explained about Emlyn Taylor's angry rages and his mother's intervention. 'I've said Ruth can stay for a while and use my room.'

'Where are you sleeping?'

'On the sofa so far, which isn't doing my back any good. I had to crawl off it this morning. I have a bed being delivered later today. It's going in my office so I can sleep there until Ruth gets organised.'

'It must be good to have the time with Branna.'

'It's wonderful. I've been practising sign language with her. She's a terrific girl. I felt so angry when Ruth said

Emlyn's shouting had upset her, made her cry. I'm glad she's out of there.'

'Ty . . .' Mary sat forward and clasped her glass with both hands, weighing her words. 'You're not going to try and get back with Ruth, are you? I just don't think it would be good for you but I know how much you still care for her. I know she's in a bad place at the moment but you're not necessarily the answer to her problems. Thing is, you always take your responsibilities so seriously. You're very steadfast.'

'Yes, and I should be.'

'Oh, don't get me wrong, that's a good quality, but you can take it too far. And I'm not sure that Ruth appreciates your loyalty, as she should. Maybe she's made use of it now and again. Oh God, now I sound as if I'm meddling and that's the last thing I want to do. I just want you to find some peace and happiness of your own.'

He saw the anxiety and love in her eyes and was grateful. She was the one person he could always rely on. He crumbled a piece of bread, ordering his thoughts. 'I've loved Ruth for a long time. I think I always will. I thought I'd accepted it was over but I realise there was part of me hoping she'd come back. But no, I know now that it's finished. I have no illusions about rekindling the relationship. I want to help her and Branna but Ruth will be getting her own place.'

Mary took his hand. 'I'm glad you've said that. Glad you can be free of old ties.'

He smiled at her, turned her hand over and kissed the palm. 'Thank you for not lecturing me that I need to sort my life out and move on or trying to line up Ruth replacements for me.'

'Oh, I think I can leave that safely to Joyce and Simone. But just to say—'

'Do I hear a "yes, but"?'

'Well, if you are available for the right woman, you could do with a hair trim and that shirt collar has definitely seen better days.'

'Message received and understood. You're lucky, I nearly came out with baby dribble on my front. But then, some women might find that attractive.'

'It would indicate you're the nurturing type?'

'Exactly.'

They talked for a while about Louis and Branna, agreeing that they should arrange a play date. He saw his reflection in a mirror over the bar and had to agree that his bushy curls needed taming. The shirt was one of his favourites, a faded turquoise, the cotton soft and smooth after years of washing. He picked a loose thread from the folded back cuff, thinking that perhaps he did need to make an effort, but he wouldn't take this shirt to the charity shop just yet.

CHAPTER 12

DS Davida Ramen took Swift's formal statement. She confirmed that Thomas Maddox had died as a result of severe brain swelling following initial concussion. She was tight-lipped about the investigation and would only comment that enquiries were ongoing. When he told her that Gabriel Maddox was still employing him, she shrugged and said as long as he didn't get in the way of the police investigation, he could do as he pleased. He decided that he would take her at her word and continue with his own line of enquiry.

He was setting up his new sofa bed in the basement and sorting out a few essentials when Stella Gath phoned. She sounded as if she had been crying again, her voice nasal and pain laden.

'I've been looking at that picture again. I'm sure I've seen a child who looks like that around here. I just can't remember the context or when.'

He sat down at his desk. Grief did strange things to people and it might have skewed her memories. 'Do you think this was someone on holiday?'

'I don't know. I don't think so. I've been wondering . . . we have social occasions for the staff sometimes. Well, used to have. They were my idea and I set them up but clearly, I won't be organising them anymore. Usually twice a year, before Christmas and mid-summer. You know, a way of saying thank you for all the hard work. That kind of thing helps with morale and loyalty. Pity the latter didn't rub off on Gabe. He bought in cheap champagne and wine and we provided a buffet. Gabe used to do a little speech about how everyone worked as a team, and so on. I'm pretty sure I have quite a lot of photos on my laptop. I don't know why I'm associating this image with those get-togethers but I am.'

'Could you look through the photos?'

'Yes, of course. Frankly, it would be a welcome distraction. Stop me moping about the house. Brooding.'

'Okay. Let me know if you see anything. Have you spoken to Sonia?'

'No. She's not answering her phone. I expect she's feeling too guilty. Good. I hope she's lying awake at night.'

Swift thought that was unlikely. He thought of Sonia and Oliver, both dodging their rightfully angry parents. 'It might be just as well, Stella. Create a bit of space.'

Her voice deepened, hostility taking over. 'Maybe. Funny, really. I'm avoiding Gabe. Sonia is avoiding me. I don't delude myself that Gabe wants to speak to me because he really misses me. I know he's in a bad way about Thomas but I don't think I can help him with that. It's too late now. I've decided he's going to find out I've become his dark star, you see.'

Coldness didn't suit her but he understood. 'I'm sorry.'

'Yes. Anyway, I'll stop boring you with my personal life and look at my laptop.'

He made the bed, set up a small table beside it with a lamp and hung the selection of clothes he had taken from his wardrobe on the curtain rail. He placed a towel by the small hand basin in one corner of the room, a relic of Lily's profession. He had hot and cold water and his coffee percolator sat on one end of his desk. It would do for now.

Ruth appeared in the doorway with Branna.

'Oh Ty, it looks like a student bedsit in here. You can't do this for long. I don't expect you to.'

He crossed the room and took Branna, stroking her cheek. Ruth already looked better. The strain had gone from her eyes and her face was less clouded.

'It's fine, Ruth. All that matters is that this little one is safe and well.'

'You're a kind man, Ty. Too kind for your own good sometimes. But thank you. Olwen rang me earlier. Said Emlyn was very upset and asking for me. I told her I wasn't going to see him for a while and I asked her not to ring me again.'

'How did she respond?'

'Cuttingly, as you would expect. I feel like a bad person for leaving him but I know I had to. I will visit him but not just yet. Don't worry, I won't take Branna with me.'

'Ruth, I never want Branna to be around him again. You do understand?'

'Yes. I feel the same way.'

Branna was staring at spots of shade on the window blinds and working her fingers furiously.

'It's the sun doing that.' He made the sign for sun. 'The sun. We've seen too much of it recently. Soon it will be raining but I haven't learned that word yet.'

Ruth laughed and put a hand out to stroke Branna's head. He watched her slim fingers cupping their daughter's crown, the diamonds in her wedding ring catching the light. Being with her didn't seem to hurt as harshly as it used to.

'Cedric's going to look after Branna tomorrow afternoon,' she told him. 'I'm seeing an old colleague about the possibility of a couple of hours' lecturing a week. Get myself back into the loop.'

'Cedric will be in seventh heaven. I'll bring her down here with me tonight, if that's okay.'

'Oh, Ty, you've no idea. It's such a relief to be able to leave her with someone who loves her and is kind and gentle with her. With Olwen, part of me could never relax. I was on watch all the time because I knew she resented Branna and me. Even the medication didn't knock me out thoroughly. I think I fought against it because I needed to stay alert. I'm sleeping properly and deeply for the first time in ages.'

'Well, get plenty of sleep in the bank, then. You need it.'

His phone rang. He saw that it was Maura and said he had better take it. He handed Branna to Ruth and watched as she danced in a circle with her before heading upstairs.

Maura was sobbing and almost incoherent.

'Someone . . . someone's been here,' she managed to say eventually. 'I came home and . . . it's Oscar's blanket. Oscar's blanket was on the table.'

'The blanket that was taken with him?'

'Yes.'

Solving this case was in his grasp now. He could sense it. 'Maura, have you touched it?'

'Yes. Yes.'

'I know this is hard but don't touch it anymore. I'm coming round now. I'll be with you as soon as possible.'

* * *

He took the car and made it to Maura's within the hour. The late afternoon traffic was building but he diverted down side roads to avoid the worst of the congestion. As he drove, he thought that for a long time the Watcher had been circling, preparing to close in. He was advancing, goading, punishing.

Maura had stopped crying when he arrived but she was trembling as she let him in. Streaks of dark mascara smudged her cheeks and her nose was pinched and red.

'I can't take much more,' she said. 'Poor Thomas dead and now this. I just can't take it.'

'Come on, let's go upstairs. You need to sit down.'

He looked at the outer and inner doors and could see no sign of a break-in. Upstairs, the blanket was on the table, lying in soft folds. The white and gold wool was finely woven, the tiny tigers picked out in orange. He looked but didn't touch it. She stood behind him, shaking. He made her sit down and pulled a chair up near to her.

'I know this is awful but tell me what happened and how you found the blanket.'

'I finished work a bit early. I was home about four o'clock. I came in and I saw it straight away. It was on the table, folded into a square. Neat.' She pleated the hem of her dress, holding it tight with both hands. 'I couldn't believe it at first. Then I picked it up and held it to my face for a long time. I started crying and I couldn't stop. Then I rang Ross. He didn't answer so I rang you. What's happening? I don't understand. Does this mean . . . Is Oscar alive?' She leaned forward and grabbed at him. 'It must mean he's alive!'

He took both her hands. They were clammy, agitated. He pressed them firmly, trying to calm her.

'I don't know, Maura. Whoever has done this is cruel and capable of awful deception. Please don't get your hopes up.'

Her eyes brimmed. 'But I have. I have now. It smells of Oscar. The blanket smells of him. It wouldn't unless he held it recently. I just know it.'

She shivered. He saw a cardigan draped on the back of a dining chair and brought it to her, settling it around her shoulders.

'I'm going to make you a cup of tea, and then I'll ring the police. I can't see any evidence of a break-in but if you don't mind, I'll look around the flat. Who has keys?'

She looked blank for a moment. 'Oh, just Ross and me . . . and Pru downstairs has a set.'

'Where is Ross?'

'He's away . . . working in Portsmouth, he'll be back tomorrow.'

He left her sitting, hunched, pleating her dress hem again and staring at the blanket. He looked in the small bedroom and bathroom but the windows were locked. It would have been difficult to access the flat except through the front doors. He made tea for Maura and brought it to her, then rang Abby Cheng and explained what had happened.

'I'll get someone round there,' she said. 'Pity she touched the blanket.'

'Yes, but that was inevitable. I've told her not to now and to leave it where it is. All these events, the emails and "accidents" are connected. They have to be. Presumably you're liaising with DI Colman's team?'

'Hmm, when I can get hold of them. Leave it with me. Thanks.'

So much of this case was about break-ins, keys, breaching a family's security and privacy, prising open their lives. Maura moved around, touching the furniture, bending to pick up an oblong box from the coffee table. She opened it and took a silver coloured harmonica from the red satin lining. There were tears on her cheeks.

'Look,' she said. 'It's a Hohner. I got it for Ross's birthday next week. The one he has is cheap. This is state of the art and has an airtight body. I think he'll love it.'

'Does he play well?'

'Oh, yes. He's very musical but he had an accident when he was young so it limits what he can play. He had a bad fall and his hands were damaged. His fingers stiffen up. That's why he focused on the mouth organ. Funny, isn't it? I seem to be attracted to musicians.' Tears were dripping from her chin but she was unaware of them.

Swift took a breath. He came closer to Maura and took the harmonica, weighing it in his hand. It was smooth and bright. For some time, he had been convinced that he had missed something in an interview. Something significant had been said that he should have explored. Now he recalled the woman in the street where Oscar had lived. She had talked about 'stranger danger' as opposed to crimes within families. Perhaps it wasn't one or the other in this case. What if the stranger was within the family, posing as a member of it, burrowing into it, accessing all kinds of information? Ross had keys, both to Maura's flat and her life. Swift hoped for her sake that he was wrong. This could just be coincidence. Plenty of people had musical talent. He handed back the harmonica.

'How did you meet Ross?'

'Oh, he came into the salon one day for a haircut. We got chatting and he asked me out for a drink. I wish he would ring. I want to talk to him. Tell him about the blanket. I expect it will be later on because he switches his phone off when he's working.'

'Has he always lived in London?'

'Hmm? Ross? Oh, yes . . . I think so.'

'And his dad, have you met him socially?'

'Just the once. We had a drink with him in town.'

'Have you been to where he lives?'

'In Bromley? No. His dad said he must cook us all dinner sometime but we've never got around to arranging it. It's difficult because of Ross's work.' She was wandering around again, going to the window, circling the table and the folded blanket. He could see she wanted to touch it.

'Could I have Ross's number? Just in case I can help in any way. This will be a shock for him too. And have you got one for his dad?'

She gave him Ross's number. She said she might have Victor's from the time they were arranging to meet for a drink. She scrolled through her phone and found it. He said he needed to use the bathroom. He slipped back to her bedroom, where he had seen a small photo of her and Ross stuck in the corner of a mirror. He eased it out and put it in his pocket.

When he returned to her, she was sitting, staring into space, pulling at her bottom lip. He wanted to protect her from the shockwave that might be coming. He took a photo of the blanket with his phone. Maura didn't notice — she was lost in thought. He needed to move, get on the road, and test out this awful possibility.

'I have to go now. The police should be here soon. Don't forget, please don't touch the blanket. When exactly are you expecting Ross back?'

'Tomorrow night. Around six, he said. At least the blanket's here now, for when Oscar comes back.'

The anxious hope in her eyes was unbearable. He felt a cold rage at the man who was tormenting this woman.

'Take care. I'll call at your neighbour downstairs, Pru, isn't it? If she's in I'll ask if she can come and sit with you.'

She nodded, only half hearing him, her eyes back on the blanket.

He found Pru at home and explained what had happened. She said immediately that she would go upstairs and keep Maura company.

'Have you got your keys to Maura's flat?' he asked.

She stepped back, checked and gestured at a set of keys on a table just inside her door. 'Yes, they're here, nobody has touched them. A pity Ross is away. He's so good for Maura, knows how to comfort her.'

Her words rang in his ears as he sat in the car. He thought for a minute, saw how this might have been set up and then rang Victor's number. He recognised the man's throaty voice when he answered. When Swift said who he was, he became instantly wary.

'Oh yeah. Why are you ringing me? Who gave you my number?'

'Maura Haskin. I'm calling you on a very serious matter. About Ross.'

'Ross isn't here.'

'You live in Bromley?'

'Yeah. Why?'

He hadn't asked if something had happened to Ross. 'As I said, this is serious. Are you Ross's father?'

'Yeah, course I am.'

'I'm not sure I believe you.'

'You what?' There was a slight slip in the voice.

'I don't think you are his father. Tell me the truth. This is urgent.'

'Look, don't you ring me and start calling me a liar. You've got no right. I've got nothing to say to you so bugger off.'

'Listen to me. You can talk either to the police or to me. This could be related to a serious crime. I'm talking criminal charges. I used to work for the Met. I know what I'm talking about. Did Ross pay you or have some kind of hold on you? Is that how this posing as his father was arranged?'

He was silent. 'Look, I don't want no trouble. I don't know about no criminal stuff, okay?'

'Your name *is* Victor?'

'Yeah.'

'Victor what?'

'Beamish.'

'I need to talk to you. Right away. You may be involved in something very serious. You might even be in danger.'

'What? How do you mean?'

'Where are you right now? I'll come and meet you.'

He stumbled over his words. 'I'm at home.'

'Is Ross likely to turn up?'

'No. He doesn't live here. Listen, I don't want trouble. I want out of this, whatever it is.'

'Mr Beamish, this is crucial. If you talk to me you might avoid too much trouble with the police.'

Beamish hesitated and then gave him the address. Swift said he would be there as soon as possible. He drove to Bromley, still hoping that he was mistaken, but he thought that maybe at last he had seen what had been staring him in the face. The Watcher had found out about his involvement, his visits to Thomas and Maura and many details about the family. Easy to do if someone was confiding in you, thinking you were her rock, unwittingly giving you all the information you wanted. Clever. Clever, warped and malicious. As yet, he couldn't see how Oscar fitted in to the picture. He drove as fast as the traffic and speed restrictions would allow, thinking of the stages of the Watcher's strategy. He thought he could piece most of it together now. And yet . . . he needed Beamish's confirmation.

Beamish lived in a poky bedsit above a chemist. The stairwell smelled of disinfectant and his door was made of cheap plywood. He left the chain on as he opened it and peered around the frame. When he saw it was Swift, he moved the chain and let him in. He was a different man to the one who had called in to Maura's, dressed in a stained shirt and trousers with several days of stubble on his face. The door opened straight into the living area. A single bed covered in a frayed blanket stood against one wall, with a small kitchen area under the window. A coffee table was littered with takeaway cartons and pocked with cigarette burns. The television was on, a blaring soap opera with two men fighting in a pub. Beamish turned it down, saying he always followed the programme because it was like real life, real people. The room was hazy with cigarette smoke. There was just one wooden chair and he perched on the side of the bed so Swift sat on it. Beamish continued smoking, a large glass ashtray on the floor beside him. His eyes were wary and he fingered the blanket beneath him as Swift spoke.

'Okay, let's cut to the chase. Ross Walker doesn't share this place with you.'

'No.'

'And you're not related to him.'

'That's right.'

'And there's no cousin called Ann.'

'No. It was my mum's name.'

'I think Ross Walker is an assumed name. He might be responsible for a number of crimes, including taking a baby.'

'You what? Ross hasn't got any kids. Why would he take a baby?'

'Just tell me how you got involved with him. How you became his "dad."'

'I never thought I was getting involved in anything criminal. It was just a laugh.'

'Okay. I believe you. Just tell me how you met.'

He sucked deep on the butt of his cigarette, stubbed it out and tipped another king-size out of a packet. Swift contained his impatience as Beamish fiddled with his plastic lighter, coaxing a flame.

'He started talking to me in a corner shop I work in. Local place, up the road here. I'd just had a couple of red bills and I was pretty down in the dumps that day. I told him I was stony broke and desperate. I've never really got on my feet since I came out of the army. He was a nice bloke, sympathetic, like, you know. He said it was dreadful that we didn't look after our ex-soldiers. He said we were all heroes. Anyway, we had a drink a couple of times and he bought me a curry. I said I was stretched for cash, struggling to pay the rent on this dump. He asked me if I wanted to earn some spare dosh. Said it was just a bit of fun, like a practical joke. All I had to do was tell his girlfriend that I was his dad and that he shared my place here in Bromley. There's nothing wrong with that, is there? Just a white lie.'

'You didn't think it was odd?'

He shrugged and tipped ash. 'Life's odd, mate. Everyone's odd. Ross said that Maura's family played jokes all the time so it was like tit for tat. It was a kind of game they all had going. He said they'd all have a laugh when they found out but he was going to spin it along for a while. I couldn't see there was any harm done.'

'What did he pay you?'

'Two hundred quid each time. So once when we met Maura for a drink and then that time I met you at her flat. Money for old rope, I reckoned. He told me what to say each time. Made me practise. Said I was a natural. Got me to spruce myself up. He bought me new togs and aftershave for when I met Maura and he gave me some fags as presents as well. He said they were my whatchacallit . . . retainer . . . in case he needed me to say he was my son again. She's a nice girl, that Maura, ever so friendly. You don't need to look at me like that. Down your nose. I work in a rotten job that pays peanuts and I was out of work for ages before that. I've got debts up to the eyeballs. I was going to get evicted from here. I like to have a flutter on the gee-gees and it doesn't always pay off. Four hundred quid is a lot to me. A real extra.'

Swift could see he was wretched and cheaply bought. He suspected that the man had a gambling addiction and that Walker had sniffed that out. 'Do you know where Ross is now?'

'Haven't a clue. I haven't seen him for a while. I haven't done nothing wrong, have I?'

'Depends on how you judge these things. Deceiving Maura was nasty, though. Did Ross ever mention anywhere else he stayed to you?'

'No. He never said much about himself, just that he travelled for work and stayed with Maura.'

'And he's never mentioned a child? You've never seen him with one?'

'No. I'd never get involved in anything nasty to do with kids. I know a bloke in the pub who's one of those vigilantes. Sets out to trap paedos. Good for him, that's what I say. Is that what Ross is, then? A paedo? If I'd known that, I'd never have had anything to do with him. Scum of the earth they are.'

'It's hard to say what Ross Walker is.' Swift stood, clearing his throat of cigarette fumes. 'I wouldn't have anything more to do with him if I were you. Understand?'

Beamish puffed away, staring at Swift, and nodded. He turned up the TV volume as Swift left. A woman was yelling at another woman, warning her to leave her husband alone.

***

He sat in the car and slammed his hands down on the wheel. Ross Walker. Ross with the usefully blank background. Ross who just happened to visit Maura's salon and meet Victor Beamish in a shop. Ross who wanted to present himself as a dependable man with a family context: a loving father, a cousin, a home base where he fixed the taps. Reliable, sensitive Ross. A fiction, a plan set up to mislead and confuse. The man had sat opposite him in Maura's flat, asking how the investigation was going, comforting Maura, looking at the picture of Oscar. How was he connected to Sam Pitford? A family member? He had no trace of a New Zealand accent but that could be altered. Had Gabe Maddox harmed Pitford in some way? He fired the engine and saw that he was almost out of petrol. He drove to a garage and thought carefully about what he was going to divulge to Maddox. He rang him and the phone was answered immediately.

'Ross Walker,' Swift said. 'Does the name mean anything to you?'

'Not sure. Hang on, isn't Maura with a Ross these days?'

'That's right. I believe he's your emailer. He's related to Sam Pitford, I'm sure of it. The ferns, remember? What did you do to Pitford back then in Highgate? You need to be honest now.'

'How have you traced a connection between Pitford and this Walker?'

'Never mind that for now. What did you do? Hurry up and tell me. Time is running out on you.'

'Oh, for Christ's sake. I didn't do anything to Pitford except give him a shedload of money.'

'Why?'

'To go away and leave Julie alone.'

'That's all? It doesn't seem a reason for someone to persecute you. There's more to it, isn't there? Oh, *come on*, Maddox. This man is dangerous. He might have Oscar.'

'Where is he?'

'I don't know. Not yet. Not far away, I suspect.'

There was a muffled sigh, the creak of a chair. 'Okay. Julie had a baby with Sam Pitford. A boy. God knows what went on in that girl's head but she got herself knocked up. I didn't know about the pregnancy until it was too late to do anything. I was angry as hell when I found out. With her, but mainly with Pitford. I had a blazing row with him. Told him exactly what I thought of him. He wasn't bothered, just sneered at me in that repulsive way he had. Bloody hell, Swift, I don't want to have to go over all this. It was bad enough at the time.'

'You haven't any choice. Not if you want to resolve this once and for all.'

Another deep sigh. 'Right. Well, Julie's pregnancy was complicated and she wasn't well. We found out she had cancer when she was about seven months gone. She was in a terrible state when the doctor told us. Pitford was hanging around, pretending to be interested. He'd come and go whenever he pleased. He'd say he'd meet her and then not show. He upset her all the time with his pissing about. I knew he saw her as a meal ticket. Julie was very ill after the baby was born. She had to go straight into chemo. I met with Pitford and he agreed to take the boy back to New Zealand for a payment.'

'So this child would now be what age?'

'About twenty-three.'

'What was his name?'

'Joe. Joe Pitford. You think he's this Walker?'

'Yes.' Swift's thoughts were racing. 'So Thomas had a younger half-brother.'

'Yes. Thomas never knew about him. He was only just two when Joe was born.'

'You handed a baby into the care of an aggressive drunkard and watched him vanish thousands of miles away. How much did you pay?'

'Thirty thousand. Listen, I couldn't look after the kid and neither could his mother. I already had Thomas to look after. I did what I thought was best in difficult circumstances and Pitford was the father.'

'And Julie agreed to this?'

'She was in a bad way. She never really got better after that. They pumped her with drugs that kept her going for a while but she just dwindled away. She saw it was for the best.'

She'd had no option, more like. Too weak and ill to protest. He thought of all the bigoted comments Maddox had made since he met him. 'It wasn't just that Julie was ill and you couldn't cope, was it? You were wealthy by then. Presumably, you could have afforded a nanny. The 30K could have gone towards looking after the baby. The truth is that Sam Pitford being part Maori didn't suit you, did it? He and his son had the wrong kind of background for your taste. A bit too foreign?'

Maddox grew belligerent. 'I had every right to protect my daughter. I'm entitled to my views. It's a free country. For now, anyway, until the chinks or the darkies take over. They all breed like flies.'

Swift clenched his jaw. 'Are you at home?'

'Yes.'

'Keep your doors locked.'

'But how . . .' It was Swift's turn to end a call. The man sickened him. Now the Watcher's anger, bitterness and thirst for revenge started to make sense. He filled up with petrol and bought a large bottle of water. The air was growing heavy and humid, the sky turning a dirty grey.

'Big storm on the way, apparently,' the woman behind the till said. 'I can't wait. I'm planning to stand in my garden in the rain until I'm soaked.'

Back in the car, he drank half of the water and saw that he had an email from Stella.

I had to trawl through loads of photos but I finally found this one, taken at Easter. It made me realise what I was remembering. The woman on the far left of the photo in the blue skirt and yellow top works at the site. She did some cleaning for me and when she called by for payment, her son was in her car with her mother. He's the child I was thinking of. He lives locally and I think his name is Neil so I must have been indulging in wishful thinking. My head's pretty woolly at the moment. Sorry.

He opened the attachment and stared at the image of a woman who was on the edge of a large group of people. They were holding glasses and paper plates of food. He closed his eyes for a moment, and then looked again. The woman had thin fair hair skimming her shoulders. She seemed familiar but that wasn't possible. Was he now imagining things he wanted to be true? He rang Stella.

'I'm sorry, I think I'm a bit befuddled right now, with everything that's happened. Sorry for misleading you,' she said.

'Who is the woman holding the child?'

'Her name is April, April Greene. She's one of our cleaners. That's her boy, and I'm sure she said his name is Neil.'

He looked at the photo again. It came to him. He had walked back to the windmill with Thomas on that first visit and they had passed near the car park. A couple had been in there, just about to leave. Thomas had waved to the woman and said she was called April and she cleaned like a tornado. The man with her — he had been a distant figure in the car, blurred by the bright sun, hidden by a hat and sunglasses. Oh, if this was true, what a player he was and how he must have laughed as he drove away. The arrogance and risk taking were astonishing.

'Are you still there?' Stella asked.

'Yes. Does April have a husband?'

'I'm not sure. I think there is someone. I haven't met him.'

'He hasn't been at the staff socials?'

'I don't think so.'

'Do you have April Greene's address?'

'She's in my address book, yes. She came here just the once to do a spring clean for me. That's when she mentioned Neil's name because it was his birthday and she was going to bake a cake when she got home. You're going to see her?'

'Yes.'

'But I don't see why. I mean, that can't be Oscar because he's April's little boy. Oh dear, I feel as if I've caused so much muddle now. Everything seems to be a mess.' She sounded despondent.

'You did right to tell me and I still need to make sure. Everything has to be checked. Can you remember when April started work at Smell the Roses?'

'Oh . . . I'm not certain. It will be on the main database. I think about eighteen months ago. Yes, about that.'

So she might already have had the child in her keeping. 'What is she like?'

'A very nice woman. Quiet, works hard. She doesn't tend to talk unless you speak first. I'd say she has a minor handicap . . . what's it called these days . . . learning difficulty.'

'And she would have answered an advertisement?'

'I'm sure, yes. I don't recruit the cleaning staff. I leave that to Marlene, who deals with maintenance. I think a cleaner retired around then so Marlene would have recruited and interviewed. You won't go upsetting April, will you? She's a really nice woman and this is just a resemblance between her child and Oscar. I only saw him through the car window and children of that age often do look alike. I can give you Marlene's number if you want, she'd be able to tell you more about her.'

He didn't think there was time. 'Can you get that address for me now?'

'Well . . . all right.' She sounded reluctant but she fetched her address book and read it out.

'Don't worry, I'll tread carefully with April. I just need to cover all the bases. Stella, make sure you keep secure in your house. I've just told Gabe the same.'

'I'm going to the windmill now. I want to collect the rest of my things. As long as there is anything of mine there, Gabe is going to think he can sweet talk me back. Time to finish things properly. It's all over. I know that now.'

'Don't mention April Greene to Gabe. I don't want to raise false hopes. I'll be in touch later.' Maddox would head straight to April's, he thought, if he had any hint of this information. He would throw his weight about and as yet, there was no real evidence that the child was Oscar. Nothing except a horrible and growing suspicion about a convoluted and meticulous plan that had been executed.

Before he drove on he wondered briefly whether he should email or text Ross Walker, but contact might precipitate some awful action on his part. Better to find April. Walker might even be there. He looked up her address, in a village called Crayton, about five miles from High Hawksford. He put his foot down on the motorway, zipping along the fast lane. A feeling of dread was snaking through him.

* * *

All this time, I've observed them and thought about them. Sometimes I imagined the other life I could have been living. That other life has been in my blood for so long. The life I was denied.

I went to look at the place in Highgate where Gabe used to live. Lovely, spacious, huge gardens. Classy. I walked around outside, picturing that life in a big house. Money, leisure, good food.

And then the windmill and a thriving business. I explored around there thoroughly. Green fields, a bit of luxury. No expense spared. I could have had a part of all that. Or something like it.

What could have been.

If I hadn't been betrayed.

If I'd been the right kind of person.

It was tormenting but it kept me fuelled. Kept me primed. Kept me hungry and satisfied.

Good to keep chipping away at the happy homestead.

But time to wind it all up now. Fun and games are over. Shame in a way but it has to be done.

A slap-up meal to set me up for it: beef Wellington, roast potatoes and mixed vegetables, followed by Eton mess and a couple of strong coffees.

I've done well, if I say so myself. Kept all the wheels turning. No slip-ups.

Energy levels high now, senses alert, eyes peeled.

You see, Gabe, it wasn't for good when you thought you'd bought off old Sam. Sam, the good-for-nothing old soak. Sam the drifter. You thought it was a neat little solution to your problem.

Money can't solve everything.

Some debts can never be repaid.

Night night. Sleep is coming.

CHAPTER 13

The evening sky was bruised with ragged clumps of mustard yellow, dull bronze and purple clouds. The light was fading, with the odd streak of gold filtering through as the sun departed. The air hung damp and suffocating. There was that deep stillness and hush that precedes a storm. Swift came off the motorway and drove fast along B roads, past woodland and open meadow. A family of rabbits scurried by a hedge and a heron drifted elegantly across a field to drink in a stream.

Crayton was a small, workaday village and clearly a poor relation of High Hawksford. There was a handsome parish church with a graveyard in the village centre but otherwise the streets were mainly drab terraces. The supermarket was small and shabby looking, kept company by a Chinese takeaway and a sandwich shop. Swift stopped the car outside the pub, The Crooked Billet, to check his location. The pub was badly in need of repair and the pitted tarmac outside was ankle deep in cigarette butts. It had a large, ragged Union Jack draped across the entrance door, drooping and dead flowers in hanging baskets and a TV blaring loudly. A group of young men smoking outside the door turned to look at him. Byfield Street, where April lived, was ahead and on the left. He moved on, parking opposite her house, near a patch of waste ground. The houses fronted the narrow pavement and looked dark and huddled but April Greene's front door was newly painted a sunny yellow and there was a pretty lace curtain at the front window.

He took a breath and knocked the brass lion's head in the middle of the door. A young woman with an anxious smile opened it immediately but the smile faded when she saw him. She was the woman in the photograph, her fair hair held back with two tortoise shell combs.

'Good evening. Are you April Greene?'

'Yes.' She stood sideways on, holding the door, glancing past him to the street.

He held out his ID. 'I'm sorry to bother you. My name is Tyrone Swift. I'm a private investigator. Could I have a word with you?'

'Well, I don't know. I'm expecting my family.' She looked out again and blinked rapidly. She was plump with what looked like adolescent acne dotting her forehead.

He couldn't detect any sound or movement in the house behind her. 'Do you mean your son, Neil?'

'Yes. Why? Has something happened?' Her eyes were a pale almond, the lashes almost invisible.

'No, it's okay. Is Neil out with your husband?'

'Husband? Oh. We're not married. He's out with Ricky, his dad.' She pulled at her T-shirt. 'They're late. I was going to ring my mum. I'm getting worried.'

'Have you tried ringing Ricky?'

'He's not answering. Do you think something's happened?'

Her face was small and smooth, her nose a little too big. She was radiating tension. Swift took the photo from his pocket.

'Is this Ricky?'

She took the photo and stared at it, then switched the hall light on and stared again.

'I don't understand. Who is this woman? Is this Ricky's wife?'

'That is Ricky?'

'Yes. I don't understand. Why are you here? Where's Ricky and Neil?'

'Ms Greene, I think we need to go inside and you should ring your mother. Does she live close by?'

'Other end of the village. Why?' She grabbed his arm tightly. 'Why?'

'I'm not sure yet. Please, let's go in. I need to ring the police.'

She made a strange, high-pitched sound and turned into the house. He closed the door and followed her into a dim lounge cum diner. It was neat and tidy, cheaply furnished and smelled of vanilla. The wall over the fireplace was lined with photographs of Oscar Maddox. Oscar from around the age of a year old. He got April to sit down and ring her mother. He went to the other end of the dining area and took out his phone. It was after seven. Abby Cheng and DI Colman were unlikely to be available. He decided to ring emergency services and spoke to a police handler, explaining who he was.

'I'm in Crayton, at a house with a woman called April Greene. She's very distressed. I believe that an abducted child has been living here.'

'Can you give me details, please? What's the child's name?'

'His real name is Oscar Maddox. He has been living here as Neil. Ms Greene seems to have been unaware that the child had been abducted by a man calling himself Ricky. His real name is Joe Pitford.'

'Where is this child?'

'I don't know. I believe he's with Ricky. This woman needs immediate help.'

He gave the address and his own details. As he finished the call, he saw that April had moved near him and was twining her hair tightly around a forefinger.

'What do you mean, "abducted"? What does that mean?'

'It means taken away. Is your mum coming?'

'She's on her way. What's happening? Where's Ricky and Neil?'

He put a hand under her elbow and steered her back to a chair, squatting down beside her. Sweat was licking her forehead, making her spots livid. Close to, her breath was milky sour. He thought she must only be in her late teens. Young for her age and vulnerable. Easy pickings.

'How old are you, April?'

'Nineteen, nearly twenty.'

'When did you meet Ricky?'

'Last year. I used to work in the pub and he came in for a drink.'

'And he's Neil's dad?'

'Yes.'

'What's his surname?'

'Wellington.'

'What about Neil's mum?'

'It's ever so sad. She died in a car accident just after Neil was born.'

'Did Ricky encourage you to apply for your job at Smell the Roses?'

'Yes. That's right. He showed me the ad.'

'How long have Ricky and Neil been gone?'

'Since about twelve o'clock. He said he would take him into Tunbridge to get him new shoes and have a play in the park and they'd be back by four. That's when Neil has his tea. He gets all upset and cranky when he's hungry. Where are they?'

The door slammed and a thin woman wearing a transparent mac came in. April ran to her and threw her arms about her, bursting into tears.

The woman stared at Swift. 'What's going on? Who are you?'

'My name's Tyrone Swift. I believe that Neil Wellington is a child who was abducted in London two years ago. His real name is Oscar Maddox. I've called the police. They'll be here soon.'

The woman cradled her daughter close. She looked bewildered and spoke angrily. 'What are you talking about? Neil is Ricky's. April's his stepmum.'

'I know that's what you've been led to believe but I'm afraid it's not true. Ricky Wellington is a false name. Ricky's been deceiving you.' He took his phone out and showed her the photo of the blanket, then held it in front of April.

'That's Neil's!' she said. 'Neil's blankie! He always has it with him.'

'Did he take it with him today?'

'Yes . . . yes. I don't understand. Where did you see it?'

April buried her face in her mother's shoulder as her crying intensified. His phone pinged and he looked at the screen. An email from Gabe Maddox's address but not sent by him.

I saw you going into Victor's dump. I was planning to pop in and give him a last handout of fags. Kill a bit of time. So you added it all up at last. You've been such a disappointment, Ty. Thought you might suss me out a lot earlier. I was sort of looking forward to working with you. There I was, right in front of you. Ah well, all good things must come to an end. An empire is about to turn to ashes and I think I must play Nero!

Yours, Ross/Ricky/Joe

'I have to go,' he said. 'Lock the door and only open to the police. Do you understand?'

April's mother nodded. April turned her blotched face to him.

'Where's my Neil?'

'I don't know.'

He heard renewed, loud wails as he ran to the door. He didn't look back.

* * *

A whipping wind had sprung up, buffeting him as he wrenched the car open. He rang the police again as he headed for the windmill. He stated that a crime was taking place and they needed to get there as soon as possible. Then he dialled Gabe. His phone went to voicemail. He tried Stella and got the same response. The sky was a brooding grey and the world had turned dark. There was a bright razor of lightning ahead, and then a huge boom of thunder as the taut sky at last gave way. Huge drops of rain started to fall, quickly becoming a torrent. His headlights illuminated blinding sheets of water. He switched the windscreen wipers to rapid but could scarcely see. In any other circumstances, he would have stopped the car but he had to carry on. He slowed, crouched over the wheel, watching for the turn to High Hawksford. He almost missed it and had to wrench the wheel, the car bouncing off the verge. He wiped condensation from the screen, clenching his jaw, hoping he wouldn't be too late.

The gates to the windmill were closed. Swift pressed the buzzer several times but no one answered. The rain hammered him, streaming into his eyes and mouth and he was already soaked, his shirt sticking to his skin. He locked the car and climbed the gates, his feet slipping. He managed to grab hold of the top of the frame and haul himself up. He dropped awkwardly down the other side and started to run up the driveway. Through the curtain of rain, he thought he could see the lamp shining in Gabe's den at the top of the windmill. Perhaps all was well after all and he was up there with a glass of whisky and Dean Martin, the stuffed creatures watching him. Thunder rolled and crashed again, making Swift shiver and duck. The trees lining the drive shook and moaned, leaves scattering. One stuck to his cheek and he clawed it away. As he drew nearer, he wiped at his eyes with his sleeve and saw the light was not coming from a lamp. It was caused by flames, dancing and shooting, red and orange. He ran, gasping, to the door. It was slightly open, the interior in darkness. He could hear the insistent, shrill beeping of fire alarms and smell smoke. He paced slowly to the kitchen, calling Gabe's name, and reached to his pocket to use the light of his phone. A blow to his back sent him pitching forwards. He caught at a work surface as he fell, striking his head on the edge, darkness merging with darkness.

He came to, coughing, the fire alarms still shrieking. Smoke was billowing around him, thick and acrid. For a moment, he was disorientated and unable to remember where he was. Then he coughed again and he knew. He heaved himself up, fighting back a wave of nausea, fumbling for his phone. He used the light to find the sink, snatched a dishcloth, soaked it under the tap and tied it over his nose and mouth. Smoke was rolling down the open plan stairs and he heard a crash of exploding glass from above. He saw a gleam from the corridor that led to Gabe's study and ran towards it, ducking low, holding the dishcloth tightly. The study door was open, a desk lamp shining. There was no fire but the smoke had snaked there, thick and swirling. On the floor, side by side lay Stella and Oscar Maddox. Their ankles and arms were bound and they appeared to be either unconscious or dead. He ran to the sash window behind the desk and wrenched it open, tugging at the frame. He lifted Oscar easily and lowered him to the ground outside. The dishcloth slipped and he breathed a lungful of smoke that sent him coughing and reeling. He leaned out for a deep breath of clean, drenched air, retied the cloth and went back for Stella. Lifting her was hard. He could feel his energy draining and knew that the carbon monoxide was working into his bloodstream. He dropped her twice, faltering and staggering but managed to heave her to the window. Somehow, he bundled her through and she fell with a thud into the howling rain and wind.

He staggered out of the study, towards the stairs, unable to see now, his lungs heaving. Gabe must be up there. Maybe at the top. Flames were licking down towards him, scorching his face. His eyes stung. Through the dense blackness, he saw a figure loom towards him and backed away, his arms up. His head was swimming, his legs like jelly. Everything was in slow motion now, dream like. He heard himself give a muffled shout as someone lunged at him and grabbed him hard.

* * *

There were fingers on his wrist and something covering his face. He tried to tear it away but a large hand stopped him.

'Behave, behave. We want you breathing. Can you hear me? Can you open your eyes for me?'

He unglued his eyes. They were smarting, weeping. A giant in green looked down at him.

'That's better. Can you tell me your name? I'll just lift the mask for a moment.'

He tried to open his mouth but his lips were stuck together. His tongue felt huge. He pushed it forward, moistened his lips and managed to croak, 'Tyrone Swift.'

'Okay, good. Now, you're in an ambulance and you've got an oxygen mask on to help you breathe. Don't interfere with it. Understand? Just nod.'

He nodded. It felt as if there was a sack of lead sitting on his head and his throat was rough like sandpaper.

'Good. We like a bit of cooperation. Here.' The giant passed something cool and wet across his burning eyes. Relief. He managed to raise a thumb.

'Good. A compliant patient. My favourite kind. My name's Gerald. Now, just stay put. I'll be back.'

He lay, blinking, trying to work out why he was there. There was a dressing of some kind across his forehead. He raised his head slightly, ignoring the dull thudding in the back of his skull. He was alone in the ambulance. Gerald the paramedic was just outside, talking to a colleague and a police officer. The night was black and filled with flashing lights. It came back to him then. He tried to sit up, pulled himself halfway. Gerald returned to him, tutting, and told him to lie down. He obeyed but lifted the mask.

'The child and the woman. Are they okay?'

'They've been taken to hospital. That's all I know. We're taking you there now. Need to make sure your lungs are okay. Smoke can do a lot of damage. Now just be quiet and do that breathing.'

The next hours were a confusion of voices, lights in his eyes, tingling in his forehead and someone asking him to cough. Someone else asked him if he wanted family contacted. He tried to think through the fog rolling in his head. Ruth might realise he wasn't back. He croaked out her name and number and said she was to be told he was okay, to stay put and not to worry. He slept for a while and when he woke, was convinced he could smell burning. He sat up, panic-stricken. He saw that he was in a small bay with curtains pulled around him. He was still wearing his jeans but a white gown covered his top. The oxygen mask was gone and his throat had eased. His lungs felt achy. He rubbed his tender eyes, winced and reached for the water by the side of his bed. He drank three glasses, swallowing with care. His phone was beside the jug and he saw that it was 5 a.m. He swung his legs down and sat on the edge of the bed, taking breaths. His head swam with woolly confusion. He texted Ruth and Cedric, saying that he was okay and would be back in London soon. His fingers seemed heavy and uncoordinated, the skin on his hands streaked with soot and grit. A nurse appeared through the curtains.

'Hallo,' she said cheerily. 'You look worse for wear but you're okay. It's good that you slept. I expect we'll chuck you out later today but there's a detective who wants to talk to you first. Let me just check your pulse and listen to your chest.'

He sat still while she carried out her checks, ordering his thoughts. Walker had been at the windmill. Walker had hit him and left him for dead.

'Can you give me a big cough into this tissue?' the nurse asked.

He obliged, holding his chest as it smarted.

'Good, no black bits,' she said.

'I was in a fire,' he told her hoarsely, realising even as he said it that she must already know.

'That's right. You were lucky. The fire brigade got to you in time. I understand the place is burned out. You got a bash on your forehead as well. Nothing so bad, just needed a couple of stitches.'

'There was a woman and a child. And the man who lived there. Gabe Maddox. I need to know how they are.'

'Okay. Let me find the police. Do you want a cup of tea?'

'Please. Can I wash?'

'There's a loo across the corridor outside. Take it easy. Smoke inhalation can leave you woozy for a while. And don't touch the dressing on your head.'

He shuffled to the men's washroom and stared at himself in the mirror. The streaks of grime on his lower face were in stark contrast to the pristine white of the dressing. He washed his hands until the water was no longer grey, then damped a paper towel and worked it around his face. He ran another over his hair. It came away black and greasy. He bent carefully and patted his red rimmed, bloodshot eyes with cold water. Bliss.

There was a cup of tea on the bedside cabinet when he returned, and a detective standing by the bed. Once Swift was sitting back against the pillows the detective found a chair and formally introduced himself as DS Norton.

'Please, tell me what's happened to Stella Gath and Oscar and Gabe Maddox,' Swift said.

DS Norton nodded. 'Ms Gath and the little boy suffered severe smoke inhalation and bruising but they're going to be okay. I'm afraid that Mr Maddox died in the fire. His body has just been recovered.'

'Was he at the top of the windmill?'

'That's right. The windmill is pretty much burned out, just the shell standing.'

There can't have been much left of Gabe, Swift thought, recalling the intensity of the heat as it rolled down the stairs. But relief flooded through him as he heard that Stella and Oscar had survived and tears pricked his eyes. He reached for the tea. The warmth eased his throat.

'And Ross Walker, the man who started the fire?'

'Nothing as yet. We're looking for him.'

'I believe his real name is Joe Pitford and he's from New Zealand. Wellington, I would guess. I don't know how long he's been using aliases. At least a couple of years.'

DS Norton was steady and quietly spoken. He took Swift through the events of the night before. Then he asked him to explain his previous involvement with the family. As Swift talked, he felt his strength starting to return. When the detective had finished, he lay back against the pillow, staring into space. Walker had got away. He had exacted revenge, left a trail of destruction and death and got away. Would he consider his business with the Maddoxes finished if Oscar was still alive?

* * *

Branna woke at 6 a.m. and lay chirruping to herself. Swift was already awake, making her bottle and brewing himself a coffee. Now and again, he felt as if he was drifting and the high-pitched, insistent wail of the smoke alarms sounded in his ears. Ruth had suggested that he shouldn't have Branna down in the basement for the night because he needed to recuperate properly. She was his recuperation, he had said. He could think of no better way to recover than to obey her every whim. He parted the blind and looked up at the day. The storm had gone, leaving the air a little clearer but it was still humid. He checked his phone and saw that Nora had sent an email. Her mother was much better, and her nursing duties completed, she would be back in London soon. He replied: *Looking forward to seeing you. Let me know your plans.*

He drank his coffee, rinsed his eyes with cold water and coughed. Although he had scrubbed his skin in the shower, he was sure that he could still sniff a lingering charred smell. Perhaps it was from his hair, which had only had a cursory wash because of the dressing on his forehead or maybe soot was still lining his nostrils. He changed Branna and put her hearing aids in. Then he sat in bed with her in the crook of his arm while she sucked her milk down, holding on to the bottle. She eyed the dressing on his forehead and kicked her legs.

'I know,' he said. 'I'm okay, tough as old boots.'

He woke from a doze a quarter of an hour later. Branna was asleep against his chest, the bottle squeezed between them. He placed her back in her carrycot, made a fresh coffee and checked his phone. He had an email from whome@randommail.org. He sat at his desk, took a breath and opened it.

Hi Tyrone.

I think we can be on familiar terms now. After all, we've been through a lot together. You were just doing a job. No hard feelings. I'm sure you can overlook the fact that I had to whack you. You'll have had worse.

I read that you were a bit of a hero at the windmill. Knight in shining armour and all that. Although . . . I'm not sure that a private eye can have much to crow about when his clients end up dead.

Not the desired ending to a case. Don't think I'd put that on your website if I were you.

You'll understand my thinking and my plan. Where do you hide a bean? In a tin of beans. Where do you hide a stolen kid? On his great grandad's doorstep.

I don't really need to use the whome address now but it's still fun and I've almost forgotten about being Joe. When you've read this, you'll understand that being Joe was hard. I might ditch him for good now.

I doubt they'll find me. I'm crafty. You have to hand me that. In the end, I thought you were pretty astute too because you did get there. Even if it was too late. I'd give you 6/10. It must grate, knowing that I stuffed my face with chicken and ice cream while you chatted to me.

And introducing you to my "dad." What a laugh that was. Masterstroke, I'd say. Having a dad wasn't crucial but given my past, it amused me and added a nice flavour to the mix. And Victor did okay out of it. He's a bit of a rolling stone, that one. Needs to stay out of the betting shop. Smokes far too much. It was like spending time with an ashtray but there's no gain without pain.

My poor old babe Maura. Tell her I did like her a bit. Although all the hours of understanding and sympathy were bloody hard work. You have to admit, I did graft for what I wanted. I'm no slacker when it comes to sheer effort and putting the time in. It was nice, knowing that she preferred me to Thomas.

That tone; taunting and insolent. Gabe Maddox had said that Sam Pitford sneered at him. Like father, like son. Swift took a drink of coffee, glad that he'd made it strong before he read on.

Mind you, she was easy company compared to April. Oh dear, where would I start with April? Very clingy. But any port in a storm and she was fond of Neil. I suppose she'll miss him. Tell her mum I'll miss her fish pie and roast pork. Tough on April, I know. Hard, losing your son. Hard, a son being taken away from his mother. Does all this ring any bells?

Now for Stella because I reckon you won't know about her just yet. There's a lot you don't know about her. Sound Stella. Slightly soulful Stella. Salt of the earth despite the starry name. So reliable with her frumpy Home Counties frocks and lady like manners. Gabe's attempt to introduce a bit of class into his life. He did like to mix it up. A bit of class with the mother, a bit of rough with the daughter. I've inherited his talent for cultivating the ladies. April told me quite a bit about Stella. Handy. Well, I decided that she could play her part for me. I contacted her a while ago and told her a sad, sad story about a man called Gabe who'd got rid of his unwanted grandson. A baby called Joe, second son of Julie Maddox. Yours truly. She was eager to listen to a sob story because she saw herself reflected in it. We met up a few times, had some country walks while I told her how I'd been cheated of my mum and abused. I had her dangling nicely, then I really hooked her in when I showed her photos of Gabe and Sonia in a clinch. That was with their clothes still on. I saved the best shots for later. Hell hath no fury etc. I told her a tale edited just for her ears. My tragic tale. You see, I had helpers everywhere. And they had no idea just how much they were helping me. Now for the clincher about our Stella. She's a bit of a goody two shoes so she might have fessed up by now but she'd already attacked Gabe before I arrived. Judging by the brass paperweight lying near him on the floor and the way he was stretched out in a lot of blood, I think he might have been dead. I didn't bother to check. I had enough on my hands with her and the boy. I was a bit annoyed with her interfering in my plans for him but I suppose she was just helping out. She does so like to be helpful to people.

Swift sat, rubbing his scalp. He felt as if he had been punched. Stella. No, not Stella. Anyone could be violent if pushed far enough but he couldn't believe that she had been drawn into Pitford's web. Surely she hadn't been party to what had been done to Thomas. Surely she didn't know about Oscar and what had happened to him. If that was the case, he would have to question all his instincts. It didn't make sense.

You'll know by now about Sam and Gabe and the money. I won't bore you with a tale of woe. Stella can fill in the gaps. Let's just say Sam couldn't have looked after a dog, let alone a child. I grew up in Wellington with a lousy old man who made sure he gave me a miserable childhood with plenty of random cruelty. He made sure too that I knew about Gabe and Julie and Thomas in the lovely house with the nice life in Highgate. The nice white life. I wonder if you knew that the reason Gabe really didn't want me around was because I was part Maori? I bet he didn't tell you that. He didn't want a strange taint in the Maddox family. At least I knew who my father was, even if he was foul. Thomas was from a random sperm. A random white sperm though, so that was okay.

So, let's cut to the chase. I got to thinking after my old man kicked the bucket. Relieved me and the world of his shitty life. I was thinking about what I might do for ages. I reckoned I was owed big time and I worked out how to call in the debt. It was easy enough to track Gabe, find out he was in Kent. Rich and comfy. Easy enough to track Thomas and his family. I came to the UK, got myself a new identity and started my campaign. I had a good time. A lot of fun and satisfaction. Right in the middle of them all. Making new friends in different places. Taking the piss, causing chaos.

What to say about Gabe? What a bastard. And he thought he was such a player. It was good, leaving him to burn. Saved the cost of a cremation as well. He emailed me earlier this week, telling me he reckoned he knew who I was, wanting to cut a deal. Agreed to meet me at the windmill. A 100K in cash in return for Oscar. He had the cash with him in that gloomy cave at the top of the windmill so I helped myself. Sadly, he didn't get Oscar.

As for Thomas. Well, he had to be helped out of his misery. And let's face it, he was a terrible wimp. No get up and go. Cutting his fingers off was hugely satisfying. I used to play a couple of instruments at school until my old man decided to break my fingers. Clarinet, mainly. My practising used to annoy him so he made sure I couldn't do it anymore. I took up the harmonica after that because I knew how much it would irritate him. He said I sounded like a couple of cats moaning. I reckoned he was unlikely to sew my lips up although I wouldn't have put it past him.

I'm okay about Oscar and Stella surviving. I left that to chance on purpose. You know, when you're godlike, you have to show mercy and all that. Let the fates decide. Stella's just a stupid cow trying to live a life she's read about in magazines. Trying to fool herself that Gabe was something special when he was just another conman in a designer jacket. In a while, when she mulls it all over, she might thank me for freeing her from that two-timing bastard. Oscar wasn't a bad kid. A bit whingy sometimes but not bad.

So in the end I made a nice bit of interest on that 30K Sam got.

Funny thing is, I think Gabe and me would have got along better than he did with weedy Thomas. We were very alike. I know what I want and I'll carve a way to getting it. I'm a mover and shaker. I'd have done well in business. We'd have made a mint as a team. He chose the wrong grandson. Shame.

Well, time to go.

It's been a blast.

Swift stared at his phone screen. His head still ached. He felt revulsion for this pitiless, damaged man. He felt fear, too — fear because he was out there in the world, still carrying his vile burden. He read the email through again. The last paragraph reminded him of Simone's great grandparents, who had rejected one son, only to find that the son they favoured disappointed them. Gabe Maddox's prejudice had produced terrible consequences. Joe Pitford's problem hadn't been his Maori heritage, it had been his legacy of abandonment and cruelty.

He forwarded the email to Abby Cheng, went to his bed and lay propped on the pillows, watching his daughter. She had her fists clenched above her shoulders. His little boxer. Abby rang him within minutes.

'Fascinating. I've never been involved in anything like this,' she said. 'What a tale of misery. Talk about suffering breeding suffering. And all that careful planning. At least Oscar is back, that's something.'

'Any sign of Walker?'

'No. We found his car abandoned near Dover. Knowing him, that could be another bluff, wanting us to think he's left the country. I would guess he probably had another identity ready to morph into. We've checked with the Border Force. He came here from New Zealand on holiday around three and a half years ago as Joe Pitford, and then vanished. Now we know why. The police in Wellington told us that his employer there had just reported a theft from his office safe when Pitford left the country. Around eighty thousand pounds. Pitford wasn't there when they arrived to question him. We're still trying to find out where he kept Oscar until he moved in on April Greene. A pity Gabe Maddox tried to make his own deal with him.'

'I suspected he might be trying to. I think that possibly, Gabe's intention was always to get me to lead him to the emailer. I don't know exactly when he realised that it was all connected to Sam Pitford but I think it was early on. Gabe Maddox was a man who was never bothered by self-doubt. That can be dangerous. If only he had realised that the woman sharing his home could have led him straight to Pitford. If only I had realised! That was straight out of left field.'

'What a bastard he was, selling his grandson. Paid the price for it though. Paid it over and over. And even Stella . . . we'll have to talk to her immediately. She hasn't said anything about attacking Gabe Maddox but then, of course, she hasn't been asked.'

'I'd never have guessed that she was involved. I've just been going over it all and there was nothing to indicate that she knew Pitford. Could he be lying? He might still want to cause confusion . . .' He knew it was wishful thinking, that he didn't want Stella to have been sucked in too.

'Well, only she can clear that up. He might be lying about part or all of it. I'll have to see if she's well enough to be interviewed.'

'Are Oscar and Stella still in hospital?'

'Yes. They'll be there for a couple more days but they're both expected to recover okay. She's in a worse way. She inhaled more smoke. Maura Haskin has been to visit Oscar but she won't be allowed to have him at home with her just yet. The kid is traumatised and, of course, he thinks April is his mum. She's in a right state.'

'Have you spoken to April and her mother?'

'Yes. It was hard going. Walker certainly had them both stitched up. April and her mum seem to have thought he was the best thing since sliced bread. He had a neat arrangement. The mother looked after Oscar while April did her cleaning shifts. Pitford had dinner at her mum's a couple of times a week and a roast on the Sundays when he wasn't "away working." Bought her flowers and cakes. She said he was such a gentleman, always considerate. We have a widow who clearly thought her daughter would have trouble finding a man. Along came handsome Ricky, a tragic single dad with his cute baby and he fell in love with April. He certainly picked his victims with true skill. April was handing over most of her wages to him.'

'Was he working?'

'We think so but we're still trying to tease that one out. He'd have had a nice nest egg from the robbery in Wellington to keep him going and of course he got free part time board and lodging with Maura. What did you think of him when you met him at Maura's?'

'He was friendly and confident. Warm. He appeared to be genuinely devoted to her. And he presented himself as a family man, fond of his dad, doing jobs around the house. I had no misgivings about him. He was so good. I'm kicking myself now.'

'Quite a piece of work. He certainly put the hours in, building up all the strands of the story. What a weasel bastard. Don't be hard on yourself. I think this guy must fit the psychopath spectrum. He doesn't seem to be bothered by moral qualms. I want to find him. I want Maura Haskin to see him on trial.'

Swift wanted it too but he had a feeling that a trial would never happen. As always, Pitford had a head start. He kept his own counsel and wished Abby luck.

CHAPTER 14

Stella was still in hospital. A police constable was stationed outside her side room. She was sitting by her bed, her eyes closed. She had lost weight from her face. Her hair was flat, held back with a clip. There were cuts and bruises on her cheek and arms from where Swift had dropped her through the study window on to the gravel. She was wearing that scent again, the one that reminded Swift of pale flowers in the dusk. He said her name and she opened her eyes, flinching.

'Do you mind if I sit down?' he asked.

She made a gesture with her hand. It could have meant yes or no. He pulled up a chair and sat near her, to one side. She reached for water and drank, then retied the belt on her dressing gown.

'How are you feeling?' he asked.

She looked at him with a deadened gaze. 'Physically or mentally?'

'Both.'

'I should think the lungs will heal first. How you must despise me.'

'That's not true.'

'You should. I despise myself. What a complete fool I've been.'

'The police have told me a few things. You were deceived, like Maura.'

'Maura! I lie awake thinking about her. Now, *she* must despise me.' She put her hands to her cheeks. 'I'm forgetting my manners. Thank you for saving my life. For saving Oscar. You could have died. I am sorry Gabe is dead. I honestly don't know if I killed him or not. That's what I've told the police. Pitford arrived just after I hit him. I was in shock. I hadn't planned to attack Gabe, I hope they believe that. When I got to the windmill, he was in the top room, looking out with his binoculars. He thought I'd come back to make things up with him. Said he knew I'd see sense eventually. The sheer arrogance of the man! When he realised I wasn't looking to kiss and make up, he started trying to sweet talk me, gloss over everything that had happened. He talked about us going away together on a long trip in the sun. When I said I could never forgive him, he told me not to be a nag because nagging women were such a turn off. I just saw red. It was like something gave way inside me. I picked up the paperweight and struck out. It caught his head. Then . . . then Pitford came in with Oscar. I suppose I'll be charged with something. I deserve to be.'

'I expect so. What you'll be charged with depends on the forensic results. It will take them time to determine cause of death because Gabe was so badly burnt.' He wondered if they would be able to determine it. It might be a shadow hanging over her forever.

She sighed and laid her arms on the chair rest. Her voice was hollow and exhausted. 'I pleaded with that man — that monster — you know. I can hardly bear to call him by any of his names. Poor little Oscar was crying as he tied us up. I begged him not to harm us but he just looked through me. He smiled. He didn't speak at all. He didn't seem like the person I had known. I can still feel his breath in my ear. When I smelled fuel and smoke, I thought I was going to burn alive. At least he laid me next to Oscar and I rolled as close as I could to him to try and comfort him.'

'You knew him as Joe Pitford?'

'Yes. I suppose the police have told you he contacted me.'

'Yes.'

'I'm sorry I lied to you. Pulled the wool over your eyes. I was distraught. Confused. Mad. There were a couple of times I almost told you. Wanted to tell you. The day you came about the ferns, I was tempted. You picked up that I was sad but I couldn't talk to you about it. I'll tell you about it now, but on one condition.'

'What condition?' he asked softly.

'That we never meet again. I couldn't bear it. I'm too ashamed. It would remind me of how much I've thrown away.'

'Stella . . .'

'Don't!' she said. 'I'll talk to you because you deserve to hear it but then I want you to go.'

'All right.' He felt a dull sadness but he thought he understood the torment this woman must be feeling.

She laced her fingers together, twisting them. 'He phoned me in early July, introduced himself as Joe Pitford, and asked if he could meet me. He said he had something important to discuss, concerning Gabe and me but I had to keep it confidential. I didn't know what to say but he sounded sincere and worried. So, I agreed. We met in a pub in Fallowfield, not far from Tunbridge Wells. He was well presented, direct, seemed a genuine person. He said he had been raised in Argentina and had been in England for just a month. He told me all about his parentage. About Julie Maddox and his father, Sam Pitford and what Gabe had done. Gabe had sold him. Joe said his father was part Argentinian and Gabe had been racist. Called him a "dago" and other foul names.' She shook her head. 'Why did he talk about Argentina when he was from New Zealand? He even put on a slight accent.'

'All part of sowing confusion, operating through the fog he created. There were elements of truth in there, enough for him to sound genuine. And it gave him protection if anyone found the New Zealand connection. He liked the risk, the game, Stella. The ferns were an emblem of New Zealand but you weren't going to associate him with them because his background was Argentinian.'

'I see now, yes. Of course. I'm still heavy headed from the smoke. He showed me photos of his mother and father with him as a baby and one with Gabe and Julie, his mother holding him. He had his birth certificate. I recognised Julie from other photos I had seen. He talked about his childhood in Argentina, how terrible and cruel his father had been. Sam Pitford was an alcoholic and a drug user. He beat Joe, kept him hungry, humiliated him, and damaged his hands. He was in and out of care homes. He felt he was entitled to something from Gabe who had sold him into that life. He said he had been deprived of his mother. He cried as he talked about that loss. I was deeply shocked that Gabe had done such a thing. I knew he could be prejudiced at times but it sickened me. I felt terribly sorry for Joe but I said he should speak to Gabe. It would be best to discuss it face to face. I offered to meet him with Gabe if he thought that would help.' She coughed, pressed her hand to her chest and cleared her throat.

She took a drink of water and continued. 'Then he took out a couple of photos and showed them to me. They were Gabe and Sonia embracing and kissing in her bedroom. Not . . . not in bed or naked. Not that time. That was later. I was devastated. He said he hated hurting me but he thought I should know the kind of man I was involved with. I felt mad with rage. Shame, too. I wept for a long time and he consoled me. At one point, we were crying together. He was kind, understanding. We talked about my feelings. He said that Gabe had been betraying and using me. Just as he had betrayed him, his youngest grandson. I could confront him but he would bluster and try to twist things. He said that if we both challenged Gabe he would fight us, blank us. It would be best to put him in a position where he would be cornered. I sat there and thought of all the hard work I had done for Gabe and all the love I had given him. He often failed to acknowledge me publicly and I had put up with that because he was so attentive in private. But betraying me with my own daughter . . .

'We went for a walk then, drifting around the country lanes. Joe told me he just wanted to know about Gabe and his family. Details of their lives. How much Gabe was worth. All the things he had missed out on. He said it would help him and when he finally faced Gabe, he would have details he could use to shame him into accepting him. He acknowledged that he wanted to punish Gabe. He needed that satisfaction. He said he couldn't bear it if Gabe tried to lie and rejected him again. His father was dead. He was alone in the world and he wanted a family. He needed a way to get Gabe to confess and make amends. He said he knew Gabe was a tough nut and he wouldn't roll over unless he was really under pressure. He wanted my help and he hoped I would give it because Gabe had wronged both him and me so badly. We were both his victims and if I could just bear with him for a month or two while he got his thoughts together, he would be very grateful. He emphasised how distressed he felt. He said that if I couldn't help him, he'd respect that but he would publicise the photos. He knew that would hurt me more but he said he had been alone in the world for so long and loneliness led to desperation. He was so articulate and his suffering seemed so genuine . . . well, of course, it was in many ways.'

A trolley rumbled towards them and an elderly man asked if they would like a hot drink. They both accepted tea. It was milky but hot and Swift was glad of the temporary distraction. Stella seemed to appreciate it too. They sat silently for several minutes. He thought of the unhappiness he had detected in her when they first met. Her control and apparent poise had been masking such turmoil. She had said that Gabe would find that she had become his dark star. Now he understood why.

'You don't have to continue with this if it's too painful,' he said.

'Oh yes, I do. It is painful but talking also helps me to sort it out in my head.' She put the tea on the bedside cabinet and sat up straighter. 'I must have been mad to go along with him but I did. I knew he was putting pressure on me about the photos — blackmailing me really — but his pain seemed so raw and honest, I forgave him that. I thought I understood his motives. I wanted to punish Gabe too. Oh, I wanted that so much! And it was a way of dealing with my feelings about Sonia. They had gone behind my back and I'd been offered a way of doing the same to Gabe and shaming her, too. I would be deceiving *him* for a change and that felt so good. I wanted Gabe to suffer horribly. And when I thought about it, I persuaded myself that talking about the family wasn't so awful, particularly if it helped this sad young man. He deserved to know about his family connections.' She took another sip of tea, moistened her dry lips. 'I had no idea at any point until that night at the windmill, that Joe Pitford had anything to do with the emails or Oscar or the other attacks. I even told him about the emails and he said it must just be another example of Gabe having abused someone. My head was storming with rage and bitterness. You must believe that. I would never have been party to any of that. I thought he had only been in the country since June so I accepted that he couldn't have had anything to do with those other events. Please believe me.'

'Yes, I believe you.'

She swallowed and continued. 'Joe said he just wanted to settle down for a while, get his bearings and think through what he wanted to say to Gabe. Then he would meet him and demand some kind of reparation. We met twice more and he phoned me a couple of times. It felt good that someone shared my pain. The last couple of months have been filled with such awful tension. There were times when I nearly turned on Gabe and told him what I knew but my secret knowledge gave me satisfaction. I drew a kind of strength from it. Joe and I were united against Gabe and I really thought that Joe was on my side, that he wanted to protect me, help me. It was all so twisted but he drew me right in.'

'That is his very special talent.'

'Yes. He asked me about how the emails were affecting Thomas and Gabe and what you were reporting. He even said he was glad that you had been employed. He hoped you would find whoever was injuring Thomas and who had taken Oscar because a child's abduction was so terrible. He said . . . he said he had tremendous sympathy for young children because of what had been done to him. We became close so quickly. I suppose I like to look after people. My son has joined a large Italian family and become absorbed by it and Sonia . . . well . . . I had lost her, and Joe needed me. I told him about the ferns. I never thought he might have brought them in. He said I needed to be more careful about my security and Gabe should be protecting me better. He must have taken my keys at some point, mustn't he? He must have got copies.'

'Or perhaps Thomas's. It hardly matters now.'

'No, I suppose not. I started to feel overwhelming anxiety when Thomas was injured in the tube. I told Joe that I was worried about what was happening, but he calmed me and I have to say that I was enjoying Gabe's agony. Oh God. I asked Joe to swear that he had nothing to do with the attacks on Thomas and Gabe and he did, on his mother's life. He looked me in the eye and swore it, said he was desperately sad about Thomas. He said he hoped he would be able to get to know him as a brother in time. All he really wanted was a full apology from Gabe and recognition as his grandson.

'He must have thought I was weakening because then he came to the windmill that morning with the photos of Gabe and Sonia in bed. That was out of the blue. He said he thought I should be reminded of the kind of man I was living with. He told me to stay strong because he was going to contact Gabe soon. I was genuinely in pieces that day. Those naked images of them were too real. The first photos had shown an embrace but the details of those ones of them having sex was too much to bear. I think that up till then, I'd been hanging on to the idea that I might salvage something with Gabe. I thought that what he had done to Joe and me was despicable but in the end, he was all I had in life. I had so much to lose. I didn't want to be lonely again and I had felt desperately alone before I met Gabe. He and the windmill were my existence. In spite of what he'd done to me, to Joe, we might make something work. But when I saw those photos, I couldn't take any more, play any more games. I knew it was all over. I packed my bag. I couldn't bear to look at Gabe anymore.'

'So, you lied to me again, when I came to see you that evening. Or at least concealed the truth.'

'I'm sorry. I've been mad for a long time. Half-crazy with rage and feelings of betrayal. I'm not the kind of person who does these things. I'm so sorry. Joe rang me again after you had gone that night. It was the last time I heard from him. He said he had been thinking about me, that he was sorry if he'd hurt me, that he'd been selfish and he would arrange to see Gabe. He said it was time to get the truth out there. He asked me to keep his secret until he'd spoken to Gabe because he still wanted the element of surprise. Again, I have to admit that gave me satisfaction. I pictured the look there would be on Gabe's face when he met the grandson he had effectively sold.

Such a despicable act. I hated him so much. And I felt pleasure when I thought about how Sonia would feel when she found out what her sugar daddy had done. Sonia with her high-minded views! Then I thought about the picture of Oscar looking familiar and tried to concentrate on that. Something to spark some hope, to help you. Something positive. And then . . . well, you know the rest. At least I did lead you to Oscar in time. At least Oscar is alive and Maura will get her son back. I did one good thing.'

'Yes, you did.'

She coughed again, her breath wheezing and bit her lip. 'I can see now how Joe isolated me from Gabe and worked on my insecurities. Divide and conquer. What I find so hard to understand is that he took such a big gamble, telling me his true identity. What if I had said something to Gabe or to you?'

'He would have vanished and he still had Oscar. His trump card. It's who the man is. Your information was helpful and by using you, he was punishing Gabe in yet another way. Ultimately, he loved the power of knowing he was manipulating and fooling so many people. All the plates were spinning. Oh, Stella, I knew something was burdening you, making you sad. I should have pressed you more to tell me what it was. Maybe you would have.'

Her eyes were glistening. 'Who knows? I doubt it. I was too wrapped up in it all. Now that Gabe is dead . . . I can't feel angry with him anymore. We did have years together, we built a lot together and no matter what he did, I loved him and his family. Everything we worked on in our home has gone up in flames. All that effort and care, now just ashes. And Joe . . . he was just playing me along, enjoying my pain, making me part of his sick scheme. What a sad, depraved man.' She shook her head. 'But I think the worst thing of all is that I'm not sure I would have confessed to hitting Gabe if Pitford hadn't passed on that information. I think I might have waited to see if everyone just thought he had burned to death. See if I'd got away with it. What does that say about me and what I've become? In the end that makes me almost as bad as Pitford.' She started crying and covered her eyes. 'Please go now.'

He looked at her bowed head. He put a hand out to touch her arm but then withdrew it, and left quietly.

* * *

Swift was making coffee in Maura's little kitchen. He had informed her about Joe Pitford's email and she had insisted on seeing it. The police had no objection and he thought on balance that it was best for her to know about the man who had treated her so brutally.

He brought the coffees over and sat next to her on her sofa. She took his hand and held on tight to him. It was hard, she said, when the map of your life suddenly altered and you couldn't read it. When he arrived, she had burst into tears, saying he had saved her son and she could never repay him. Her face was free of make-up, her skin sallow with exhaustion. With no earrings or other jewellery, she appeared younger. She was telling him that she had been allowed to see Oscar the previous afternoon.

'He's with foster parents in Tunbridge Wells for now. The social worker explained to me that I will have him back but it has to be done gradually. She's nice. She said she'll help me every step of the way but what can she really do? Oscar calls that woman, April Greene, his mum. She's being allowed to see him too. It seems that she treated him well. She told social services that Ross wasn't unkind to him and left most of the care to her and her mother. The social worker said that Oscar was checked out and shows no obvious signs of any abuse. He's the right weight and everything.'

'That's something. At least you have the small comfort that Oscar has been looked after properly,' Swift said.

Her breath caught on a sob. 'He didn't know me at all when I saw him. He was scared of me. I gave him back his blanket and he ran off with it and sat under a table. The foster mother said he's anxious and upset, keeps asking for his mum. The social worker said I should meet April, talk to her about Oscar. She said it would be the best thing for him because April will know his routines, what he likes to eat, and his favourite toys. All that. I don't know. I feel sorry for her and I know that she's a bit . . . you know . . . disabled. I realise that she must be in a terrible state after what has happened but I don't know if I can bear to see her. Do you think Oscar will ever accept me as his mum?'

Swift had no idea. He thought there would be fraught years ahead. 'I expect it will take time,' was all he could say. 'You all need time. Joe Pitford caused so much turmoil and pain to all of you.'

'I still can't think of Ross as this Joe. I can't believe he did all that. Found me on purpose and pretended to fall in love with me. Told me how much he would always love me. He would always be there for me, by my side. Pretended to have a dad. He was so caring and kind to me. I think of all the things I told him . . . confided in him. My darkest thoughts. How I'd contemplated killing myself. I cried in his arms. And he had my child. And when he wasn't here, he was using Victor or living with April, telling her other lies about how his wife had died in a car crash and he had been left with his baby. He was having meals at her mum's. He didn't sell solar heating at all. That's what he told her too but the police reckon he worked at odd jobs around Kent and London, whatever he could pick up. And Stella. To think that she was helping him, meeting him. I can never forgive her for what she did.'

'She knows that.' Swift reached for a coffee with his free hand. 'So many people got caught up in the aftermath of a deal Gabe made. He traded a baby and it backfired. Julie Maddox must have suffered terribly when her child was taken but she was ill and weak and her father was a bully.'

Swift handed Maura a coffee. She took a sip. She was staring vacantly ahead.

'All that time after Oscar was taken I thought I would go mad,' she said suddenly. 'Now I feel like that again. I feel as if I'm living in a new nightmare.' She got up and paced around the room, moved a dining chair, leaned on it, came back and sat.

'You'll be offered help, counselling,' Swift said. 'You will need it. Maybe for a long time. What has happened to you is unusual and terrible. More than you'd think anyone could bear.'

'I don't know if I can bear it,' she whispered. 'Thomas gone, Gabe gone, my son thinks another woman is his mother. God knows what that man was doing to him while he had him, even if he didn't actually hurt him. He might have been whispering terrible things to him, things that will only come out with time. Everything has his horrible, filthy mark on it. Everything is spoiled. I feel so dirty. Oh God, to think that he lay in that bed in there with me and all the time he had my child. He was playing me, laughing at me, getting information from me. What am I going to do? I can't stay here. I'll have to move. This flat feels disgusting.'

'You have Oscar. You have him and you will work out a future with him. You have to start there.'

'Yes. But they haven't caught him, have they? What if he comes back? What if he takes Oscar again?'

'Hopefully, the police will find him. I think it's unlikely that he would come back.' It was all Swift could say and he knew it wasn't enough. It was ten days since the fire. With every day that passed, the likelihood of the police catching Pitford decreased.

Maura turned, shaking her head. 'You don't know that. He's clever and they haven't caught him yet. He might lie low for years. I was thinking that last night. He might want more revenge and plan to do damage all over again. He might come after Oscar when he's older.'

'Maura, there are no guarantees. But he got a lot of money and left Thomas and Gabe dead. He probably feels he's had his payback for what was done to him. He could have killed Oscar but he didn't, he gave him a chance. Slim, but a chance.'

'That's what the police said.'

'Yes, so listen to them. You have Oscar back.' He took both her hands and held them.

She bit her lip, looked down. 'I'm sorry. I'm sorry. I shouldn't take it out on you. You nearly died too.' She sank back into her seat. 'I just don't know how I'm going to do this. Get through. I feel so alone.'

'Have you any family?' Swift asked.

'My dad lives in Hull. We're not close. I have a brother but he's in Newfoundland. *He* was my family. That's what that brute used to tell me.' She jumped up and went to the bathroom, slammed the door. Swift drank his coffee and took a painkiller for the dull thudding in his head. After a while, she came back, carrying a wad of tissues.

'I suppose Ross learned how to abuse people at his father's hands.'

'Don't feel sorry for him, Maura. Not for one moment. There's no excuse for what he did.'

'No. I understand that. It's just that . . . I suppose people who've had pain inflicted on them inflict it on others.'

'Not necessarily and Joe Pitford might have been a criminal even if he had had a decent upbringing. Don't waste any sympathy on him. Save it for yourself and the people who matter to you.'

'Sorry. It's just . . . and there was some of his shaving foam in the bathroom. I binned it. I thought I had got rid of everything of his. I never want to hear the word "babe" again. I expect he called April Greene that as well. I've been realising how much he took over my life and arranged it for me. The more I think about it, the more I see how he did it. I stopped seeing other people. I relied on him so much and everything was built around his comings and goings. He made sure of that, didn't he? But I made it so easy for him.'

Swift turned to her as she sat down. 'Maura, the man was subtle as well as vicious. You were so adrift in life and he was so kind. Why wouldn't you have trusted him, listened to him? The first time I came here, you told me you realised that you had to stay well and strong for Oscar. You said he might come back to you one day and you had to be here for him. Do you remember?'

She nodded silently.

'Okay. Well, despite everything that has happened, he is your little boy and he's going to need you. So please, stay well and strong. I think that's what you have to try and focus on.'

'Yes.' She sounded doubtful.

CHAPTER 15

He was woken by the noise of twigs falling down the chimney and a familiar *coo coo*. He could hear Ruth's footsteps upstairs. She was singing to Branna. Calm, domestic sounds.

He sat up, holding his head. It was still full of Pitford — how he had infected every part of the Maddox family, an invisible virus that worked quietly, lethally. So much of his strategy had been risky and had depended on his victims' frailties or their need for concealment. He was angry with himself for taking too long to establish the truth and kept going over the path of the investigation. He had failed and it hit home. He saw Pitford in Maura's flat, smiling, chatting, urging her to eat more. Pitford was right about one thing: ending up with dead clients was hardly a success. He knew that taunt would stay with him for a long time. He remembered Stella's tormented face. They had all suffered but Maura at least would have a life with her son. Stella had been stripped of everything. Livelihood, dignity, her daughter, perhaps her liberty if she faced prosecution. She was so alone and hating herself, convinced that everyone would scorn her for colluding with Pitford.

He thought of Pitford's engaging manner, the apparent honesty in those eyes beneath the arched brows. His skill at drawing people in. His ability to change his identity and become whoever he wanted to be. He worried that the man was still at liberty. He worried too about what Pitford might do in the future. He had a nagging fear that if the man got bored and ran out of money he might seek to persecute the Maddox family again. If Oscar had inherited his great grandfather's businesses and properties, he would be a wealthy target. Oscar might end up like his father, always looking over his shoulder.

He went to the basin, ran the cold tap and splashed his face. He was weary of other people's secrets and emotions. Drained by them. He longed to take his boat out and row for miles on a full tide. He needed to stretch and challenge his muscles, work up sweat and speed. Clean his head of the taint Pitford had left. Try to leave behind all the distress and deception. Maybe he could take his daughter on holiday.

But there were two things he had to do. First of all, there was a man he needed to meet and deal with face to face. He had been thinking about loyalty to someone and not being able to let them go. There was a fine line between the two. There was never going to be an easy solution but it was time to look to the future. Give it a shot, anyway.

He was in Brighton by mid-morning and parked outside Emlyn Taylor's house. Ruth had had several phone calls from him, asking her to come back, asking to see Branna. He rang the bell and a woman he didn't know answered. She was wearing a name badge and told him that she was a carer. Mrs Taylor was out shopping. He was relieved and asked to see Taylor, showing the carer his ID. She left him at the door and went back inside, returning quickly to say that Mr Taylor would see him.

Taylor was sitting in a wheelchair in the conservatory at the back of the house. He held a book in his lap and was wearing sheepskin slippers despite the warmth of the day. He was a slight figure, skinny, with thinning grey hair cropped short. He looked up as Swift came through and nodded.

'Sit down. Would you like coffee?' He spoke hesitantly.

'No thanks. I won't be long. This isn't a social call.' Swift sat on a cane chair opposite Taylor.

'I hardly thought it was. How is Ruth? And Branna?'

'They're both okay. Much better for being out of this house. I've come here to say that what happens between you and Ruth in the future isn't my business. You have a marriage. But Branna is my business. She is never coming to this house again. Never. You won't see her and neither will your mother. Do you understand?'

Taylor looked down and away. 'I suppose you're poisoning Ruth against me now.'

'Hardly. Not everyone operates the same way as you. I don't care if Ruth comes here or not. Up to her. But maybe you should consider why your wife has left you twice.'

Taylor shook his head. 'I miss her. I miss them both. Don't do this to me. It's not fair. I'm sorry for what I did. Will the punishment ever stop? Please, I'm a very sick man.' He started to weep loudly, holding his forehead in a trembling hand.

Swift watched him, refusing to be moved to pity. 'Just remember what I said. You're not seeing my daughter again.'

He walked back into the house. As he reached the door of the next room, Taylor let out a piercing howl and found the strength to throw his book at the wall. It caught a vase of flowers and glass shattered, flying through the air. The carer appeared, running. Taylor was shouting hoarsely, a stream of obscenities. Swift left them to it. As he started the car, he saw Olwen Taylor arrive and park. He wound down his window and spoke to her.

'Your son's in one of his rages. I've told him that neither of you will ever see my daughter again. I mean it so don't try to have any access to her.'

He closed the window as she went to speak and accelerated away. He could see her sour, pinched expression in his rear-view mirror and was glad that his daughter would never have to be near her again. He headed for the motorway and Gatwick airport.

* * *

It was raining again, a light, warm drizzle. Swift left the car in a short stay car park, wincing at the extortionate fee. He held his face up to the rain, shielding the small plaster that now covered his forehead. He'd had his hair trimmed and ran a hand through it to check that the charred smell had finally gone. He realised that there were threads hanging from the right cuff of his shirt. He didn't think she would mind.

He headed into the airport, checked the time, and made it to the arrivals hall with ten minutes to spare. He stood among the ranks of drivers carrying name cards and watched as the passengers from the Dublin flight started to drift through.

Nora wasn't expecting him and he saw her first, moving fast, her dark cap of hair looking newly cut. His heart lifted and he smiled as he waved and called her name. She looked, saw him and laughed with pleasure.

THE END

Thank you for reading this book. If you enjoyed it please leave feedback on Amazon, and if there is anything we missed or you have a question about then please get in touch. The author and publishing team appreciate your feedback and time reading this book.

Our email is office@joffebooks.com

www.joffebooks.com

ALSO BY GRETTA MULROONEY

ARABY
MARBLE HEART
OUT OF THE BLUE
COMING OF AGE
LOST CHILD

TYRONE SWIFT BOOKS
THE LADY VANISHED
BLOOD SECRETS
TWO LOVERS, SIX DEATHS
WATCHING YOU

Printed in Great Britain
by Amazon